JENNIFER KROPF

In case you're dying to know all the copyright details…

This is a work of fiction. All characters and places are made up. (Though, let's be honest, we all secretly wish Winter was real.)

ISBN PAPERBACK: 978-1-990555-18-3
ISBN EBOOK: 978-1-990555-17-6
ISBN HARDCOVER: 978-1-990555-19-0

For Phil

Thank you for believing I could do this.

For Mom and Dad

Thank you for reading me books when I was young.

For Grandpa John

Thank you for being so excited about my stories. What a treat.

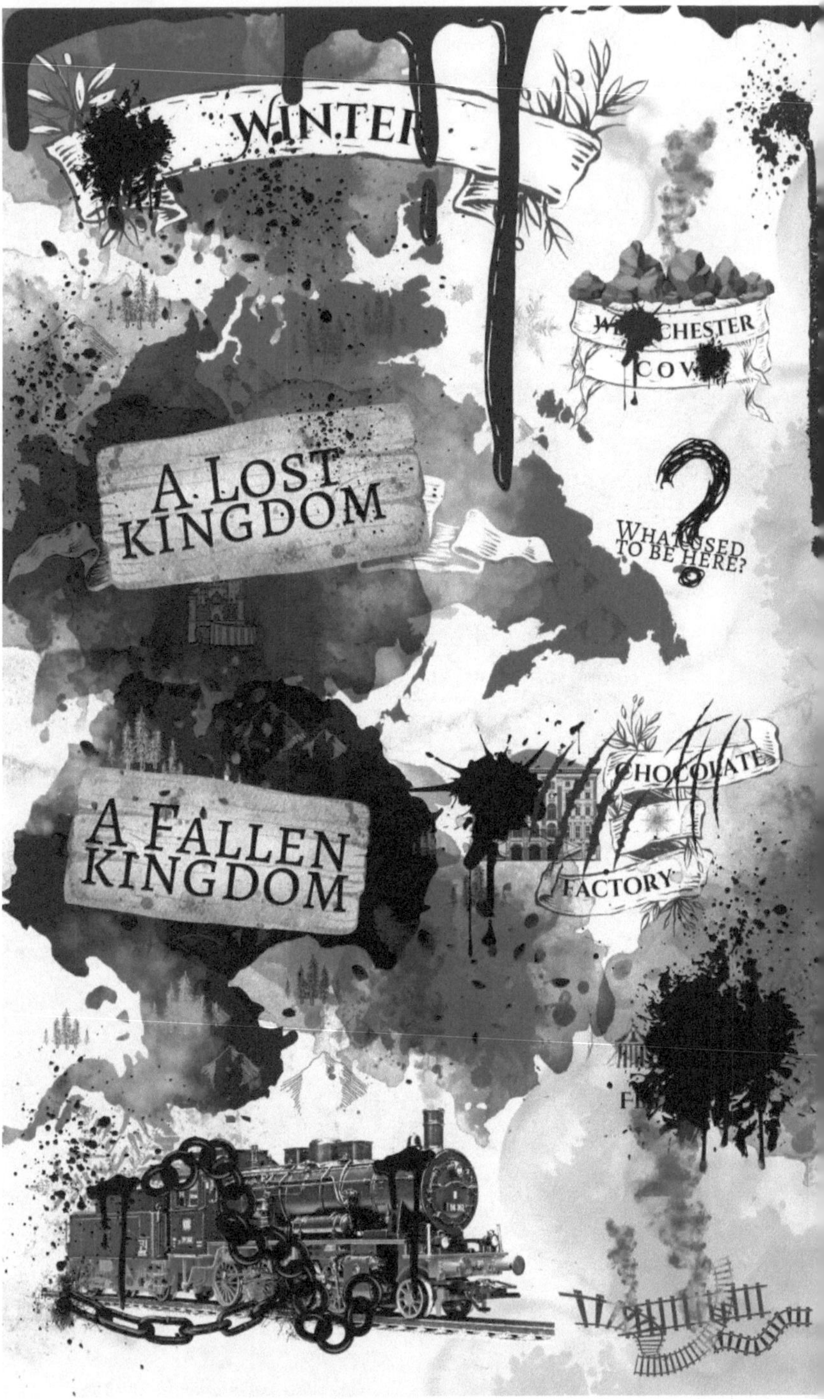

A LOST KINGDOM

WHAT USED TO BE HERE?

A FALLEN KINGDOM

CHOCOLATE FACTORY

POLAR
TERRITORY
THE THREE
KINGDOMS OF
THE EAST
DWARVE'S
COZY
COTTAGE
MIKAL'S
OME
THE
LIBRAR
THIS
KINGDOM
DOES NOT
EXIST
THE DUNES
NORTH (ISH)
LEFT
OTHER LEFT
TRY TURNING
AROUND

Deep within a cupboard,
hiding in the world of Trites,
a Volume of Wisdom whispers
a parable of great insight…

"These signs shall follow the believers:
They will survive when they **drink deadly poisons**.
They will triumph over **the bite of serpents**.
They will **speak in new languages**.
They will **lay hands on the sick and see them healed**."

Penned by Mark, the Ink Whipper,
in his sixteenth chapter

PART I

PROLOGUE

A blessing is how this story begins.

'Twas a single fleck of gold, no heavier than a feather, floating along the Winter skies, searching for a shoulder to land on. The whistling wickets were not amused at the sight of it bobbing along, taking its time, twirling upon the gales, and waving to the galloping prayers in the clouds as it passed. A prayer sneezed in the sky's darkened chill, and the blessing offered a "*Bless you!*" before descending from the skies and entering the darkest hollows of Winter where there was wailing, aching, hunger, and gnashing of teeth. There, a war raged with clashing instruments, shouts of the folk, and blood speckling the snow.

The blessing landed on the wood pauldron of an

infamous once-prince whose eyes blazed burgundy, his mahogany hair stained with Rime blood and frost. Feeling the tiny weight touch his shoulder, the prince paused his slashing to listen.

"Hang on a little longer, for the time is near," the blessing whispered in the once-prince's ear. "Be courageous. Do not be afraid."

Cane Endovan Crimson-Augustus wiped the grime from his chin, the drips from his cheeks, and the snow from his emerald cape. "Do not be afraid," he repeated. "Do not be afraid." He breathed in the offering, imagining the One it had come from and the old allies these Reds before him had stolen away.

Cane hardened his jaw and stared across the battlefield where Red clashed with Green, copper swords and Ruby Legion spears sliced at silver Host axes, and arrows fired from both sides. The Queen of the Pines was tossed from her polar bear, her iron blade skidding o'er the snow. Cane scooped it up and hurled it back.

Ever Green caught it with pale fingers, narrowly blocking a descending Ruby Legionnaire blade. Cane charged the Legionnaire, tossing him aside as the queen's iron sword turned the folk into a puff of snow.

Ever's sharp gaze darted to Cane's, and Cane offered her a nod. "Hang on a little longer," he pleaded. And, as the blessing had whispered, the once-prince added, "Do not be afraid."

But a speck of worry tilted the queen's brow as she panted. For nearly the entire Evergreen Host had been turned back into snow.

The army in Red stretched far o'er the hills, spotting the

plains like crimson and obsidian rose petals; a thousand Legionnaires mixed among fowl, dark beings emitting smoke and vile whispers. Cane swallowed and tightened his grip on his sword.

"Do not be afraid," he murmured to himself a time again.

Still, the Red army marched on with growls and hisses, surrounding him, and closing 'round the Greens that were left.

"Do not be afraid."

But let us slip back to the beginning. It started with a letter or three, you see, tied to the ankle of a silver-winged bird:

Cane,

Something is wrong with Forrester.

I know you and I have not spoken in a good measure of seasons, but our father has fallen ill. The eve the mediciniers announced that the Crimson King was on his deathbed, Forrester killed Tegan and lied to the Court about it. He doesn't know that I saw him with blood and snow on his hands.

Vile creatures have joined the Ruby Legion ranks, and Forrester has welcomed them with open arms. With the imminent fall of the Green Kingdom, I believe Forrester has set his greedy sights on the Kingdoms of the East with hopes to conquer them next.

This is why I mean to challenge Forrester in a Quarrel of Heirs: to fight for the title of Crimson King and to stop Forrester from destroying what's left of the Red Kingdom.

Brother, never in my timestring did I expect to do a thing so mad. But I have been trained by someone for a situation such as this one (though, I cannot say by whom).

However,
I cannot make a move while our father is still alive, or he will overrule me with his dying breath. You know how our father feels toward me.
This is why I seek your help.

- Driar

Driar,

What do you need?

- Cane

Cane,

I need to ensure no one in the Crimson Court sees this coming. If Forrester gets wind of my thoughts, I'll be turned to snow before I can challenge him. To be blunt, I need his attention far away from me until our father passes. I need a rather large distraction.

Do not tell a soul. I can trust no one else.

- Driar

CHAPTER, THE FIRST

It wasn't that I didn't *like* our new barista. It was just that I didn't get why Emily had insisted we hire him.

Emily and I interviewed seven hopefuls in our search to find an employee capable of helping us run The Steam Hollow Corner Café. It was a risk; we didn't know for sure we'd make enough money to pay someone else, especially in Waterloo where nicer cafés than ours populated the downtown core. So, it was a happy surprise when customers made a habit of coming back.

In the beginning, I thought they preferred our café because of the Christmas garland and fairy lights we kept up all year 'round and the shelves filled with charming books we'd scored at garage sales—books we always let our customers borrow while they sipped their coffee.

But after a few weeks I realized it was our new barista that customers were returning for. He juggled coffee mugs up to the ceiling, he whistled pitch-perfect tunes through the café, and he danced his way through the tables while he swept. Our customers couldn't get enough of the handsome "coffee guy" who fashioned bright coloured contacts. I was skeptical of him at first, but he started making me laugh, and once or twice, I caught him glancing over to see my reaction when he did something impressive.

During his interview, he'd told us through a thick accent that his name was *Zane*, but he wouldn't say where he was from. I asked him how he liked his coffee, and he admitted he'd never had coffee before. When I kindly set one before him, he took one big gulp and spat it back out into the cup. After an apology, during which he muttered something about it being "*a good measure too bitter*," he informed us that coffee wasn't for him.

Obviously, I decided we weren't hiring him. But unfortunately, Emily decided we were. She offered him the job on the spot, completely ignoring the loud objections of my facial expression.

But Emily had been right about him. It didn't matter that he hated coffee and detested tea even more. Zane ended up being our best worker. He was always the first to clean off a table or fill the napkin dispensers. He stayed late and was always in the shop before anyone else in the morning, whistling to himself at all hours. The old ladies who came in flattered him—and he loved it. He did everything I asked, sometimes even before I asked it. He twirled while juggling mugs in one hand and carrying a full-to-the-brim coffee pot in the other, getting a rise from any girls waiting in line. Our sales had steadily grown because word spread that the barista in The Steam Hollow Corner Café did tricks.

Over the months, Emily and Zane snuck around,

whispering, and even arguing once. I tried not to get involved, but when I walked upstairs to the storage room this spring, I overheard Emily say,

"You said you didn't bring anything magical across!"

"I didn't! I found it in her room," he'd replied.

"You snuck into her bedroom? You creep!"

"She wasn't there! The Volume has been calling to me every day and eve since I got here. It was driving me bloody mad, so I went and got it."

They both jumped when I appeared; Zane slammed a closet door shut. The two of them stared at me wide-eyed—two beautiful deer caught in headlights. I didn't care to ask what they were up to, but I trusted Emily to keep her shenanigans to a minimum at work.

I spent days at the beginning of summer staring at the lamppost on the street corner where the dead, cold bulb never turned on at night. The city crews hadn't bothered to change it and our corner got pitch dark after 10 p.m. I finally went out to replace the bulb myself, realizing too late that I'd picked a bad day to climb a teetering ladder. The wind picked up so fast, I could hardly see through my flailing hair. I was wrenching the dead bulb free when something warm came against my back. I shrieked when Zane reached around me to get the bulb himself. "Are you trying to get yourself killed?" he snapped. "Get your scotcher down and let me do it." He stole the good bulb from my fingers. I hobbled down the ladder without objection.

Zane attended church at Kaley's invitation. I sat in my favourite building in Waterloo, listening to the pastor-in-training, Stephen, give a sermon. I nearly had a heart attack when Kaley commented on how nice the service was, and

Zane said loudly from his seat, "Are you bloody joking? This is *boring*."

Things only got weirder when David Boram strode into our café. I'd assumed the bully from my high school had come to see what had become of Emily since graduation. He marched up to the counter where I was placing fresh muffins behind the display. When I recognized him through the glass, all I could see were the years he spent shoving grade nine boys into lockers and pointing out all the holes in my thrift store coat to his laughing friends. He started muttering a coffee order when I stood, and I didn't know what came over me, or why in a million moons I felt brave enough to talk to him, but my mouth started moving. "Sorry, but I actually don't have Supergirl-level hearing," I said, cutting him off. "So, if you can speak up, that'd be great."

He halted his order, hazel eyes settling on me. "Helen Bell?" he asked, gaze roaming. "Wow…you look super different." I would have accused him of forced flattery, but there was genuine surprise on his face. I curled my toes in my running shoes, thinking about my morning jogs by the river. I'd never been the jogging sort, but lately the sweet morning air had been inviting me outside.

It took David all of three minutes of small talk and loud laughter before he said, "When do you get off work? Do you want to grab a coffee?" He paused and looked around as though realizing coffee was probably the last thing I wanted after a day of work. "Or dinner?"

I waited for my cheeks to heat, but to my own bewilderment, they didn't. Apart from one time with Stephen last year, I'd never been asked out on a date. My curiosity stirred, and I wondered what it would be like to date the most popular boy from my school. David wasn't even pretty; he was just mean, and that had given him power. But still.

"Sure."

I realized Emily had come out from the back when she released a heavy breath beside me. "You don't have to say yes," she said to me, not quietly enough.

"I know." I shot David a look of apology. "I want to go."

For a reason that eluded me, Emily and Kaley both became annoyingly invested in the upcoming date. Kaley appeared at the café out of the blue and began interrogating me about it. Emily refused to help me find something to wear as though I was being punished.

"I can take care of myself. Good grief, you two, I'll be fine." I shewed them away until only Zane and I remained in the café.

Zane hauled a log onto the fireplace in the corner and took the broom from the wall, gripping it like it was a walking stick. The crowd-pleasing barista glanced over his shoulder toward the counter as he swept. Finally, I couldn't take it anymore.

"What's the matter?" I finally asked.

He chewed on the inside of his cheek. "Nothing, boss. Just be careful with him."

Be careful?

I chuckled.

"Why do you care? Aren't employees supposed to hate their bosses?" I shoved the rest of the napkins into the last dispenser and set it on the counter with the others. I expected Zane to disappear into the back now that his shift was over, but he came over to collect the dispensers for the tables. He didn't take two at a time like a normal person; he wound his arms around the whole batch and hugged eight napkin dispensers to himself. His bright blue eyes settled on me, and my chest fluttered when his gaze traced my features.

"I care," he said. "Differently than he does." He nodded to the door where David had left hours ago. He turned toward the tables. "And I can see it in his face; the fellow is a bland, boring saltslug who won't treat you well," he added.

"That's a lot of insight from someone who only saw him for three seconds," I mumbled. But I sighed. It wasn't like I disagreed.

If Zane hadn't become so vital to our café's survival, I would have scolded him for meddling in my personal life. I thought about what he'd said for most of my date with David. Not only because Zane had a way of leaving his voice in my head after we parted ways each night, but because David Boram was just as awful as I'd always imagined. I had to sit for *five hours* and listen to him brag about himself. And frankly, I didn't have the patience for show-offs.

I shook my head at myself when I came back to the café afterward to get my coat. The glowing lamppost on the corner illuminated the stairs as I dragged my tired legs up. I paused when I noticed a light was still on inside the store even though it was past midnight.

Zane paced by the light of the crackling fireplace; his apron was tossed over the counter. "Have you been here all night?" I asked, setting my bag on a table. He whirled, his nutty-pecan hair standing on end.

"Helen." His voice was dry, and it cracked on my name. I stopped walking.

Zane's bright eyes flickered between mine as he approached. He didn't stop a respectable distance away; he came until he was close enough that I could smell whatever peppermint candies he'd consumed. His blue gaze dropped to my mouth.

"I thought you liked Emily," I blurted, because with the way he was looking at me, I was sure this was going to end in a betrayal of Emily's trust.

But Zane blinked in surprise.

"What?" The horror that crossed his face made me feel guilty for even suggesting it.

"You two are always whispering and sneaking around," I said.

Suddenly I felt like a monster, and I didn't know why. I asked him if he was all right, but he closed his mouth, sealing away his surprise, and took a step back with pursed lips.

I had to ask myself what in this freaky clown-house-world was going on? First David had dragged me to dinner, and now Zane was interested?

"I'm sorry, but I can't do something that would hurt Emily." I backed up a step, but Zane followed. I didn't know what he was doing until he reached for my bag on the table and handed it to me. "Go get some sleep, Helen. Today isn't the day."

After I took my bag, Zane disappeared into the back of the café and returned a moment later.

"Good grief, I don't need you worrying about me too," I muttered at the sight of my coat in his hand. "I have enough people going out of their way to worry about me, you know. But I'm perfectly capable of spotting a shallow jerk asking me to dinner, and changing a light bulb, and getting my own coat."

Zane's mouth moved once or twice before he finally

said, “I know. I’m not used to you like this.”

I walked to my car with a puzzled expression.

Zane showed up at Sylvia’s front door the next morning. I bit down on a smile when I saw him marching up the porch stairs through the front window, guessing he’d come to apologize. My phone rang, and I answered it as I swung the door open. Sylvia’s voice came over the call, her words hitting me along with the cool morning air from outside. “She’s gone.”

My breathing stopped.

My thoughts tipped into a spiral.

I barely realized when Zane’s face changed, when he caught me as I crumpled, and when he pulled me against his chest. His other arm scooped up my legs to carry me back inside. Beats of quiet passed where I just breathed. Fought to *keep* breathing. I was carried to a chair, and he sat down, my silent tears soaking his shoulder.

Grandma.

“She’s gone…” I whispered to myself, or him—I wasn’t sure.

How will I tell Kaley?

Winston…

The clock in the living room released quiet ticks; the only thing telling me that time was still moving forward.

“Do you want me to tell you a story?” Zane asked after a while.

When I didn’t answer, he began murmuring a tale about a girl who’d once rescued a handsome guardian from a prison below ground. I only half-listened.

“There’s music in your chest,” I interrupted. Even in the fog of grief, I was fully aware of a hum of striking chords seeping through his shirt.

"Yes," he said. "There are colours too."

I didn't remember when I fell asleep on the couch, or when he left, or what happened the next few days until the funeral.

I hated funerals.

THE FIRST INTERRUPTION

Behind a sprouting tree, a young Patrolman stood dressed in the colour in which he felt the most comfortable. He stayed a good measure away from the burial site, not wishing to intrude as he pondered the curious circumstances which had brought him to the Trite world to gift a Rime kiss in the first place. But he watched; the bronze and violet hues in his chest dipping to a starry navy as the family gathered 'round to witness the final celebration of a woman's timestring. *Wendy Wilsmurther* was her name, good and faithful. Zane had only met Helen Bell's beloved grandmother a time or three, but the lullaby in his chest recognized her even now.

Zane tugged at the button-up Trite shirt's collar, which was a good measure more uncomfortable in the heat of this summer quarter. He watched Wendy Wilsmurther's offspring, noting how cold and standoffish the Trites were to each other.

"What a gloomy gathering."

Zane stilled. His fingers tingled with the impulse to reach for a weapon that would not be at his back. He turned to find a Rime Folk dressed in black also, as though he had come for the funeral.

"Stay away from her, Cheat. Don't do this now," the Patrolman warned.

Jolly Cheat rolled his eyes. "You're such a squatch, Cohen. Come now; I'm not here for your beloved Trite. I came to find *you*."

"I don't believe you." Zane folded his arms.

"Aww. Is that because your unmerry mother-problems have made you incapable of trust?" Jolly guessed, and Zane's jaw tightened. "And I go by Nicholas now. Just jolly old Nicholas Saint. No more bells, as you can see."

"What do you want with me, *Cheat*?" Zane asked.

A bothered speck pinched Jolly's brow, but he sighed. "You and I have a common problem, I'm afraid. Do you see that iridescent speckle in the sky?" He flicked his gaze toward the heavens and Zane twisted to look. "That is *not* a cloud," Jolly finished.

Zane turned fully, a muddle bending his colours as he studied the white slash above the burial site. "Ragnashuck," he muttered, smoothing down his suit as he prepared to storm the funeral after all.

"*Ragnashuck* doesn't even begin to cover it," Jolly said. "Your little sweetheart over there is almost certainly the one they're coming for."

"Why are you warning me?" Zane adjusted his collar

and looked toward the Trites in black.

"Well, I need you to lead them off. I have a thing or three of my own to lose now," Jolly stated as voices lifted from the funeral:

"Is that...*snow*?"

"Snow in July?"

"Where is it coming from?"

A chilly wind rustled the trees and Zane felt the old magic of Winter slip into his veins as snow billows began tumbling from the slash in the sky, sprinkling the common world. "We're too bloody late!"

"No, *you're* too late. Move your scotcher, Cohen. Tick tock."

Zane jogged for the crowd, weaving through sputtlepun Trites hopping on their toes to catch snowflakes. The Trite minister, Stephen, paused his nattering to look around.

A dollop of snow rested on Helen's held-up palm. She watched it melt with a perplexed look, but her gaze flickered up when Zane reached her.

"This is going to sound spinbug-mad," Zane said. "But you and I...we're..." He bit his lips. He wrung his fingers and looked to the ground. "Well...this is scotchy tidings, but I need to...ragnashuck—"

"Oh, for the *love of Winter*."

Zane was shoved aside, and Jolly Cheat swept in. He took Helen by the waist and pressed his lush, lunatic lips against hers. Zane's colours tumbled into turmoil, but he waited, frozen in place, eyes on Helen as Jolly's mouth released her.

"I'm going to bury you in snow for that," he whispered to the Court jester.

"Please. Try." Jolly's smile tugged.

Helen's lashes fluttered as she looked at Jolly Cheat with flushed cheeks. "You taste like butter tarts…" she said, and Zane grimaced. But when her brown eyes narrowed upon the infamous Court jester, she tore back. Her fist flew toward his face, and Jolly dodged it.

"Ragnashuck, sweetheart." The madman grinned. "Welcome back."

CHAPTER, THE SECOND

Kaley was holding a necklace toward me, and the sky was dripping crystals of snow that left cool dots on my bare shoulders. Somewhere in the distance, a shrill train whistle blasted a song of warning through downtown. I shook the fog from my mind, and when I looked up…

Zane.

Something doubled over in my chest. A thousand cries flooded my mind, all carrying the weight of pilfered time and sealed memories. But when I opened my mouth, all that came out was, "You let him kiss me?"

No matter how Zane's mouth twisted, an explanation didn't surface. He finally shook his head and shoved past Jolly Cheat toward me. "Helen, we need to hide."

A glimmering cloud bloomed against the summer blue sky, casting my extended family in shadow. The flesh on my forearms tightened to bumps as my stare fired to Kaley where a familiar necklace dangled from her fingers. I blinked at the glass sphere on the chain, the ivory and gold inside it bursting like a sprouting flower, and suddenly I wanted nothing more than to be wearing it against my heart.

Kaley reached to fasten the necklace around my throat. I could hardly form clear thoughts as reality swooshed in.

But…why had I forgotten everything until now?

The whistle of the train blasted through the buildings like a metallic lashing, prickling my ears. My gut tugged toward it.

"Someone has broken through, Helen. We have to leave before he realizes all these Trites are your beloveds."

I stared at my Patrolman, a dozen memories of the past months slamming into my consciousness.

Emily's dark hair tossed in the wind as she approached. "Are you all right?" She glared at Jolly Cheat. He glared right back, and Emily lifted her chin like she was about to verbally slap him across the grass.

But Jolly turned to me. "Since I've done you a merry good deed, I'll be off—"

"I have to go back. Right *now*. Something is wrong," I interrupted as warmth trickled down to my fingertips.

"Farewell then." Jolly scurried across the grass toward the sidewalk, and I realized he was in city clothes.

Kaley cleared her throat, nodding to our staring relatives. My cousin Quinn gaped after Jolly, and Aunt Sylvia was scowling at Zane for interrupting the funeral proceedings.

The squealing of tires filled the cemetery, and cameramen climbed from news vans with their lenses aimed at the mysterious cloud of pale flecks and gloom.

"Wait…Can those people see what we're seeing?"

I'd barely asked the question when a tongue of red

lightning plunged through the tear in the heavens, and a newswoman pointed and screamed. The bolt spiralled through the haze and pierced the grass like a blade.

Everyone panicked at once; my relatives shouted and pushed each other out of the way.

"I'm going to assume they bloody can." Zane pulled me and Kaley toward the road.

"Wait!" Emily appeared in front of us and grabbed our hands.

"Hide," I told her.

"I will. But make sure you come back to me." I realized she was shaking. "All I ever wanted was a family. You two are all I have. Don't leave me forever."

I pulled my friend into a hug. "Don't wait up for us." Her hair brushed mine. "We'll come back; I promise."

Wind yanked at our clothes and picked up fallen leaves. Cold crept into the gales, subtle whispers filled the whistling wind, and a thrill brushed over my knuckles.

Baseball-sized hail plunged into the news vans, striking trees and shattering against the road. Serpents of white snow descended from the sky with monstrous faces, and my Aunt Sylvia screamed, racing on wobbly heels toward her corvette.

"Can I really leave them like this?" I asked.

"Helen, this is exactly why you *should* leave them." Zane propelled me toward the sound of the train screeching through the blizzard, but I craned my neck to watch Stephen guide Emily into the church. Others followed.

Zane was torn from my grip, and I spun to find him on his back below a wild snow serpent with an ice fang caught on his sleeve. My Patrolman kicked his shoe through the serpent's face, and white flakes spurted across the sidewalk. The monster swivelled back with a warped half-face as a baseball bat burst through its fang. Kaley swung the bat again and again until I grabbed her arm and dragged her past the *Toys and Things* storefront where a dozen other identical bats lay scattered over the sidewalk.

We rounded a building and Zane grabbed my waist, pinning me back against the wall. He shielded Kaley and me as the serpent roared through the alley and blanketed us in silver-blue dusk. Cold claws stunned my bare arms, and I gritted my teeth so I wouldn't scream until soothing heat rushed into my fingers, and through the dusk, gleams of gold and silver appeared on my wrists. I reached around Zane, fingers stretched toward the raging storm. "Stop!" I shouted at the snow.

The roaring ceased. The serpent shrieked, tearing back and solidifying into an icy white snow sculpture glistening in the summer sun. My vision flickered with light as Zane pulled back, his cheek brushing mine. His mouth was parted. His gaze dragged over to the frozen serpent.

Kaley tipped forward with her palms on her knees, the bat tumbling from her fingers and clattering over the asphalt. "Helen, we're not going to make it out of here," she said from a dry throat.

The howling train horn grew louder in my ears.

"Yes, we will." I jogged out of the alley, searching the skies and counting at least thirty more snow serpents hissing on the funeral hill.

A large shadow passed over the street, and the train's massive boxcars, gold arches, and glittering violet dust drifted over the buildings of Waterloo. But my face fell.

The train dipped, the entire vessel falling toward us on wildly spinning wheels, knocking bricks out of an office building before coming to a loud, screeching halt in the middle of the road. Trite people ran away in fear, but I gaped at the cavalcade that had once proudly boasted *Britley Steam Corporation*, now scrubbed of its name.

The wheels were bound by chains.

The windows were lined with iron bars.

The train was painted *red*.

The doors swooshed open. A few candles were lit, illuminating dim rows of figures in crimson robes and scarlet jackets. Zane took my shoulder.

"They're asleep," he said.

Dozens of Rime Folk had their heads tilted back on the deep blue cushions. Some snored.

"Helen, look." Kaley nodded to a billboard in the train car. On it, sketches on ivory paper rustled in the wind from the open door. The word "*WANTED*" was scrawled across each one in gold script.

I blanched, recognizing my face. I saw Zane's face too, and I saw Kaley's. Lucas's. Cane's. Apple's. Theresa's. Dozens of sheets covered the board.

A shadow moved by the door, and someone stepped out into the light. Husky, inset turquoise eyes looked at us from beneath black hair and pale skin. A long scarlet coat wrapped his stooped shoulders.

"Ragnashuck..." Zane breathed. "What have they done to you, Cornelius?"

Cornelius Britley's dismal gaze drifted between the three of us. "What a tale that is," he said without a hint of his usual smile. His small mouth pulled into a frown. "They took my mum, you see."

"Who did?" I asked.

Cornelius didn't answer. He nodded into the train car behind him. "I put them to sleep when I saw you on my schedule. But they'll wake in a pinch." His throat bobbed. "I hope you've brought rings, Peg," he said to me. "This train is now the property of the Crimson Court, and therefore I cannot grant you passage without payment. Those are the *new* rules."

"I've been in the dead world for nearly two full quarters. I don't have any rings," Zane said, and I glanced back toward the funeral where the serpents rounded in our direction like something had alerted them. They crept through the buildings toward us.

"This door is guarded by the rules. You cannot pass through without payment. As much as it pains me, I must enforce it." Cornelius looked at the ground.

A voice lifted behind us. "I suppose I can share my rings. But I'll expect plenty of hugs and kisses for them."

We turned to find Lucas Leutenski standing behind us with raised fingers; every one of them was stacked with gold rings. "I think the treasury in the Scarlet City had a leak," he added before glancing warily back at the hissing snakes crossing the street.

Cornelius swept aside, glancing up at the darkening skies. "Hurry, then." He ushered us in with a gloved hand.

"You bloody thief," Zane said as Lucas dropped a few rings into a pot by the door and grinned.

"This way." Cornelius strode past the sleeping Rime Folk. We followed him to the end of the car, through a gate, and into a dark hall of cabins. He stopped at a slender door with a thick lock and a sign that read: OFF LIMITS.

Sounds of yawning rose from the car ahead as Cornelius pulled out a key. The lock fell away and he stepped aside. "This is the best I can offer. But they do unannounced cabin checks every day or three, you see. They will arrest you if they find you, and I cannot stop them," he whispered.

"Thank you, Cornelius," I said.

Cornelius dipped his head into a nod. "I wish you safe travels, Peg. May the forces of Winter save you from what's coming. Here, take this for the ride." He lifted a silver tea tray from a cart and passed it over, then ushered me into the cabin after the others. As soon as I was inside, Cornelius closed the door, and the lock clicked shut.

"Sit, Trite. You look like you're going to faint." Zane slid over.

"I'm fine." I flexed my free hand into a fist. The buzzing warmth hadn't left my fingertips since the alley.

Zane paused. "Of course you are," he murmured, releasing a heavy breath.

So, I sat, tossing the tray onto the opposite bench where the teapot and cups clattered.

"Why did that have to happen at Grandma's funeral, of all places?" Kaley rasped.

I stared at the cushioned seats until Zane lifted my wrist.

"You froze that snow serpent in the street." His electric gaze darted up to mine. "You couldn't do that before."

The train's vibrations rumbled under my dress shoes. "I feel different," I admitted.

Zane pursed his lips.

"What?" I asked.

"I'm sorry you had to...*touch* Jolly's mouth. You know.

With *yours*. Ragnashuck, he wasn't supposed to kiss you like that. I was going to do it."

"You still could," Lucas mumbled from his seat. Kaley reached to swat his leg, but he swerved.

"Don't get involved," she scolded.

Zane's dimples threatened to show. "I just mean, it wasn't what I'd planned. I'm sorry about your grandmother too. I'm sorry about everything. I wanted to tell you that before, Trite, but I knew it wouldn't be the same coming from your measly floor sweeper."

"You were a barista, not a floor sweeper," Kaley corrected.

"I thought we weren't getting involved," Lucas said to her.

"Technically, Jolly's kiss brought me back, so I'm glad. But if you ever let him do that to me again, I'll…" I tossed a hand in the air, at a loss.

"Kiss him back? That would punish Cohen," Lucas suggested with a grin. When Kaley swatted at his leg again, he wasn't fast enough to dodge it. "Ow! Oh, don't muddle your buttons, darling. I've missed you all a merry measure and I'm painfully overdue for a few improper comments." He reached across Kaley to the tea, squishing her against the seat. When he lifted the pot, he made an odd face and shook it from side to side. Finally, he flipped open the lid to peer in. "Cornelius Britley must be losing his mind," he said. "It's empty."

"Let me see that." Kaley took it, and a smile spread across her mouth. "It's not empty. It's a blessed teapot." She took a cup from the tray, and when she tilted the pot, hot, steaming liquid trickled from the spout. "I saw stuff like this in the Volumes. They talked about a feather pen that never runs out of ink too. These things are hard to come by." She passed me a cup of steaming tea.

"I've never seen a teapot do that." Zane eyed it.

"Maybe you would have if you ever *drank* tea." Lucas accepted a filled cup from Kaley. "In Mikal's house, if you didn't drink tea, the girls would frown at you."

Zane laughed. "In Mikal's house, the girls frowned at *you* anyway."

Lucas made a slurping sound as he drank. "Ah. Yes. That's true."

But Zane's smile faded. "What's happening, Lucas? How did you get to us when the intersects aren't open? And what about those serpent snowsquatches?"

Lucas took a deep breath and rested his tea on his lap. "Our enemies opened a good measure of doors. I was the only one brave enough to try and slip through one when they weren't looking. It'll be a frostbitten catastrophe in the common world now."

"But everyone in my world could see it all," I said.

"Yes. Well. I suppose when you meddle with things you shouldn't, a bad thing or three can happen." Lucas's topaz gaze dipped to rust. "You must have guessed by now that Asteroth is back."

I thought of the red lightning in the sky. I thought of Emily at the church. I wrung my fingers.

"What about the Patrol and captured believers we left in Winter?" Zane asked.

"They're still trapped in the Dungeon of Souls," Lucas said. "I don't know who's alive, or if anyone still has hope."

My mouth parted. "No one saved them?"

"There is no one left to save them, Trite." Lucas looked out at the snow brushing the window. "The only reason I haven't been turned to snow yet is because I was gone when…"

We waited on the edge of our seats for Lucas to finish. But he seemed more interested in the blizzard outside. I slumped back and covered my mouth with my fingers. "How did so much happen in just a few months?"

"It's been two long and dreadful quarters." Lucas drew his attention back to us.

Zane pushed up his sleeves and clasped his hands. "And Elowin still hasn't returned?"

The sheen in Lucas's eyes dulled. "No." He lowered his voice when chatter passed by outside our cabin. Then he leaned forward with his elbows on his knees to whisper. "Winter is a lost cause. There's no point in Elowin saving it now."

"What?" I shook my head as the columns of symbols on my wrists warmed. "Lucas—"

"Decide for yourself when you see it, Trite." After a beat of silence, Lucas slouched back against the backrest. "The end is near. For all of us."

WELCOME
TO
THE END

THE SECOND INTERRUPTION

Jolly-as-pie Nicholas Saint was a folk made for games, secrets, and sage tea. The scent of the steeped herbs drifted up the staircase and tickled his nose in the nursery where the tiniest of babies lay beneath a knit blanket. The rocking chair swayed back and forth where Nicholas sat, singing a light tune to carry the child into her dreams. A storm clamoured outside the window; a concoction of plain Trite weather fighting the forces of changing magic temperatures. Cold rain spat upon the glass, staining the view of the approaching eve with tears.

The rocking chair slowed when the baby's soft breathing filled the room, and Nicholas brought his song to an end. He leaned to spy on the girl's soft curls, splayed arms, closed eyes, and open mouth.

"You are positively lovely, Posineon, my sweetheart. You will make all the boys swoon." Nicholas paused at the thought. "I'll have to teach you to throw a merry punch. It's the only way I'll let you leave my sight, I'm afraid."

Thunder cracked o'er the city, and Nicholas sighed as he stood and tugged the child's blanket up a pinch higher. "Ignore the unimpressive weather of this world. Someday, I'll show you what a real storm looks like, with snow that growls and wind that screams. Now, sleep well so I can drink my tea in peace. And don't even think about waking me again tonight or you'll be in all sorts of trouble." The girl released a snort in her slumber, and Nicholas smiled. "Dream of pretty things," he instructed, "and wake up with cheer."

Nicholas slipped from the room, closing the door with quietness. But he paused when the latch clicked, realizing he no longer smelled the sage tea. Rather, something much sharper and fruitier had taken its place.

His nickel eyes darted to the hall closet. There were exactly three hops between him and the closet door.

Nicholas sprang for it and drew out a hooked staff which he held before him as he descended the stairs.

Nothing moved in the shadows. Yet, Nicholas crept to the middle of the living room with his staff poised.

"I smell you," he said into the darkness.

Ten plus three white-fleshed beings sprang from the corners, snatching at his clothes, his wrists, his ankles. Nicholas managed to slash only one before a glowing staff-point touched his throat. Sparks of red snapped at his flesh, but Nicholas refused to lift his gaze to the shadows as he was pushed to his knees by oily Greed hands.

The room went quiet, apart from a slow set of footsteps. Long diamond-white hair appeared before him.

"It seems you've discovered a thing or three that I have done," Nicholas dared to say.

"I have." The voice was cursed, and Nicholas's gaze drifted toward the staircase where, to his relief, the child had not awakened.

"Did he at least survive? Or has he been turned to snow too?" Nicholas pulled his gaze away, lest he give away what was up those stairs.

A chilling silence followed, filled with distant thunder and the scent of sour cranberries that had stained the lovely sage aroma of the house. When Asteroth did not answer, Nicholas finally lifted his eyes. The once-prophet's hair nearly reached the floor now, patched with black burns. But the hollow stare in his eyes did not register Nicholas's question, and a crease formed between Nicholas's brows as he realized that Asteroth did not know *who* he was asking about.

And perhaps…

Perhaps...

Maybe, possibly, conceivably, *probably*, there was a chance that Asteroth Ryuu had not discovered all that Nicholas had done.

"No folk escapes the Night Beast." Asteroth's smooth and scarred tone was a cavern of emptiness. Nicholas bit his lips as Asteroth's silver eyes slid to the Greed breathing hungrily in the room. "Bring him."

Pale limbs shifted through the dimness of the house, and Nicholas was forced to stand as a Greed whispered in his ear, "Wicked folk aren't gifted merry endings, *Jolly Cheat*." The being's pale finger pointed to Asteroth pulling a thing from the pocket of his long bloodred coat.

Nicholas swallowed at the sight of his wiry, noisy, bell-decorated hat.

CHAPTER, THE THIRD

The train came to a jarring halt; Kaley flew from her seat, and Lucas sprang to catch her before she collided with the window.

A rustling sounded in the hallway, and Cornelius's voice drifted through the door, bringing our chatter to an end. "This cabin is off limits, you see," he said. "I don't permit folk to ride in there—"

"We will search every cabin." The collection of whispers was sinister, and goosebumps plagued my skin.

"Feastbeggars," I warned the others.

Lucas waved to get Zane's attention. Both boys stood at once, and Lucas passed Zane his Patrol staff who aimed it at the door as the lock clattered. Lucas flicked the latch on the window, and cold air rushed into the cabin.

The door's lock fell off with a *clunk* and we froze.

Kaley grabbed the blessed teapot and Lucas grabbed *her*, hopping out the window with both. Zane kept the Patrol staff poised. "Jump out, Helen. I'll be a pinch behind you."

Below the open window, Lucas raised his arms to catch me.

"I'm not leaving you here to get arrested!" I whispered.

"Do you think you can hold these things off better than I can?" he shot back. But the unoiled handle squealed, and both our gazes flashed to the door. Zane whirled, grabbed me, and soared out the window. I landed on top of him in the snow. He sprang up and pulled me against the train's side, concealing us from the window's view.

Lucas leapt up and clasped the window shut behind us just as the door of the cabin burst open and darkness entered.

My heart thudded in my ears as we waited, trying to soften the sound of our laboured breathing. The feastbeggars' whispers filled the cabin, and I squeezed my eyes shut, willing the terrible sounds to vanish. Seconds went by. Minutes. None of us moved a muscle.

"They're gone." Lucas's whisper reached us. "That..." he pointed up to the cabin, "scared the snow out of me."

I jumped when the train horn blasted, the pipes fired glitter, and the golden wheels began to move with the chains around them screeching.

"We need somewhere to hide," Zane said. "Ragnashuck, that was too close."

But I was staring down at my feet—not because my toes were freezing in my summer shoes—but because the ground below me was *quiet*. I dropped to a knee and leaned with my ear toward the snow, blocking out the sounds of the screeching train rolling away. I sorted through echoes, wind, and breathing, searching for a quiet tune that was missing.

Nothing.

I stood again. I peered through the crisp flurries making wild patterns in the air, seeing more than just dunes and snow. I saw hearts, and the last sparks of hope left in them wilting to embers.

When Zane trudged past, my attention moved to his tense back where a tear in his dress shirt made the fabric hang limp.

"Do you think you can hold these things off better than I can?"

It had sounded like a challenge.

As if Zane could feel me watching him, he stopped and turned back. His shoulders relaxed. "Come on, Helen." He held out his hand.

Rubbing my forehead, I followed my sister and the two Patrolmen through the whisking snow. Zane wrapped his arm around me, his warmth seeping into my cold skin.

We avoided the forests—nothing in them seemed welcoming. Not the black shadows coiling within the trees; not the branches decaying up to their trunks; not the nooses of smoke quivering at the roots. The forest colours had disappeared, and everything was left grey and cold.

By the time we reached a village, my flimsy funeral clothes were frosting at the hems, my black dress shoes were soaked through, and my fingers were blue. Kaley passed me the teapot, and I sighed in relief. Steam flitted out the spout, getting lost in the wind as I clutched it to myself, absorbing its heat.

We stopped walking at the village's edge.

"Where is everyone?" Kaley looked at Lucas, who looked at Zane, who looked at me.

Torn ribbons hung limp along the rails of houses and bridges. Gems and paintings had been scratched off the dark-windowed storefronts. It was so dark, it looked like nighttime.

Tall red banners with the Red Kingdom royal family crest fluttered on high posts down the empty village street. Another star had been stroked off from each emblem. An ivory sheet was posted below every banner, and I moved for the nearest one to read it:

Official Summons of the Crimson Court
For: The Folk and Foes of Winter,

I invite you to join the ranks of the Ruby Legion.
I shall accept every folk regardless of status, history, or criminal record.
All who wear a crimson cape shall be equals.
Honour and glory and power await those who register at the Hall of Knowledge in the Scarlet City this quarter.

Sincerely,
Prince Forrester,
First Red Prince, and Heir to the Crimson Throne

I tugged the page off the post.

"Careful," Lucas said. "Removing a summons is a crime."

I folded the paper against my thigh and slid it into my

dress pocket. "I'm already wanted. What difference does it make?"

A dismal smile cracked Lucas's face. "That's the spirit."

I crossed the street to a seamstress shop and peered in the window. I saw no life, not even a flickering candle. The sill inside looked like it had been collecting dust for a while.

"You shouldn't be walking around in the open street, Trite. There are things watching," Lucas called after me.

My hand slid off the glass.

"Elowin," I whispered into the cold air. "Why didn't you return like they all believed you would?"

"I've been asking the same question since the train," Zane said from behind me.

I turned to my Patrolman. "He wouldn't abandon Winter. Lucas is wrong."

"I don't know what to think. The Patrol are still trapped. Who's supposed to save them if not him?" Zane's nose was pink. We were all going to get hypothermia if we didn't get somewhere warm.

A wisp of black shadow curled around a building, creeping below a sleigh and sitting there like it was watching us. Another one rose from inside the seamstress shop and I propelled back from the window on wobbly feet. Zane reached to catch me, but I raised a hand to stop him, finding my own balance.

A limb of black smoke slithered into a chimney pipe across the street.

"We shouldn't stop." Lucas appeared, pulling off his coat and extending it toward Kaley. Kaley looped one arm in and pulled me into the coat with her. I held the teapot between us.

"This is unreal," she whispered.

"Let's move our scotchers." Lucas led the way through an alley, keeping to the shadows.

"If only we'd found that iron star," Kaley said. Zane slowed his walk, tilting his ear toward us. "We had the wreath and the drum. We were so close to completing the Triad of Signs and being able to make more Carrier of Truth orbs. Is this what the Volumes were warning me about? Is this what we were supposed to keep from happening?" She glanced up at a shadow following us along a rooftop. "What's the point of trying to finish what we started if the worst has already happened?"

I tugged Lucas's coat tighter at my shoulder.

Lucas opened the door of an enclosed wagon and waved for us to get in. "I'll pull you," he said, and grinned. "Like a robust reindeer."

"You're going to pull us in this?" Zane made a face.

"I have a Patrol staff. It'll be like butter gliding over hot bread."

Zane chuckled. "Ragnashuck, Lucas. It will *not* be like that." But he climbed in anyway, and Kaley and I followed.

The ride was nothing like butter on bread. It was so choppy I had to close my eyes to fight nausea until Lucas slowed to a stop. When Zane opened the door, Lucas was laying in the snow panting with an arm flung over his face. Zane cast me and Kaley a knowing look as he hopped out to take over, and Lucas stumbled into the wagon, collapsing on the opposite bench.

It was over an hour before the wagon stopped again, and the whole ride, soft light flickered on my wrists. Kaley stared at the silvery words gliding over my skin.

When I climbed out of the wagon, Zane was staring off in silence. Kaley appeared beside me, tightening her clutch on the teapot.

Lucas had the decency to keep himself from saying, "I told you so." He waited for one of us to speak. Waited for one of us to comment on the smoke-stained walls of the factory, on the boarded-up windows indicating those inside had been trying to keep something out, and at the long, deep claw marks scratched into the metal walls like that same something had been trying to get in.

"Ragnashuck," Zane whispered. "Are they…Did anyone survive this?"

Lucas's mouth tipped into a frown. "Barely."

Kaley's green eyes glazed. "How did *you* survive, Lucas?"

"What in the world did this?" I asked at the same time.

"I wasn't here when this happened." Lucas hugged his arms to himself. "And I don't know who to blame for this horror," he said, nodding to the factory. "Asteroth, or that frostbitten Beast controlling his tongue."

"Someone's there." Zane skated to a hooded figure who was approaching the factory, dragging their feet in a listless amble.

"Wait!" Lucas's call was lost in the howling wind as Zane placed the hook of the Patrol staff against the figure's stomach to halt them.

"Who are you?" he said. When the figure turned her head, her face lit up at the sight of Zane. I broke into a run as Zane lowered the Patrol staff and took an uneven step back.

"Apple…" I rasped, taking her into my arms. Slowly,

she dropped the bags in her hands and wrapped her arms around my middle. I pulled back to see my friend's pale skin, uncoloured, dry lips, and her sunken topaz Rime eyes. It was like seeing a stranger.

"Please...tell me," Apple whispered, studying my face then looking over at Zane, Kaley, and Lucas. "Am I dreaming?"

Something sank in my chest. "You're not dreaming, Apple."

Lucas wrapped an arm around her and turned her in the direction she'd been travelling. "We'd better get inside before something sees us."

Apple grabbed my hand as Lucas moved her, gripping with all her might like she was worried I might disappear. Kaley collected Apple's bags from the snow.

We bypassed the front doors and came to a narrow, dug-out snow tunnel behind the factory. Lucas ducked in, leading the way down the passage until we reached a basement window. He knocked on the glass.

After a shuffle, a set of beady eyes appeared on the other side. The window was thrown open. "By the sharpest wind! We hadn't expected you sputtlepuns for another quarter, at least! Come!" Old Jymm whispered, his eyes darting to the tunnel behind us.

We took turns crawling through the window. When my numb toes hit a solid floor, there were no sounds of gears turning or the rush of the chocolate waterfall upstairs. I smelled dust and dim corners instead of sweet cocoa and hazelnuts.

"It's good to see you, friends," Apple said once the window behind us was sealed. "Your arrival will bring good tidings on this dark eve." She lifted a candle from a dust-covered table and struck a match to light it. When she turned, her topaz eyes fell to the glowing symbols on my wrists and fingers. "Bad tidings have befallen us, I'm afraid. But you're here now. Perhaps there is hope after all."

By her tone, I wondered if she believed it.

She swung open a closet door and began pulling out knit sweaters. Zane politely declined, but Kaley and I wrapped ourselves. I lifted the collar to smell it, inhaling the faint fragrance of sugarmelon, burning firewood, warm stories, and good memories.

"This way." Apple led us into the hall, and Old Jymm waved goodbye. My damp dress shoes squeaked over the floor as I followed. "It seems the factory has been preparing for these days—shifting itself into what we needed at the end." Apple's voice was strained.

None of the hallway's lanterns were lit, and some walls were black and smelled of old, rotting smoke. We followed Apple's flickering candle as she led us around turns and down a winding metal staircase.

Chatter lifted from a room tucked into the basement. The faint aroma of warm bodies and friendship was enough to make me want to run in when we reached the door. Dwarves were nestled beneath heaps of knit blankets, but they all sprang up when they saw us. I saw Scarlet Strange among them.

"Is that our little Cohen?" Bertra pushed her way through the others with her arms out. She collided with Zane like a stone, nearly throwing him over.

Kaley set the teapot and Apple's bags on the table in the middle of the room. I looked from face to face, but I didn't see Porethius or Cane. Gathadriel sat in a chair in the corner, his wings tucked in around him. It was strange to not see Patrolmen fill the gaps, making all sorts of noise. Lucas was the only one wearing a Patrol uniform, and I tried to ignore the heat that returned to my fingers at the thought. Theresa appeared with a knit blanket raised, and I gladly stooped so she could put it around my shivering frame.

"At your service, Carrier." A boy with fiery orange hair bowed, and Apple gave him a little shove.

"My cousin, Ginger," she said in introduction. "He's blessed because he wasn't born," she told me, and I raised a brow. Apple waved her hands like she needed to start over to explain. "My aunt and uncle—the *bakers*—couldn't bear children. So, my uncle made Ginger out of gingerbread." She nodded toward the boy. "And one marvelous day, Elowin's spirit breathed life into him and he could walk and speak. But you see, when Ginger began to run, he was dreadfully fast. My uncle and aunt couldn't keep up with him."

"Oh. All right." I took an awkward gander at the boy again, trying to imagine that.

"Run, run, as fast as you'll go," Apple sang. "They can't catch you! You're the gingerbread folk!" She patted his orange hair, and I had a creeping fear that Apple had lived in isolation too long.

"Where's Porethius?" I took another look around, but Apple's face fell.

"Well, friend…She's here. She's just…" She glanced toward a pitch-black hallway off the room. "Well, you see, Cane scuttled off. He left a week or three ago when he received some letters." Apple darted to a chest of drawers and came back with a handful of crinkled papers. She stuffed them into my hands. "He wouldn't tell us who they were from, but we found these in his belongings after he left. He told Porethius not to follow or rescue him." Apple scratched at her hairline, but her eyes widened when they fell on the table. "By the sharpest wind! Is that a *blessed teapot*?!" She moved past me before I could read the letters. Across the room, Scarlet Strange's gaze dropped to her hands as she twisted her fingers. A gold band wrapped her wedding finger.

Good grief.

A large map hung on the wall. Sections were burned off, scribbled out with ash, or painted over with cherry-coloured ink. Dread moved through me when I realized what it was.

"Look at this, friends! When was the last time we drank tea?" Apple yelled, opening a cabinet and pulling out every teacup she could find. I should have been relieved to know we'd arrived with something that would bring our friends joy. Apple began pouring tea—she stuck a steaming cup into my hands, but I didn't drink it.

Tightening my grip on Cane's letters, I moved for the lightless hall, fighting Lucas's voice in my head:

"Winter is a lost cause."

THE THIRD INTERRUPTION

Kaley Bell was certain her ears were on fire. Try as she might—rubbing them, patting them, covering them up—she could not stop hearing the soft tinkling of a bell that began ringing the exact moment she had entered the factory. As the tea was passed 'round, she shook her head back and forth to clear it, yet still the bell rang.

"None for me, thank you," Zane said when Apple offered.

"Oh, have a bit of cheer, Mr. Zane. Drink some! You might change your mind about it!" Apple took his hand and put the teacup in it. Zane made a face as soon as her back was turned, but he did slowly, reluctantly, and with a horrid scowl, raise the cup to have a taste. A deep cough escaped his throat, and he set the cup on the table.

Kaley heard him mumble a thing or three, along with the

never-quitting tinkling of clapping metals in the distance filling her ears.

Finally, when she could take it no longer, Kaley crept for the door she had first come in. She found herself glancing up the spiral staircase as though the answer might be waiting for her just a step or three up. She climbed one, then ten plus four more, until she entered a hall of ash walls and caved-in floors. The tinkling sounded to her left, and she turned, following it 'round corners. She climbed another staircase to a wide, rectangular room with slivers of dull light peeking through nailed-up boards over the skylights. Shattered balconies hung tilted above, and litter and metal spindles carpeted the floor in uneven heaps along with shredded bows and ruined memories. Kaley inhaled deeply. But when the tinkling resumed in her ear like a button-sized church bell, she followed it across the room to one staircase more.

Down the hallway she found a dust-covered door marked: STORAGE. When she pushed it open, the bell sang crisper; for along the far wall, past clutter and debris, a rocking horse tipped back and forth with a handbell braided into its mane. Something seemed to be rattling inside it.

Dust dirtied her knees as Kaley crawled 'round the wooden creature. She pressed her face to the floor, and her eye caught on a hatch on the horse's underside. She tugged the lever, and the hatch swung open.

Out fell a ring of keys, hitting the floor with a clatter and splaying. She lifted them to read the keyring's inscription:

For such a time as this

Kaley ran her thumb along the words, wondering who

the keys belonged to. She flipped the ring over to see the other side, but as soon as she did, she dropped them. She sprang back to her feet, staring down with wide forest-green eyes.

For, upon the other side of the keyring 'twas scribed:

Kaley Bell

CHAPTER, THE FOURTH

I almost didn't notice Porethius sitting at the corner table in a darkened room down the hall. I took a step in, but bit down on my *hello* as my feet came together.

Her wings…

My mind swam, trying to come up with something to say. I stared until she spoke instead. "I was struck out of the sky," she explained as though she could feel my gaze on her back. When she turned in her chair, I closed my gaping mouth. "A serpent of smoke and snow snapped over my wings. I wrestled free, but I still fell a good measure."

My hands grew oven-hot. I clasped the teacup, sure I was going to boil the tea inside. "I didn't know. I would have come back sooner—"

"You needed rest."

She folded her hands on the table, lifting her pale eyes that matched her blurry, blotted out tattoos.

"Can't we come up with another plan now that I'm back?" I inched closer and she turned away again, her shredded wings bristling.

"We?" There was almost no sound in the word. "It's not up to *us* anymore, Carrier. Gathadriel and I have failed our assignments."

My fingers tightened around Cane's letters. I crossed the room to set the steaming teacup before her. Her purple eyes wandered over, but she didn't touch it.

"You're not alone, Porethius. You need to remember that when it's dark," I said. "An ancient war fairy once told me that."

Her head tilted. I turned to leave, but the sound of her chair sliding out stopped me.

"You've brought a thing with you, Carrier," she said. Her purple gaze dropped to my glowing hands as she walked around me. "A thing different than the last time. It smells a pinch like hope," she said, and a bleak, doubtful smile tugged at the corner of her mouth. She slid past me to leave first, her feet dragging over the grainy stone floor.

But her eyes had said something else,

"*It's too little too late.*"

The letters grew heavy in my hand. Swallowing, I unfolded them and began to read.

I marched back to the others with the letters just as Kaley burst into the room shaking a metal ring of keys above her head.

"What are these?" she shouted, and all the chatter ceased. "Why is my name on these keys?"

Lucas reached to take them. "You have cobwebs in your

hair," he told her.

Theresa hobbled over. She tugged Lucas's sleeve down and squinted at the metal ring.

"Maybe they're a gift, love," she said. "When one gives a gift, the name of its intended recipient is usually put upon it. Isn't that right?" she asked the others, and a dozen dwarf heads began bobbing up and down.

Lucas handed the set to Zane, but Zane's gaze darted up to mine. His mouth twisted to the side, and he made an odd face. My Patrolman looked away, giving the keys back to Kaley.

"I'm going to find something to wear." It was the last thing he said before dragging a hand through his pecan hair and heading for the door.

My feet were moving before I realized it. I slipped out after him and looked both ways, but he'd already disappeared. I darted up the spiral staircase into a blanket of shadow. After a few minutes of searching, I realized I didn't know my way around the factory basement. I came to a dead end.

"Zane?" I called, but everything behind me was still and quiet. I peered into the nearest room, seeing only stacked boxes and piles of broken furniture in the darkness.

I turned to go back, checking the other rooms as I did. After venturing down several more hallways, I sighed. "I'm lost, Zane," I admitted, deciding I didn't care that I was talking to empty factory hallways and dust mites.

The scents of brittle stone and decaying wood tickled my nose and I sneezed, taking another step back the way I'd come.

His voice sailed through the darkness. "You've never

been subtle, noisy Trite."

I swiveled, but I didn't see him. "I just came to see if you're okay. Good grief, come out of hiding before I fall through this rotted floor trying to find you."

Two hands took my waist and spun me around. I inhaled a mouthful of dusty air, along with pine tree aromas and cool peppermint. Zane's eyes practically glowed in the dark. A new Patrol staff leaned against the wall with a raven-black jacket draped over the hook.

"Why did you follow me?" he asked.

I shrugged, and his mouth tipped down at the corners. "I was worried something was bothering you."

"And you think it's your job to worry about me?"

"Zane," I sighed, "I've been annoying since the day we met, and you still worried about me. Maybe I *want* to worry about you too." I rubbed the dust particles from my eyes. "Are you okay? Because you're lurking through the dark like a bat—"

Zane's thumb came against my bottom lip, stilling my words. He stared, and the beat changed in my chest. He dipped toward me and put his warm lips against mine, taking my waist and gently holding me against him, robbing me of the ability to breathe until he eased away, keeping his hands where they were.

It was an eternity of feelings, yet too short of a moment.

Zane stared at my mouth a second longer. "I owed you at least that," he said quietly. "For what Cheat did at your grandmother's funeral. And because I promised you I'd kiss you when I knew you wanted me to."

I took a deep breath to steady my thudding heart.

When he dropped his hands back to his sides, his warmth

left. "But that's the last time. I wanted to pay my dues before things get worse."

I had to deduce whether I was hearing him clearly. "Your *dues*?" I folded my arms. "What's gotten into you?"

Zane looked at the floor. "There are consequences for me doing a thing of that sort, Trite. And I'll be dead before I'm caught muddling up the heart of the last Carrier of Truth at a time like this."

I shook the haze from my mind, and I laughed. "And you said I was wishy-washy."

He hardened his jaw. "I'm a Patrolman, and it's my duty to protect you. Nothing more. You need to remember that," he stated. "We need to stop letting things turn backwards. I know I've let things go too far with you."

I slammed my mouth shut and cleared my throat. "I didn't expect anything more from you." My toes curled in my wet shoes. "I know there's a lot at stake. Zane, I only just got my memories back. It's not like I want to run off to get married in the middle of this dark factory basement..." I looked off as a blush hit my cheeks, wishing I hadn't said that out loud.

His eyes were pointed when I looked back, and I wanted to sink into the floor.

"Sorry, that was a stupid joke." His continued silence only made me talk more. "Can you just forget I said that?" I muttered. And then, when the quiet was practically strangling me to death, I added, "I don't even know if you're my type."

I winced.

I was glad it was dark because I knew I was beet-red.

Why was he still staring?

I clapped my hands in front of me. "Okay, well, I'm going to go navigate these halls and see if I can find my way back without getting lost." I moved to swerve around him, but his arm came across my stomach, and he pulled me back to where I had been. I couldn't look at his face.

He tapped the necklace at my throat. "Trite, I'll say it again. My *only* focus is on protecting you and this orb. Nothing more."

"Good," I agreed.

"Good."

Zane took my hand to guide me out of the labyrinth of halls, picking up the Patrol staff and jacket on his way.

I followed without another word and tried to settle the chugging of my pulse that had started the moment he'd looked at my mouth.

THE FOURTH INTERRUPTION

A Week or Three Ago

The haze clouding the Scarlet City had thickened since Cane had seen it last. He tugged the claret hood down further o'er his eyes, lest his mahogany sheen be spotted, and he pressed his princely back against a cook-house emitting spirals of white smoke. There he peered through the mist, watching.

At a registration table in the city's middle circle, Sullen Sprit-Spellborrow waved the next folk forward. A poorly dressed sputtlepun approached and offered a shallow bow to the renowned ink whipper.

"Pen your name here," Sullen directed with a flicker in his yellow eyes, barely visible beneath the darkened skies above that had not allowed even a speck of light to reach the kingdom in days.

The folk leaned to scribble on a glistening page. Halfway through, a stamp came down on his hand and he jumped. Lifting his pale arm, the sputtlepun studied the black crescent moon marking his flesh. Sullen pointed to a Ruby Legion training house nearby where a good measure of folk waited, and the sputtlepun turned to go. Cane slipped from his spot to follow.

Through the crowds waiting in line he weaved, his gaze set on the sputtlepun until a startled cry sounded to his left, and Cane glanced to a tetrad of horrid-faced creatures in torn burgundy robes drifting through the folk with low whispers. Red Kingdom dwellers rushed out of their path, appearing pale-faced and sickened. Cane picked up his pace, anger warming his blood at the sight of such detestable things in a street once beautiful and proud.

"What have you let into this kingdom, Forrester?" he muttered beneath his breath.

The sputtlepun reached the training house and Cane crept through the gate after him before it closed. There, the once-prince rounded the building to avoid being drawn into the front entrance with the others. He kept his head high like he belonged, but once in the shadow of a thin spruce, he ducked and crawled to a low-set window.

'Twas so dark inside, only vague shapes could be distinguished. But as Cane's eyes adjusted, he saw an elf with a crescent moon stamp being led to a black curtain. Once the creature stepped behind it, a shrill cry escaped, and Cane's skin tightened. Black smoke seeped from beneath the fabric as Cane waited.

And waited.

And *waited…*

The curtain was torn back and out came the elf. Cane scrambled back in horror as the creature's eyes flickered with black ink, his head twitching to the side as though he were adjusting. With freshly tousled hair, the elf straightened himself and marched from the room.

The next folk came in—the sputtlepun Cane had seen register at the table. But Cane could not watch; he scrambled backward. His chest rose and fell, but he forced himself to brush the snow from his knees and keep moving.

"Kingsblood," he rasped as he moved for the gate and climbed it to escape. He hopped o'er the metal spokes and landed in the busy street, hands trembling. He stopped only when he reached a pearl lamppost upon which a notice was pegged. He was so sickened; he tore it down after reading only the first few lines:

Official Summons of the Crimson Court
For: The Folk and Foes of Winter,

I invite you to join the ranks of the Ruby Legion.
I shall accept every folk regardless of status, history, or criminal record.
All who wear a crimson cape shall be equals.
Honour and glory and power await those who register at the Hall of Knowledge in the—

Cane crumpled the paper in his hands, wishing he could crumple Forrester as easily.

For glory, honour, and power awaited no one.

All who signed up were being deceived.

Presently…

A great distraction.

At first, Cane had wondered how in all of Winter he might grant Driar's request.

He looked 'round the city for the place that would suit him best, and when he spotted the great monument of the witch who had hunted down Carriers of Truth for many seasons, a satisfied smile found the once-prince's face.

To that statue he went, passing a sign of tribute to the late First Prince Tegan where ribbons and presents were stacked like bricks. Folk lit candles; some even hummed low songs of sadness. Cane spared the sign a glance on his way, noticing the whispering monsters in burgundy cloaks passing by, making the mourning folk cringe and duck their heads.

When he reached the statue, Cane studied Mara Rouge's stone eyes glowering down upon the city. Collections of flowered wreaths and garland rested at the base, left there by Red Kingdom dwellers who had adored her. Cane removed the floral offerings with one great swipe, and the buds tumbled onto the obsidian city streets.

"What is that fool doing?" someone nattered as Cane climbed onto the statue's base, dragging his muddy boots o'er the witch's sabatons.

"Folk of the greatest kingdom in Winter!" he called, and when enough city folk had turned, Cane pulled down his hood, instigating cries of alarm and pointed fingers. "I come with bad tidings. This kingdom is on the verge of destruction as my once-brother, Forrester, is a pinch away from ascending to the Crimson throne. But take heart!" He paused to wink at a nearby lady and she blushed. "For I see that ring-hungry whipsteamer for what he truly is: a coward who has killed the true heir in secret rather than facing him properly in a Quarrel of Heirs. And now he is tricking you into joining his army! Resist him and his whispering monsters if you do not wish to be turned into a monster yourself!"

Gasps and murmurs rumbled through the crowd, and more folk gathered until Cane could no longer count the measure of them.

"Arrest him!" A Ruby Legionnaire tried to push through, but the folk were too congested in the street.

Cane flashed his lovely, princely smile; the one that had once won these folk over and caused his name to be spoken with fondness. "This is why I have aligned myself with the Queen of the Pines in an effort to overtoss Prince Forrester. Spread the merry news if you can. I'm calling upon my brother to come meet me in battle at the border. I shall fight for this kingdom since he will not!"

As the Ruby Legion shoved through the bodies of elves, folk, and Greed, Cane fluttered 'round the statue's base and vanished into the throng that had gathered at the other side. He tugged his hood up, moving faster than the undecided consciences of those who had heard his speech.

A pinch and a dip and a palace away…

THE PEBBLE PAPER

AS THE QUARTER OF MOURNING FOR OUR BELOVED PRINCE TEGAN COMES TO AN END, THE CRIMSON COURT WISHES TO THANK THOSE WHO HAVE DELIVERED GIFTS TO THE PALACE FOR THE CRIMSON FAMILY DURING THIS DIFFICULT TIME. WE ARE CONTINUING TO HUNT DOWN THE RADICAL BELIEVERS OF THE OLD TRUTHS RESPONSIBLE FOR BREAKING INTO THE PALACE AND TURNING PRINCE TEGAN TO SNOW. PUNISHMENT AWAITS THE MURDERERS.

IN OTHER NEWS, THE CRIMSON COURT MEANS TO DEDICATE THESE NEXT QUARTERS TO INVESTIGATING THE TRAGIC AND MYSTERIOUS DEATH OF THE POLAR KING IN POLAR TERRITORY THIS SEASON PAST. IF ANYONE HAS ANY INFORMATION ON THE STRANGE OCCURANCES IN THE NORTH, PLEASE DO NOT HESITATE TO BRING YOUR FINDINGS TO THE COURT. BUT ABOVE ALL, DO NOT TRUST THE BELIEVERS. THE COURT HAS REASON TO BELIEVE THEY ARE BEHIND THE FLOODING OF THE POLAR KING'S PALACE WHICH ULTIMATELY LEAD TO HIS UNTIMELY DEATH.

AND FOR THE LAST OF THIS MORN'S NEWS:

THE CRIMSON QUEEN IS ENJOYING HER VACATION AND DOES NOT PLAN TO RETURN THIS QUARTER, DESPITE THE FACT THAT OUR DEAR FIRST PRINCE HAS BEEN RETURNED TO THE SNOW AND THE CRIMSON KING REMAINS ILL—

An ivory-haired prince in a crimson cape glided past a tetrad of stained-glass windows that cast shapes of red onto his pale skin. He moved as smoothly as the wind, sailing into a dark room.

Youthful Prince Driar watched his oldest living brother enter their father's bedchambers. He stuffed the Pebble Paper into his book and slapped it shut as he followed, creeping down the hall until he stood outside.

"Out." Forrester's cold word came through the dark, and a palace attendant shuffled from the room with a wobbling tea tray in her fingers, paying Driar no attention.

"Son." The Crimson King's airy voice crackled as deeply as the fireplace inside. "What have you come to tell me?"

Driar heard Forrester's light palace slippers pacing over the tile floors. "Cane has returned to the Scarlet City."

A rough cough and a creaking of bedsprings filled the room. "What?"

Driar squeezed the bookmark in his hand. He moved to leave, certain he would be turned to snow if he was caught listening. But Forrester's next words stopped him.

"I have a way to trap him. Fear not, Father."

"What are you brewing?" the Crimson King asked.

"I'm going after what he treasures most in all of Winter. And I will steal it from him."

Driar inhaled as he left. He trudged on padded slippers to the stairs and descended toward the theatre. When he entered, he caught the unusual fragrance of fish. He stopped behind a chair and leaned his palms against it, flexing the muscles he hid away beneath the loose sleeves of his robe.

He started when a pecan-haired woman in the back row turned her head. A flit of dread filled Driar's stomach at the sight of her pure-white eyes. Her cherry-red lips curled up.

"Would you like to see the future, Prince?" she invited in a cat's-purr voice.

"N…" he swallowed. "No, thank you. Do you happen to know if the magician has returned yet? I'd very much like to fill my head with some senseless entertainment." Driar clutched his book to himself, and the bookmark slipped from his hand. He rushed to scoop it up and wiped a bead of sweat from his brow.

"Is there something on your mind you wish to forget for an hour or three?" the prophetess guessed.

Driar's knuckles turned white 'round his book.

Suddenly, the woman laughed. It was loud and wild, and it echoed through the empty theatre.

"That bloody magician has been avoiding me this entire quarter past. I do not think he's coming back. But I would be happy to entertain you, Prince. I can sing a merry tune if forced," she cooed.

Driar's mouth dried. "Uh…well…no, thank you." He stooped into a bow of farewell, then felt foolish for bowing at a woman who could not see it. "Pardon me. I'll be off, then."

Though her eyes were white and void, Driar could not help but feel her gaze on his back as he left.

CHAPTER, THE FIFTH

Nighttime consisted of people spreading out on knit blankets in the rooms down the hall. I could hear echoes of snores and quiet chatter as the dwarves drifted to sleep. The windowless basement didn't distinguish between night and day, so my perception of time was lost to the constant darkness.

Beside me, Kaley stared at the ceiling.

"You can't turn it off?" She glanced at my wrists.

"No." I raised my hands where gold and silver columns of text ran along my fingers like rippling underwater patterns. "I don't get it. I spent over a year wanting these words to show up when I needed them, and now I can't get them to leave."

Kaley scrubbed her eyes. "I can't fall asleep. It's like having a light turned on beside my face."

I stuffed my hands beneath the blanket, but cracks of

light spilled through the holes in the knit pattern. Kaley laughed.

Two empty teacups rested between us. We'd drunk ourselves warm as we listened to the others chat over tea in their rooms.

"I've never seen them like this," I said.

Kaley was quiet for a moment, but she rolled over to face me. "The tea helped."

I smiled weakly. "Not enough."

Buzzing energy trickled over my arms, sailing over my shoulder and up my neck to my ear. Kaley sighed and flopped onto her back. "They're getting brighter," she said. "Anyway, you should try to get some sleep. We'll figure out what to do tomorrow."

I nestled in and closed my eyes, but she spoke again a moment later. "You understand why I did it, right? You know why I asked Elowin to take away your memories for a little while?"

"You don't have to explain. I think Elowin was preparing me for the ending. I think he knew what I needed, and that was to be sidelined for a while so that I'd have the strength to come back into the fight when it mattered." My fingers drummed against my stomach as I thought about Porethius's broken wings and Apple's washed-out appearance, both of whom had been fighting since I left.

After a few minutes of silence, my sister's eyes slid closed. Her breathing turned heavy, and a quiet snore left her lips. My gaze stayed on the ceiling where I imagined constellations of sparkling Winter stars above the factory. I imagined dunes of snow, broken villages, and forests crumbling to ash by their branches. I imagined beating hearts past all of it, and believers who were barely hanging on to the last shard of hope they had left.

When I lifted my hand, the symbols flickered like Porethius's tattoos always had until they'd paled into the dull marks I'd seen on her today. I wondered if that was what could happen to a person's light if they hid it under a bushel for too long. Or, in a dark basement.

My light wanted to get out.

"Elowin," I whispered into the dark. Kaley didn't stir, so I lifted my arm to talk to the symbols, somehow sure the Truth in my veins could hear. "What am I supposed to do?"

I started when a tingling sensation flooded my wrist. My light grew brighter, and Kaley did stir this time. I quickly tossed the blanket over myself and peered at my wrist where the glow was the hottest.

Within the light, a word formed. I squinted to read it as the glow dimmed and left me with an inked word like a tattoo. I scrubbed it with my thumb, but it didn't smear. It didn't go away when the rest of my symbols faded either.

I sat up and flung off my blanket, staring down at the word in plain English that had marked itself down my wrist:

HOPEBRINGER

Hopebringer.

It went through my head a dozen more times. It was a new word—one that by the English language wasn't a true word, but maybe it was a true word for me. And suddenly I knew why Elowin hadn't come back to Winter yet.

My gaze fired up to the dark hallway. Winter was waiting for me to do something. The believers were waiting for *me*—even Porethius had seen it.

I tossed the knit off and draped it over my sister whose dark hair splayed across the cold floor, her deep lashes fluttering with dreams. "I'll be right back," I promised.

I was relieved my dress shoes had finally dried and stopped squeaking as I passed closet-sized rooms full of dwarves huddled together in slumber. I came out to the empty gathering room. At least, I thought it was empty until a large, dark-skinned being with golden eyes shifted in his chair.

"The hour is late." Gathadriel's voice was low. "And you're still up."

I paused and scratched my ear. "So are you."

"I'm keeping watch."

I nodded. Light returned to my fingers, and I pulled them into fists. "I'm going to go get the Patrol back." There was no sense in hiding it—as a fairy, he could probably sniff it on me. "And the believers," I added.

Gathadriel didn't react. His golden eyes dropped to my wrists though. "And what of your Patrolman?" he asked.

"I don't need him for this." My own confidence surprised me, and I fought the impulse to look toward the hall. Maybe I should have woken Zane up. I thought of the snow serpent I'd turned to ice in the street.

The fairy leaned back and folded his muscular arms. The silence dragged on, letting me feel the coldness of the basement all over again.

"I can see them, you know," I said as my fingers ran over the bumps on my arms. "I can see the believers' hearts fading." A small part of me felt foolish for admitting it, but Gathadriel's expression remained unfazed.

"What of the Night Beast? What will you do when you cross him?" he asked.

My symbol-columns cast faint hues of silver on the walls before sinking back and leaving us in darkness again. This was the moment I was supposed to break down and tremble. But I looked at Gathadriel in earnest. "I'm not afraid of him." The words quickened my pulse.

I headed across the room and took off my sweater, replacing it with Lucas's Patrol jacket that had been hanging up to dry. My eyes fell on the staff sitting along the wall beside it.

"You *should* be afraid, Carrier." His voice was a low rumble in the dark. But I turned to Gathadriel one last time, locking onto his golden irises.

"No. I *shouldn't* be. Can't you see that?"

His face changed.

"We need a win right now." I glanced back at the dark hall. "Tell the others if you have to. But enough is enough. I'm getting our people back."

No one was guarding the window when I made my way back to the hidden basement entrance. I began rifling through the closets until I found warm raven-black pants to change into and ribbon-laced, curled-toe boots. A smile threatened my mouth as I kicked off my dress shoes and slid my feet into the fur lining. The contraption of belts I'd found should have confused me, but I'd seen Zane put his on enough times to know where my arms were supposed to go. I buttoned up Lucas's jacket the rest of the way to my throat and picked up the Patrol staff I'd leaned on the wall.

The window wasn't locked, so I slipped out in silence.

The blueish glow of the snow tunnel was brighter than the basement had been, even under a hazy midnight sky. I appreciated the warm boots as I met the frigid Winter wind at the end of the tunnel. Diamond stars struggled to peek through the grey coils of cloud. I placed the Patrol staff in front of me and jammed the end of it into the ground.

It threw me forward so fast, I shrieked and scrambled to catch my feet before my whole body plummeted into the snow.

"Sweet mother of pearl…" I brushed the flakes from my face and tugged my hood up to keep the snow out of my ears before I tried again. This time I did it slower, and when I balanced myself well enough, I managed to glide over the next few hills. A laugh boiled in my stomach.

I fell again a minute later.

After an hour I stopped to take a break, heaving for oxygen and tugging at my wild hair sticking out from the hood. I looked ahead to the hundreds of hills before me. The trek to the Red Kingdom seemed further than before, but I climbed to my feet and dragged the Patrol staff off the ground.

An earth-rumbling thud made me scream. I reeled backward into a tree, swinging the staff and catching a branch above my head. I blinked up at the marble-statue figure standing in the breeze. The fairy stepped into the moonlight.

"It'll be faster if we fly," Gathadriel said. His large hand came out, his tattoos like glowing embers in the night.

I pushed myself off the tree to stand. Without a word, I latched the Patrol staff onto the contraption on my back, and I took his hand.

We were skyborne in a heartbeat.

AN INTERRUPTION

A heavy shade of dark thickened the air within the great cave and in the winding tunnels of the cliff. Seasons of lost souls cried from the darkness, beckoning Nicholas Saint to join them in a luring trap. The once-jester of the Crimson Court closed his eyes, wishing to plug his nose against the stench of decaying dreams and crushed spirits. He did not dare try the nose-plugging, however. Not in front of…

No, no, no, no, no, no, no.

He could not whisper that dreadful name, not even in his mind.

When the scent of burnt hair filled his nostrils, Nicholas bit his lip to stifle a grimace. He heard Asteroth's slow steps as he passed by, but the old prophet did not finish his passing. Nicholas was tempted to peek an eye open to see if Asteroth was still there, but that wild smell of singed hair and sacrifice had not yet left.

"You're asleep." The once-prophet's tangled voice crept into Nicholas's ears.

"Just resting my eyes. It's rather bright in here, wouldn't you say?"

'Twas only silence that responded. So, Nicholas peeled his eyes open, but kept them on Asteroth's hollow gaze, fighting every temptation to look 'round the room so he would not happen to spot…

No, no, no, no, no, no, *no*.

Asteroth showed no amusement. When the once-prophet tilted his head, Nicholas felt a crawly or three skitter up his spine.

"If only the rest of these creatures enjoyed sage tea," he offered in another untimely jest.

Truthfully, he could go for a decent pie too.

Asteroth removed his dark gaze from Nicholas. The prophet continued journeying into the shadow to meet with…

"Ragnashuck," Nicholas swore, certain he would utter that name in his mind before the eve was through. What a complicated game this was. Closing his eyes a time again, he hummed a whispered poem to himself to pass the seconds:

"'Twas the eve before darkness, when all through the house,
Not a creature lingered, not even a spouse.
A child's stockings were hung by the fire alone,

In hopes that Nicholas Saint soon would come home.
The child was snuggled deep in her bed,
While dreams of sugar and tea danced 'round in her head.
But when she would wake, she would learn of the fright,
So…merry evening to her, and to her a good, blessed night…"

Screeches erupted, and Nicholas's eyes snapped open to a shifting light in a nearby tunnel. The shrieks grew louder, and the witch's great black dogs snapped their teeth from the corner.

Coal-black mist shuddered in the cave's creases, inching downward to flood the cave and turn the floor into an obsidian lake. Nicholas felt the thud of panic arrive in the side of his neck. He slapped his hand against it, holding his throat as he stared wildly at the tunnel where the light was rounding a bend. He backed up until his rear hit the cave wall. The creatures 'round him shuffled toward the disruption until light burst into the cave and creatures covered their unadjusted eyes.

Nicholas blinked at a tall being with hills of muscles, dark skin, and the old power of the ancients.

What in all of Winter was a war fairy doing down here?

Tremors brushed o'er Gathadriel's spirit as he grew conflicted in the presence of such wickedness. In the shadows, dogs snarled along with a hundred plus a hundred more creatures of evil gnashing their teeth. Looking upon them, the fairy reached for the dual-bladed weapon at his back.

Beings recoiled, slithering backward as he drew his sword. Others rushed for him with violent screeches.

'Twas a swift show of bloodshed and snowshed, and the voices of a thousand creatures more lifted from the tunnels and crannies where they watched. Hunger crept into the cave, and Gathadriel's golden eyes darted from one being to the next until he spotted a diamond-white-haired false prophet gliding o'er the floor with a red spark on his staff.

Gathadriel straightened as the creatures scuttled away. "Tell your master to face me himself." The command boomed through the cave, silencing the growls.

Asteroth Ryuu stared. When he spoke, the voice was low and beastly, so much so that Gathadriel hardly recognized it. "Bow to me, old brother, and I shall give you back all you've lost." Whispers and shouts of lost friends filled the fairy's ears. Gathadriel's wings bristled, his tattoos burning o'er his flesh as he shook away the temptation before it took root.

Black cloud sprang from the floor and pressed in around him. Gathadriel's bearings wobbled, and he spun just as Asteroth burst through the blackness with a red flame. Gathadriel lifted his sword; the clash created a thunderous boom down the tunnels.

"Jolly Cheat," the voice of both prophet and Beast called, and the clouds whisked away to reveal a nickel-eyed folk in a jester's hat at the back of the room. Asteroth stepped aside as his flesh greyed in patches. "Kill the fairy or be turned to snow," the prophet instructed.

Gathadriel watched Jolly Cheat's hands tighten on the staff at his side. "Ragnashuck," the jester grumbled, dragging himself forward. "I can't beat a war fairy," he said, coming to the middle of the cave. The Court jester settled his ferocious eyes on Gathadriel and aimed his staff. "But I will try. I do have a thing or three to live for, after all." The last part rang in Gathadriel's ears. He twisted the sword in his grip.

With a gaze 'round the cave, Gathadriel called, "Meet me yourself, Night Beast! Will you hide while I turn each of your servants to snow?"

Cold wind rippled across the floor. Jolly Cheat's eyes rounded, and he spun, turning his back to the carved archway where evil appeared in its true form. But Gathadriel did not glance away. He looked upon his fate, knuckles white 'round the handle of his blade, and he swallowed.

A glimmer slid o'er the arch of a metal helmet in the rippling black haze; a warped reflection of Gathadriel's light. But it disappeared as the clouds in the room thickened, and Gathadriel lowered his sword when he could no longer detect where Nightflesh was.

From the cave's edge, Asteroth's neck snapped to the side, his face darkening. "There's been a shift in the atmosphere!" He lifted a set of pure black eyes to Gathadriel. "He's a distraction. Someone came here with him."

Gathadriel's flesh tightened; he stole a look back toward the tunnel.

"Let all see and know." A low, beastly voice seeped from every direction, and a single drop of moisture fell onto Gathadriel's wrist from the shadows above. The fairy lifted his arm to study it, brows tilting in. The black speck looked like paint, but it *sizzled*. His thudding heart sank.

Poison.

The fairy closed his mouth, accepting his fate. A flood of black ink spilled from above, consuming his body and stealing his breath. With his last heartbeat, the fairy hurtled his weapon toward the tunnel where it spun ‘round the bend, chasing the wind like a bird in flight. There, Gathadriel submitted to his end, his body tumbling to snow.

The poison smothered the fairy’s pure white ashes, his snowflakes dissolving into black pools, as the voice of Nightflesh uttered from the darkness, “Turn the believers to snow.”

CHAPTER, THE SIXTH

The Dungeon of Souls brought back nightmares. Thick mist curled off the walls, suffocating me with the smell of smoke as I moved through the tunnels, trying to remember which way was which. I paused to cough and catch my breath before I made the last turn to where the Patrols were imprisoned.

I waited and listened, but I couldn't hear them. Why wasn't a single person making noise?

I rounded the corner with my hand raised, ready to melt their ice prisons, but I stopped short at the sight of still bodies sprawled over the floor. A well of terror sprang into my chest.

"No…" No, they couldn't really be—

"Trite?"

One of them shifted. A mop of chopped fuchsia hair appeared at the bars of a cell.

Timblewon.

My hand shook, my symbols flickering in and out. I opened my mouth to tell him I was there to rescue him when the hall filled with whispers, and bumps formed on my skin.

"Wake up!" Timblewon shouted, and the rest of the bodies in raven-black stirred.

Frizzy hair appeared at the bars of the cell beside me, and I started, barely recognizing Wanda. She stared like she thought I was a delusion.

The curtain at the end of the tunnel shook, and I flattened my palm toward the dozens of feastbeggars brushing through. All too quickly, I realized there was no snow in the tunnel for me to use in my defense like I'd done with the serpentine snowsquatch before. My gaze flickered to the ice of the cages, but I didn't know how to make ice obey.

"Wanda—"

Her name barely left my lips when the feastbeggars rushed, thrusting me to the floor. My vision was blocked by burgundy cloaks and snapping teeth. They tried to pry the Patrol staff from my grip, but I screeched and clung to it with all my strength.

Patrolmen began shouting; Wanda screamed from my right.

Claws scratched my skin.

The Patrol staff broke free from my fingers.

But a low swishing sounded below the chaos, and I opened my eyes as something silver spun into the hoard like a boomerang, ripping them off me. A dual-bladed sword clattered over the floor. I grabbed the Patrol staff and hurled it toward Wanda's cell. I saw it land at her feet before the feastbeggars lunged again and I was smothered in robes.

Popping ice sounded. And a female screech.

A Patrol staff plunged through the hoard, and I gasped as fresh air hit my face. Wanda drove the staff into a feastbeggar's gut, and I scrambled backward, clutching my throat. Tattered fabric hung off me, and cuts burned through what was left of my Patrol jacket. I rasped as I inhaled and looked for the dual-bladed sword. A Patrolman was straining to try and reach it through the bars of his cell.

Wanda was thrown against a cage, but a pair of thick hands reached around her and took the Patrol staff. The spindles of ice at Wanda's back shattered, and Mirkra stepped through, catching Wanda before she fell. He swung the staff at a feastbeggar, sending the creature across the hall where Patrolmen reached through the bars to grab it, trap it there, and finish it off.

I lifted the silver sword from the floor and smashed it against the spindles of the nearest cage. The ice chipped, but it didn't break, so I grabbed the pole with my bare hand and willed it to combust.

It shattered. I blinked.

Patrolmen began squeezing through the gap as I turned and swung at a feastbeggar, nearly tipping off my feet from the sword's weight.

The tunnel floor shook, and every being stopped moving. I put my arms out to steady myself and looked up at Wanda whose bug-eyes drifted to the tunnel I'd come through. It felt like an army of footsteps thundering over the ground.

The feastbeggars slinked away, crawling behind their curtain to make way for what was coming.

"Go!" A Patrolman from the back shouted.

But I reached for the bars of the next cage where a Rime

woman blinked up at me. A young boy was beside her. Across the hall, Mirkra blasted another set of ice spindles, and two more Patrols tumbled out of their cage—Timblewon being one of them.

"Go!" the Patrolman at the back shouted again, and this time, a chorus of voices screamed the word alongside him—Patrols and believers alike. "Go! Go! Go!"

But how could I leave them?

I moved to the next cell and freed another family. Then to the next one, and the next, ignoring the screams of protest from the cage at the back that told me to leave. Mirkra followed on the other side, dissolving the icy spindles with the Patrol staff.

"There's no time left, Trite!" Timblewon's arm came around me, and I stumbled backward as he tugged me through the sprawled feastbeggar bodies.

A limb of black mist burst into the tunnel, blocking those in the last cage from our view. Those in the back continued yelling, "Go! Run! Go!" Tears glistened in Mirkra's eyes as he turned to follow us, racing out of reach of the black mist. It burst after him, flooding the back cell at the same time, and silencing those who yelled.

Timblewon thrust me into a hallway. As soon as Mirkra rounded the corner behind us, the mist lunged into the tunnel as well, scurrying up the walls and racing ahead to cut us off. Wanda shoved through a door, and my symbols ignited. I didn't know what I was doing when I raised my hands, and a thick wall of ice formed up the hall, trapping the mist behind it. No one stopped to question it; everyone rushed through the door and came out to the gaping arch of the reindeer landing entrance.

Mirkra tossed the Patrol staff to Wanda, who leapt from the platform and landed on a jut of the cliff, thrusting the foot of the staff into the snow. Crackling filled the ravine as a bridge of ice formed, so thin I could see the dark pit through it. I slid over the ledge and landed beside her, looking into the deep, dark ravine.

Wanda released quiet sobs as she led the way across. The others slid down to follow, but I stayed behind, keeping my eyes on the entrance, certain something would follow.

I counted twenty-five Patrolmen.

Twelve believers.

Such a small number crossed the bridge to safety. Everyone else had already been gone before I got there, or had been left in that last cage…

I swallowed as I followed the group, realizing Timblewon had picked someone up and was carrying him over his shoulder. The young boy's light hair swayed in the wind, and I recognized Kilen. His thin arms dangled down Timblewon's back. In front of them, the Rime woman and the little boy rushed over the ice.

My arms and legs burned with cuts from the feastbeggars' claws, and my chest swelled as I realized I wouldn't have survived if I'd gone into the Dungeon of Souls alone.

I looked down at the dual-bladed sword in my hands.

"Thank you, Gathadriel," I whispered to the wind, feeling his sacrifice so deeply in my soul that it took everything inside of me not to burst into tears. I'd expected him to meet me at the cages, but only his sword had made it.

Only a sliver of the pink and fire-orange sunrise had broken through the muddy grey clouds shadowing Winter. We'd been forced to stop a few times so the weakest bodies could rest. I glanced over my shoulder every few minutes.

"Is there anything to eat, Trite?" Kilen's high, scratchy voice reached me, and I spun in relief to see him awake.

"I'm sure Apple will make whatever she has at the factory." I tried to smile, but I'd never seen a boy with such sunken eyes. He looked slightly grey against the white landscape.

"I can't wait to eat chocolate." When Kilen surprised me with a dull smile, all of Winter seemed to light up around him. I patted his shoulder.

Wanda hadn't said much on the walk, but she sat down beside Kilen and used the Patrol staff to lift the snow into the shapes of birds and elephants. Kilen leaned his head against her shoulder to watch. A moment later, he was asleep again and Wanda reached around him to pin the buttons of his jacket together at his chest. When her large eyes lifted to me, I was surprised to find no blame on her still-stricken face.

"Thank you," she whispered.

I nodded, but half my heart was still in the dungeon with those I didn't save. And with Gathadriel, who was the one she should be thanking.

A low frequency slipped over the hills at our backs, and my hand tightened around the dual-bladed sword. When I saw what was coming, I grabbed Kilen's collar to shake him awake.

"Everybody, run!" I shouted over the group that was in no condition to fight. The Patrolmen followed my gaze, their weary eyes dulling as they locked onto the crackling red flames snapping around the long red coat gliding over the hills.

"I should stay—"

"Don't stay. Get them home, Wanda." I pushed up my sleeves to show the glowing symbols on my wrists, and I stole a glance at the word tattooed on my arm.

Hopebringer.

I took a deep breath.

Wanda opened her mouth like she planned to object, but when her eyes settled on my glittering arms, she turned to the others and began shouting raspy orders.

I didn't watch them go; I focused on Asteroth Ryuu's black eyes as he approached. The last time Asteroth Ryuu had come for me in the burning library, I'd run away. And I had kept running for all these years.

My fingers twitched, fiddled, clenched. Nausea pinched my stomach, but I dug my heels in and lifted Gathadriel's sword.

The hills quivered, and a hundred Greed crawled over the shallow dunes on all fours. The hoard rose to their feet with long bows, and my eyes widened when I realized they weren't aiming for me.

The sword dropped from my fingers, and my hands whipped out at my sides. The snow sprang to life, spiralling into two pillars of ice on my right and left. The Greed fired their arrows across the sky, but they smashed into the pillars and grains of ice tumbled down. I gritted my teeth and pushed all the energy I had into growing the shield to protect those racing away.

The Greed lowered their bows. Their violet eyes turned

up toward the height of the enormous ice towers thickening like tree trunks. The ice pressed in against my shoulders, but I waited, forcing the trunks wider. When it felt like the pillars were going to snap my bones, I let go and tumbled out of the gap, landing on my knees in the snow. I whipped my head around to see, and a beat of triumph moved through me to find that the Greed's arrows would never find their way through the narrow slit I'd left.

Red fire snapped over my fingers and I shrieked, tearing my hand back. Asteroth Ryuu appeared before me, and I reeled backward, smacking up a measly puff of snow from the ground that bounced off his coat. His thin fingers whipped out and caught my neck, and I gasped as he lifted me from the snow by my throat.

I reached for the snow anywhere, *everywhere*, slapping only tiny beads against his cheek with what I managed to muster. Asteroth didn't move a muscle apart from tightening his grip. I flung my hand toward the mountain in the distance, and I tried with all my might to bring the snow down upon him.

But a cruel, unnatural smile formed across his face.

"Shall I show you how it's done, Carrier?" My gaze shot back to him in surprise—I didn't hear the beastly tone in his voice this time.

Suddenly the ground trembled, and the mountain cracked above us. Asteroth threw me into the snow as half the cliffside unclipped from the mountain and came tumbling down in an avalanche. The waves thrust in every direction, and when I tried to stand, Asteroth shoved me down again with his boot and held me there as the river of snow and ice channelled over me.

I thrashed below the snow. My body slid from beneath his heel, and I tumbled right, then left, then up, then down; until I was *falling*…

A hand snatched me from the air, and I went to scream, but a hat was stuffed against my mouth. I released a deep, tear-filled moan instead, biting down on fabric.

"Shhhh. Hush now, sweetheart. Do you *want* him to find you?"

I stilled. That voice wasn't Asteroth's.

My scathed eyes focused on a pair of curled-toe boots and a black and red coat hem. The subtle tinkling of bells mixed with the scent of sage, and I lifted my gaze to where Jolly Cheat stood over me with kohl-painted eyes.

"My, my, my. Look at the trouble you've found yourself in," he said dryly.

I looked around and pain shot through my neck. Jolly nodded upward, and I turned to see that we were tucked behind a high hill. I could hear the Greed scurrying on the other side.

Jolly held a finger against his lips to hush me as he took his hat back and slid it onto his head.

"I thought you'd abandoned Winter," I whispered, lightly touching my swelling throat. All the cuts from the feastbeggars began to burn, and my knees shook. I was sure I would faint.

"Well, we all do what we must." Jolly wasn't smiling. "And on that note…Alas," he sighed. "I've been sent to kill you, I'm afraid."

My jaw tightened. "Try it."

Hot pain lifted in my eyes, but I didn't blink. My trembling fingers uncurled, aiming for the snow I wanted to use to send this clown flying over the hill. But Jolly Cheat didn't make a move.

"Try it," I said again, and a sob slipped out. One of my legs buckled, and I dropped to one knee.

"I assure you, I will," he promised. "But I need you to live for another eve or three. There is no one else to face that *Beast*, I'm afraid."

I glared at the madman that had just been at my grandmother's funeral in plain Trite clothes.

Jolly smiled down at me, wide and ridiculous. "Of course, taking you to him now would just get your timestring snuffed out in your condition. And I can't have that."

"You really are mad," I muttered.

Jolly inhaled a deep breath. "Truly. Irreversibly. Consumingly," he agreed, then tilted his head. "Attractively?" he tried, and I made a face. So, he went on, "Hurry now, common-blood. You'll have only a pinch to scuttle off after I send Asteroth searching in the wrong direction."

"First tell me why you're doing this." I slumped back in the snow.

"Isn't it obvious?" He raised a brow. "For you. And, well, maybe mostly for me. For you in order for it to be for me."

My dizzy mind found a memory of him dressed in all white, wearing a mask and doing a juggling act at a Red Prince's seasonal birth celebration when I was pretending to be Scarlet Strange.

"Why did you give me that white apple in the orchard outside the palace if you knew who I was? I know what it means to pass someone a fruit here, especially the way you did it."

“Ragnashuck, what a *terrible* time to ask me such a thing.” He glared up the hill where sounds of the Greed drew closer. “I’ve always liked women who surprise me. But don’t get your hopes up, sweetheart. I’m taken now.”

I made a repulsed face.

He scowled in return. “Now, hit me with your fanciest strike before they see us so I can say I tried to stop you from getting away.”

“I’m not doing that.”

His jaw tightened and his silvery eyes narrowed. “Fine. Don’t you *dare* let them kill you before you’ve done your job, you common thing, or…” He began stomping up the hill. “…or I’ll kill you.”

Jolly Cheat broke into a slide and shot over the hill to where I couldn’t see. The air filled with the sound of my own heavy breathing, and I hauled myself to my feet, quieting to listen. When I heard nothing, I dragged up the slope on my knees, collapsing when I reached the top, and I stretched my neck to see over.

By the pillars of ice I’d created, Jolly spoke with Asteroth. I saw Jolly point in the opposite direction of where I was. I shrank back down behind the hill.

Was I imagining things, or had Jolly Cheat just helped me?

I scooted back down the hill and stumbled into a lazy jog in the direction of the factory.

CHAPTER, THE SEVENTH

Earlier this year, I'd expected Grandma to walk out of the hospital and get back to baking blueberry muffins. I wasn't sure why—maybe it was because the old woman's brain never failed her while she was commenting on her favourite soap operas from her hospital bed.

I remembered coming up with the idea to mix butterscotch and lemon to put an extra zing into a whipped-cream-covered coffee concoction I was testing out. I'd spent the afternoon in Aunt Sylvia's kitchen in an apron stained with coffee grinds, squeezing a fresh lemon and spraying whipped cream over my masterpiece.

When I brought it to the café the next morning, Emily had loved it. I worked late that night and tucked the last lemon into the back of the fridge so it wouldn't get used. I'd planned to make one of my new drinks for Grandma in the morning. I would have taken it to her at sunrise if things hadn't gotten so crazy the moment I arrived at the café.

Apparently, Emily had done a feature on our new drink on social media, and customers had lined up down the sidewalk to try it.

Things got so busy that I never had a chance to go see Grandma. It was the next day that David Boram had come into the café, and I'd gone on a late-night date.

It was the morning after that Sylvia had called me.

Looking back, I realized it was Zane who'd carried me into Sylvia's house that day when I learned the news.

It was Zane who had made excuses to show up to Sylvia's house every day after that until the funeral. I hadn't even remembered all that until I saw raven-black and electric blue eyes amidst the shifting hills, and felt his arms slide beneath me to carry me the rest of the way to the factory.

PART II

AN INTERRUPTION

Cane awoke with a pinch of crinky in his back. He grimaced as he untucked himself from the narrow cupboard in the sweets shop's basement. Rolling out from the cabinet, he stretched, offering a snort when the crinky did not go away. He'd have to find a new place to sleep before eve approached; he could not bear to be crumpled into a folk-ball again.

As he sniffed his way through the tables of cloth-covered pastries, he selected a jam-filled stuffy bun, a sugar nugget, and ten plus four poppy pebbles, bowing his thanks toward the upstairs where the baker's light footsteps could be heard through the floor.

It had been a measure since his address to the Red Kingdom dwellers. But he had a merry plan for this glorious morn'. Cane strolled to the closet and flipped through the cleaning supplies, the baking supplies, and…

Yes. There it was.

Carefully drawing out the heavy metal bat—meant for shewing away wild animals and local thieves from the sweets—Cane did not make a peep of noise. He tucked the bat beneath his arm.

Tugging up his hood, he took in a deep, shaky breath and slipped from the back door into the crowds dully pushing past to gather their morning hot drinks. All eyes were cast down to the onyx roads, seemingly worried about what they might spot in the Scarlet City streets if they dared to lift their heads. Cane emerged through drifting puffs from the smoke shop, inhaling that old scent of spruce and cinnamon that carried memories of his boyhood, along with the potent aroma of illness, smoke, and darkness that crept between the buildings.

The once-prince did not stop until he reached that same momentous statue at the city's edge where he had made his first announcement. Gazing up at the solid stone eyes of the witch, Cane stretched his hands, his wrists, his arms.

He wound up and took a swing.

The shattering stone exploded, echoing o'er the streets, and bringing sleighs to a halt on the black roads. Cane struck again, taking out the witch's gauntlet and sending it plunging to the street where it smashed. He climbed the statue's base, staring levelly into those wicked, solid eyes, and he swung to take off her head.

A chorus of screams lifted from the city, and Ruby Legionnaires shoved folk out of the way. Mara Rouge's marble head plummeted from its high perch, shattering against the roadside, causing an eruption of snow and stone.

Cane's chest heaved with exertion as he turned to face his former underlings.

"Let the dead witch stay dead!" he shouted. "And let those who revere the dead witch…" A glint of silver tore Cane's focus from the crowd. A feather fell, and the once-prince reached out to catch it. He turned it over in his fingers, his brows tugging in as he glanced up at the sky, ignoring the gasps in the street.

A white bird with silver wings descended in an arch, and through the haze that lingered o'er the Scarlet City, Cane spotted a tiny scroll of parchment tied to the bird's ankle with string. Dropping the bat into the rubble, he reached to catch the creature with gentleness.

A Ruby Legionnaire shouted at him to come down from the statue as Cane freed the note. He unrolled the paper and read quickly.

A moment later, he lifted his burgundy gaze, his tantalizing merriment falling flat. He rerolled the note and stuffed it into his mouth to swallow it so no other soul might spy its words.

Feeling the colourful hues of his Rime blood sink to ash, he pulled the golden ring from his most important finger and slid it into his pocket. Cane set his jaw and looked upon the Legionnaires who had come to fetch him, seeing their smoky souls, their dark eyes, and their tricked minds.

"Take me, then." The once-prince hopped down from the statue and held out his arms to be tied so he might be dragged back to the home he had run from, all the while thinking of the note with Driar's writing:

Cane,

Forrester has found Scarlet.

The lobby in the Red Kingdom palace came alive as Cane was brought through. Nobles he barely recognized cheered at his capture. Creatures of a different sort were among them too—ones that would never have been allowed in the palace a season ago; black-eyed beings with slithering tongues and misty monsters that belonged below the ground.

Folks in olive-green huntsman clothes and emerald capes watched from where they were trapped behind cage bars. Cane had spent little time noticing the Greens in his early seasons, but he gazed at them now. He wondered if he would meet his fate alongside them in the arena.

The hallways were as white as ever, but the air smelled different; darker, heavier. Instead of glowing sunlight burning through the stained glass, charcoal clouds blanketed the windows, bringing the halls dim. Cane tried not to relive memories of chasing Scarlet down these very halls and tormenting her in them. He tried not to imagine her here at all.

His nerves tumbled when the Ruby Legionnaires opened the doors to the throne room, and the potent smell of torture and decay seeped out.

"Have you truly aligned yourselves with Forrester, the murderer? I may be your only hope at a merry future," Cane tried with the Legionnaires.

But still, they shoved him in.

The throne room was cold and quiet even though it was filled with folk. Down the line of thrones, the Red Princes sat in their proper chairs, apart from one.

Forrester sat on the Crimson King's throne. His ivory hair was neatly pushed to the side, his silver coronet warming the place where the real crown would soon rest.

"How arrogant of you, Brother, to sit there when our father has not yet passed," Cane braved. "Do the rest of you not feel insulted by this?" he asked the younger Red Princes.

Cane's burgundy gaze flickered down the line of his brothers and landed on the other light-featured Red Prince. Driar looked like he might faint; he gripped a book between white fingers, but he did not cast Cane an expression of sympathy or speak up to answer the question.

"Ember?" Cane moved on. "Have you lost your mind too? What if our father were to recover and walk in on such a sight?" He nodded to where Forrester sat.

Prince Ember adjusted himself in his seat, twisting his heart-shaped mouth as he looked away from both Cane *and* Forrester.

"I see. Kingsblood, what a ridiculous bunch you've all become." Cane dared to look directly into Forrester's purple eyes as he said it, and a noble or three 'round the room murmured.

When Forrester rose, his crimson cape slid o'er the armrests of the highest throne in the kingdom. There was a tone in his demeanor that Cane had not seen in this brother before. It muddled Cane's heartbeat, twisting his thoughts as he recognized a dark thing he had once run from.

He straightened himself. "I hear you're hunting for your

former fiancé."

Forrester's cold eyes narrowed. "That I am, Brother. And I know exactly where to find her."

It both pained Cane and quickened his spirit to hear the words. For it confirmed that Forrester did not have Scarlet. *Yet.*

"Perhaps Lady Kissing no longer wishes to be your betrothed. Perhaps that's why she left." There was no jest in Cane's tone. All he could see was the moment Forrester would capture her and discover she belonged to someone else by Winter's rules. He would turn her back into snow. He would do worse things to her first.

But Forrester's thin mouth curled into a cruel smile. "Perhaps we shall duel for her, you and I."

Cane opened his mouth to invite the chance, but he closed it again. He shut his eyes instead, willing the Winter winds to warn Scarlet to run. All Cane could do now was hope and pray that Driar—the flimsy, book-loving sputtlepun whom Cane had never seen touch a sword—would do the miraculous.

"Put him in a cage," Forrester said, his sweet rasp filling the throne room, and Cane felt his arms be taken by two firm, smoke-scented Legionnaire hands.

CHAPTER, THE EIGHTH

Through tired, watery eyes, I watched Zane's teary reunion with his brothers, and I saw Porethius's longing gaze drift toward the Dungeon of Souls we'd left behind. I wanted to tell her what had happened to Gathadriel, but somehow, I think she already knew.

I watched the dwarves race around to pack. The factory grew smaller as we left it behind. I heard Apple say, "It's all right, friend. Sleep now."

As if they just needed permission, my eyes slid shut. Within the folds and hours of deep sleep and quiet, I tasted orange tea and sugary bites placed on my lips. I smelled Apple's hazelnut fragrance.

After a while, I smelled peppermint, and I heard Zane whisper, "I'm bloody relieved you made it back. But, Helen, I don't think you need me anymore."

After that, I dreamt.

It became so dark; I couldn't make out what stood before me. Shadows bled together, mixing like a cauldron of ink. The faint glint of a helmet appeared amidst the darkness, and a dented gauntlet reached from the blackness, its fingers opening toward me. I tried to scramble backward, but it caught me, squeezing my spirit in its grip. White puffed out of my chest like a cloud and burning poison spilled in its place.

I writhed.

My hands flashed up to try and peel his fingers open, but when my knuckle struck the gauntlet, a faint, metallic echo arose. An echo…as though the metal was hollow.

A cry in the distance chilled my blood; I could feel the exact moment a folk lost hope. I jumped when a spark barrelled through the darkness, its light flickering out, and thumped into the being in the shadow. It looked like a spot of flesh patching a body of smoke.

My wide eyes shot up to the darkness where I could see no face. And as soon as they did, his fingers uncoiled, and I was dropped.

I fell forever.

I awoke to the fragrance of pine trees and peppermint, mixed with the smell of herbs and a chemical scent that reminded me of Grandma's hospital room. I blinked at a dark wood ceiling.

Then I tossed off my quilt and stood up.

Soft snoring lifted from the bedside chair. Zane's legs were crossed, his head tilted against the backrest. I didn't mean to stare at his peaceful sleep, but my own dream beat against the inside of my head.

I left him like that. I pushed through a thin door into a hallway lined floor to ceiling with wood beams.

"Porethius?" I rasped.

I didn't know what to expect when I emerged from the hall, but I hadn't expected a wide room of bubbling potions or shelves lined with various liquids in bottles like a wizard's lair. I eyed the bowls of multicoloured powders, the piles of measuring spoons, and the various bunches of herbs drying out on a line of string overhead.

"Hello?" I called.

A large window filled the far wall where bright sunlight spilled onto two white cots. A face appeared through the window; the boy's wild orange hair glowing in the light. I had to sort through my memories to remember it was Apple's cousin, Ginger. But he didn't come in to say hi, he grinned and sped off instead.

"Trite."

I turned to find Zane blinking sleep from his eyes.

"Where are we?"

"We're at the Medicinier's." Zane nodded toward the shelves.

The front door suddenly flew open, and I barely had time to catch Apple as she rushed in. She grabbed my arms, her topaz eyes glossy. "By the sharpest wind!" She fanned her cheeks. "Something dreadful has happened! Scarlet has been taken! I don't know how they found us. She and I were sneaking through the village when twenty plus five Ruby Legion guards surrounded us! She barely had time to pass me her ring before they apprehended her in the name of Prince Forrester."

"And they didn't recognize you?"

"I'm not the fashionista I used to be, friend. Not many recognize this bland face." She poked her cheek. "But the Ruby Legion...they're *different*. I don't know how to explain it. Their eyes..." She swallowed. "Anyway, they've been patrolling these streets every hour or three—I imagine they'll find us next."

But I made a face. "How many days have we been here?" I glanced over at Zane's clothes, his dry boots, and his dishevelled pecan hair.

"A pinch over six days, and you seem as sturdy as a sputtlepun. The Patrols told us what happened to you in the dungeon, friend. How awful!"

My jaw dropped.

Six days?!

"Where's Kaley? Where are the believers? Is everyone...Did everyone make it to the..."

"They're in hiding. They made it. We ran from the factory before Asteroth caught up," Apple cut in. "But it's been difficult to gather food. Only yestereve one of our young couples got stopped in the street and arrested on suspicion. I fear what will happen to them, and...Oh, *Scarlet*. What are we to do about her?"

"Season's g-g-greetings!" A voice entered, and I startled at the sight of a large-eyed man with a wild butter-gold beard. "I'm D-D-Doctor Tubby Spoot."

"Doctor, thank you for your help!" Apple reached to shake the man's hand. "I know it'll cost you greatly if anyone discovers what you've done for us."

"Oh, pish posh. I never ch-ch-chose Red; *they* chose this village. And I'll never w-w-withhold my help from a follower of the True King of Winter. That's a Winter promise."

The man revealed a twisted tooth when he smiled.

"I pray good tidings come your way. Thank you for hiding us," Apple said.

"Do you have any idea where we should go?" Zane asked the man. "Have you been in contact with whoever is left from the underground cathedral? Is there anywhere left in Winter that's safe for us?"

The Medicinier's chest deflated. "I'm afraid I haven't any suggestions. Not g-g-good ones, anyway. Not since the villages have been taken." He tapped a thick finger against his belly.

Apple looked to the floor, and Zane's hands tightened to fists. "We'll figure it out." He forced a smile. Without another word, Zane ducked back into the room where I'd been asleep and came back out with a Patrol staff.

"Where in all of Winter can we hide a large group of dwarves, believers, and not to mention a flock of Patrolmen who eat as much as ice pigs?" Apple whispered to me. "There's nowhere on the map left for us."

The map that I'd seen on the wall of the factory basement filled my mind. To survive, we couldn't be on that map. And I only knew of one place in Winter that didn't show up on any maps.

Apple held my arm as we crossed a bridge and passed dark-windowed townhouses. The sky had grown darker, stirring with ashy wisps of cloud like it was preparing to unleash a violent hailstorm. The heavy air made it hard to breathe. We stayed in the alleyways, ducking behind wagons as black shadows crept around corners and into homes, slipping through cracks and beneath doorframes like mist. Rime Folk turned their heads numbly when they heard us, and my skin tightened at the sight of pure black eyes.

We reached a forest of trees with charred bark like they were dying from the inside. Piles of ash littered the white snow, and I wondered how many trees had given up completely.

"We had to run for the hills," Apple whispered as we crunched over the snow. "So, we made what we could with what we had. It's all thanks to that blessed teapot, friend. Every time we shuddered from the cold, we sipped on tea to warm ourselves and we kept working."

My mouth parted at the dozens of igloo-like snow forts spread across a clearing—some two stories high.

"Did you *make* these?" I asked.

"Well, the dwarves did, mostly. The Patrols helped too, of course. It really wasn't hard with so many staff wielders."

Patrolmen, dwarves, and believers travelled through the village of igloos carrying firewood and hauling buckets of water from a spring nearby.

I thought of my dream. "I need to meet with everyone," I said.

"Yes! We must meet now that Scarlet has been taken. Your beloved sister is in the main ice house with Mr. Lucas." Apple pointed past the dwarves patching up holes in the igloos.

We marched into the valley, easing through crooked snow walls and narrow gaps. Kaley's voice drifted out to meet me, but her words paused when I stepped into the crystalline room.

Lucas flashed me a wide grin. "Looks like Asteroth loses again," he said.

I chuckled and thought of Jolly Cheat but quickly shook the thought away. "Has everyone heard the news about Scarlet?" I asked, and a few heads nodded. "If Cane finds out she's been taken, he's going to abandon his mission," I said. "And based on what I read in his letters, I think we need to help him in any way we can—"

"Cane doesn't want our help." From the back of the ice house, Porethius leaned against a doorframe with her arms folded. I felt the sting of Gathadriel's sacrifice seep through the space between us.

"I know Cane said he doesn't want to be rescued, but he didn't say anything about us going after Scarlet," I said. "This might be the only way we *can* help him."

"Agreed!" Hope filled Apple's eyes.

Wanda raised her cup of tea in agreement then tipped her head back and guzzled. I wasn't sure if I was supposed to keep watching when drips ran down her chin, so I shot Kilen a smile, happy to see colour returned to his face. Someone had given him a proper haircut.

"Anyway, there's something else." I scratched my hairline as the dream of the squeezing gauntlet flooded my mind. "I think I know what Nightflesh is trying to do."

Kaley paused while pouring her tea, and Zane's head turned toward me in surprise.

I wrung my fingers, stealing a look at that word: *Hopebringer*. It hadn't made sense until now.

"The Night Beast is crushing hope and somehow using it to form himself with flesh. Whenever a soul gives up hope, he takes on a piece of his physical form. He's transforming from mist into a real monster with a body."

Shudders lifted through the ice house, and I pulled out the summons I'd been carrying in my pocket since passing through the first village.

"He's been gathering in the souls of Winter to extinguish their hope and make himself stronger. Once he's a physical being, I think he plans to rule over Winter."

"By the sharpest wind," Apple breathed with a hand against her chest.

"That must be why he's used vessels until now," Kaley said, dropping her tea onto the tabletop. "And why he's been chasing us as mist."

"But he's not a body yet. That means we still have a pinch of time; isn't that right, Trite?" Lucas asked.

I folded the summons and slid it back into the pocket of my torn clothes. "We have to stop him before he crushes enough souls to turn. I don't think he needs many more—his transformation has already begun."

"How do we stop him?" Kaley asked. Patrols gathered around the table, quiet and listening.

My gaze flickered to Lucas, then back to Kaley. "We need to make new Carriers. We need to start spreading the hope back across Winter, to stop the spread of darkness and to open people's eyes to the Truth so they can see what Nightflesh is doing."

"We don't have time for that, love." I realized Theresa had led the dwarves into the gathering.

"Probably not. But there is one place in Winter that's equipped and already filled with young hearts ready to learn. Didn't you say Orphan Island was surrounded by a time pocket?" I asked Kaley, and Lucas spat his tea.

"What?" He craned his neck. "Absolutely not. I'll not be responsible for leading Nightflesh's armies to destroy a pack of sputtlepun children."

"Helen, the island isn't on Winter's maps for a reason. We should leave it off the maps," Kaley pleaded.

"I know. But if Nightflesh rules over Winter, the island will get taken too." I glanced at the Patrols who were bruised, thin, and ill. "The Carriers have fallen, and now the Patrol is weaker than ever. This was Elowin's plan; to raise Carriers and Patrols to go into Winter and share the Truth. You have the knowledge of the Volumes of Wisdom inside of you, Kaley! And Lucas, who better to teach kids how to fight and defend themselves than you? You lived with Mikal most of your life."

Lucas huffed and spun away, tugging a rough hand through his dark hair. "There's no point in nattering this nonsense, Trite." Lucas's doubt was contagious, and I glanced off. "Elowin's hope has already left Winter."

My hands grew warm, and I fought the impulse to look down at them.

"Then why did the Volumes tell me how to find the pieces of the Triad of Signs?" Kaley asked Lucas, and Lucas spun back with an agonized face.

"Darling, it burns my scotcher to point it out, but you never found all the pieces of the Triad of Signs. And bringing children into this muddle is cruel. What do you think happened to the last measure of sputtlepuns that were trained to be Carriers of Truth?!"

A harsh silence followed, and from the back, Kilen sniffed and started to cry.

"Leutenski, what other option do we have?" Timblewon

piped up from among the Patrolmen. "We failed our Carriers. Perhaps it's time for a new generation to try."

I clasped my hands so I'd stop wringing my fingers. "You did find the island, right? Is that why you weren't at the factory when it was attacked?" I asked Lucas, and his fist tightened around the handle of his teacup. He slowly lifted the cup for a long, loud, angry sip.

"Yes," he said. "To answer the question your beloved sister never even *bothered* to ask me; I did find it. But if either of you ever make a request for me to do such an outrageous thing again, you can bet your merry scotchers I'll say no."

"What?" Kaley slammed her own teacup on the tabletop, spilling it onto the ice. "You found it?!"

"Frostbite, darling. You never *asked*."

"Where is it, Lucas? Tell me." She came around the table, but Lucas wouldn't look at her. He buffed his nails on his shirt.

"Do you mean where was it when I found it? Or where is it now? Those are two very different locations."

"Ragnashuck, Leutenski," Timblewon huffed.

Lucas's topaz gaze finally thwacked into Kaley. "In case you're riddled with concern for me, you should know I had to rob a treasury in the Red Kingdom to be able to afford passage on a merchant vessel, and those fowl merchants might as well have been frostbitten snow pirates for how terribly they smelled."

Zane suddenly snorted a laugh. It made a small, cold part of me warm to see him finally smile.

"But even after I paid the snowseas captain handsomely to take me to where you predicted the island might be, it was still very much invisible by some ancient Winter magic. I had to search for ten plus six days before I found the door to the frostbitten place, and what do you know—a *fairy* was there guarding the entrance, and she wouldn't allow me to pass through. It was all a waste of time, Trite. Orphan Island cannot be reached. It wants to stay hidden, even from us."

Kaley shook her head. "If we had the Triad of Signs—"

But Lucas raised a finger to cut her off. "But we don't. It was all a merry, jolly plan before, but as you can see, we have nothing and no one. This is all we are now." Lucas raised a hand toward the fragile ice city.

Kaley's jaw tightened. "I want to see it for myself," she said.

Lucas threw his hands up. "Ha! Good luck finding it!"

"I can find it."

We turned to the fiery-haired boy in the doorway. Ginger kicked snow when he came in.

"Ginger, not now," Apple scolded. "This isn't just pebble talk, this is serious."

"I am being serious. I can find the island, even if it's moving. I can chase it over the water." The boy scratched behind his ear. He looked at me. "I'm supposed to help you," he said, scratching his hair next.

I turned to face him. "What do you mean?"

"I had a dream two seasons ago that I had one of those." He pointed to my throat, and I untucked the Revelation Orb necklace from beneath my shirt.

Ginger nodded. "Mine looked just like yours. That's why I've been following you around. I'm supposed to help you do a thing or three, I think."

Zane's peppermint aroma appeared at my side. In this

moment, Ginger looked exceptionally young: his wild hair, his uneven stance, his scratching.

He started picking his nose right in front of us, and Apple reached to smack his hand away.

"Apple," I said, eyeing Ginger's worn boots. "Is he crazy or is that true?"

Apple clasped and unclasped her hands. "Well, friend, my cousin may be horridly impolite, but…He's not a liar." She turned to Ginger. "Show her."

In a whiff of snow, Ginger disappeared, and I staggered backward into Zane. In the same second, the boy reappeared again at the back door, skidding to a halt and spraying all of us with snowflakes.

Kilen and Wanda clapped.

I blinked away my shock. "Ginger," I said, stepping toward him. "Were there others in your dream too? Were there other kids who had these?" I lifted the orb on its chain.

"A few," he shrugged. "We were in a school. There were classrooms with colourful windows, and there was a big clock on the wall, and there was a man there with black pictures on his neck, and there were books…a *good measure* of books."

"Well. Frostbite," Lucas muttered, tossing away his teacup.

"Can you run ahead and tell the fairies to keep the island still long enough for us to get there?" Kaley asked, and Ginger nodded again.

From the back, Porethius watched in silence. After a moment, she lifted off the doorframe and headed away, her torn wings dragging through the snow behind her.

"We don't have orbs, Trite," Lucas reminded Kaley.

"I'm staying to get you the orbs," I said, and Kaley shook her head.

"You're not coming? Helen—"

"No." I looked around the room. "But the rest of you should go and hide there. There's nowhere else in Winter that's safe."

"Helen, you're *not* staying behind," Kaley stated.

I glanced down at my flickering symbols.

Hopebringer.

I thought of Jolly Cheat's words to me by the hillside. *"There is no one else to face that Beast, I'm afraid."*

"I came to face Nightflesh," I said. "So that's what I'm going to do."

"Well, ragnashuck. The Patrol won't abandon you now, Trite. You're all that's left of the Carriers, and we're all that's left of the Patrol," Timblewon said. "We'll stay with you and distract Nightflesh to give those on the island time to learn what they must."

"Yes. We'll go into the streets in uniform every now and then to stir up gossip. If Nightflesh thinks the Patrol are in the villages, he won't be looking elsewhere," Mirkra added, tapping his staff along the wall in a slow beat. "Besides," he chuckled, "Cohen will never leave your side."

Zane's greying blue eyes slid over to me.

I smiled and walked toward the back entrance of the ice house, patting Lucas's rigid shoulder as I passed. "Come on, Lucas. We need you," I said.

I found Porethius gazing out from a cliffside deep in the forest. Shadows turned the white snow grey below. Every so often, a patch of pure black stained the landscape like it had been burned at random.

I paused when I came up behind the fairy. I didn't want to interrupt, though Porethius wasn't whispering to the wind, or mouthing anything like I'd seen her do in the past. She also didn't acknowledge that I was there if she'd heard me coming.

"We would have heard about it if Cane was dead. It would have turned up in the Pebble Paper," I finally said.

Her head tilted slightly toward me.

"He's alive, at least."

She tilted her face away again, back to the landscape.

"He won't be for long, Carrier," she said. The breeze ruffled the brittle, burned trees, sending blowing ash up her calves. I clasped my hands behind my back and took a step closer.

"Cane wasn't trying to hurt you, Porethius. He just had a job to do alone," I said, and the fairy released a light grunt.

"You can see all that, but you cannot even see that your own Patrolman is struggling?"

My feet came together.

I looked back toward the camp, then back to Porethius. And I set my jaw. "I don't know what's going on with you, but you're a leader to those who are left. And when you lose hope, they start to as well."

She still didn't move.

I huffed, my breath steaming in the chilly air. "Get it together, Porethius," I said, and this time she did flinch. "My sister is about to go on a hunt for Orphan Island which just *happens* to be guarded by fairies. I have a feeling you knew where it was the whole time we were just talking about it, and you didn't bother to say anything."

"I don't know where it is. I've hidden nothing from you."

I chewed on my lip. "All right." I dared a few steps closer until I was almost beside her. "What are you going to do now? Are you going to stay with me or go with the rest of the believers to the island? Or will you go somewhere else?"

Her tattoos faded. "I'll obey Cane's command and stay away, like he's asked. I cannot fly to him anyway."

Something shifted in my stomach, and my hands grew hot. I stuffed them in my pockets, but it made it even worse. A sound escaped me when I yanked them back out again, and Porethius did look over this time. Her violet eyes narrowed on the silvery symbols slinking down my wrists.

"Can you read those, Carrier?" she asked in an odd tone.

I lifted my hands. The symbols were a mix of circular shapes and embellished lines. "No," I said. "Can you?"

Porethius's hair fluttered as she turned. "They utter truths," she said.

"What are they saying?" My brows scrunched.

"It says…" Her eyes darted up to mine. "Heal the sick and heavy spirited." She tilted her head with a new look in her eyes. "The spirit of Elowin is with you."

When the words left her mouth, my throat constricted. Porethius looked like she'd turned into a statue.

But which one of us were the words for?

I reached for her wings before she could react.

"Carrier..." It was the most frazzled I'd ever seen Porethius as I grabbed a handful of her delicate wings. I felt the warmth leave my arms and hands as the scraps began to pull together—new, sparkling fabric forming.

Her mouth parted. We watched the length of her wings strengthen to a shimmering hue of violet, like fields of lavender blossoms sprinkled with sugar.

I dropped my hands. I didn't know whether to feel flustered or to start cheering. She was gaping at her wings in complete silence. So was I.

I folded my hands and mustered a sentence. "If you need to leave, Porethius, then leave," I said. "Go figure out what Elowin wants you to do next."

Porethius remained still, staring at me. I started when she suddenly leapt off the cliff, violet wings spanning out. She sped against the wind, tattoos flaring, and she disappeared into the clouds.

A PRINCELY INTERRUPTION

The nights were filled with darkness. Cane rested his back against the lobby prison, feeling more constrained in this birdcage than in the cupboard where he had slept so many eves past. All through the night, growls had lifted from the palace where things lurked in the hallways. After a while, Cane pressed his palms against his ears to drown the noise out.

Not one of his brothers had come to visit and gloat. Not even Forrester.

Cane wished for sleep that would never come. During the dark hours, he thought of Scarlet in Forrester's grip. Cane had promised her he would hide her in the cracks of Winter. But then he had fled from her for this task. What a lying ashworm he was.

"Psssst!"

Cane's eyes flew open. He rolled his head against the

bars to look upon a figure in the shadows inching toward his cage. When he realized it was Driar, he scrambled to his knees.

"Kingsblood, Driar!" Cane scolded. "I didn't endure all that whipsteaming just to have you get caught like *this*."

Driar tugged down his hood with a wobbly hand, and the moonlight from the window bleached his cheeks. "You've been handed over to the Directors of Tournaments," Driar whispered. "There was nothing I could do."

"*Obviously*." Cane huffed and fell back to sit. "I wasn't expecting you to slay the Crimson Court in one evening," he muttered.

Driar looked over his shoulder at the cages where the Greens slept. 'Twas a sight Cane wished he could unsee, for Driar did not look a pinch like the warrior the sputtlepun claimed he had become under the guidance of some mysterious trainer. And Cane released a tortured laugh as he realized that shy, little Driar was still shy, little Driar. Cane was certain now that he had thrown himself away for nothing.

"Have you heard a thing of Scarlet?" he asked, desperate for a shard of news before Driar was forced to leave. "Has Forrester…"

"He has her."

Dread filled Cane's belly.

"But she's alive. She's fooling everyone, for now. She's released a story to Sullen for the Pebble Paper in the morning about how she was kidnapped by a band of believers and locked in a basement all this time. Naturally, Sullen ate it all up."

But Cane released a heavy breath from his tight chest. "Kingsblood," he cursed, tugging at his mahogany locks.

"I've doomed her."

Driar's throat bobbed, and Cane's burgundy gaze fell upon where the boy fiddled with the lace at his cloak's collar. "I cannot go through with it alone, Cane."

The words struck Cane like a slap—fast, searing, and begging for retaliation. "What did you just say?" He articulated the words for his socially crippled, book-loving brother. "There must be frost in my ears, Driar!"

Driar shook his head in apology. "You've been scheduled to meet your fate in the arena at dawn. As soon as you're dealt with, Forrester will turn his sights on me and become paranoid because I'm next in line. He'll kill every one of his brothers if he must, to ensure his spot is safe. I will not be able to take a breath without him noticing."

Anger flashed through the once-prince's fist, and he slammed his knuckles against the bars, not caring if it awoke the Greens. Cane pointed a sharp finger at his brother.

"I have sacrificed a good measure too much for your plan, Brother. You *must* go through with it now."

Driar wavered on his feet. "You were my best hope at entertaining him."

"Then let me out of here, Driar! Let me go and I'll create the greatest diversion this kingdom has ever known so that you can stop that ivory-haired saltslug before he *kills my wife*!" The words came through Cane's teeth, and Green huntsmen began to stir in their cages throughout the lobby.

Driar closed his mouth, and his posture straightened. After a measure of silent heart thuds, he said, "I'll be back." Cane might have snatched the boy if he could reach, but Driar slipped into the shadows.

"You'd better come back," Cane whispered, leaning his

forehead against the bars.

When a moment or three passed, Cane was certain he had scared his brother away for good. He pulled at his hair, scrubbing his scalp with his nails. “Kingsblood. Kingsblood. *Kingsblood*,” he whispered until his tongue was sick of the word.

A soft clank brought the once-prince’s head up. He blinked at where Driar stood outside the cage. The boy slid a metal key through the rungs. “I cannot help you more than this. They already suspect me after the mess I made in Polar Territory, so your escape will only add to their suspicion,” Driar said, and he shoved a claret cloak through the bars too. “You’re on your own to find a way out. But keep your promise, Cane. Time is what I need now. Keep Forrester’s eyes off me until the Crimson King breathes his last.”

“I’ll do it,” Cane promised, grabbing the key and clutching the cloak to himself. He fought the impulse to fling wide his cage door and go charging through the palace in search of Scarlet.

“You can use the servants’ tunnels—”

“I know how to get out.” Cane looked upon his brother, certain that if given this same choice a season ago, Driar would not have helped him the way he just did. ‘Twas the first speck of confidence Cane felt toward the young Red Prince.

“Do not fail me, Brother,” Cane warned.

“Likewise.”

Driar headed back for the shadows.

CHAPTER, THE NINTH

I splayed my fingers toward the valley's slope and winced as I lifted the snow into a dance of flurries. But my symbols flickered, and I released a moan as the flurry scattered in every direction. I let the flakes fall again.

How had I created an ice wall in the Dungeon of Souls and those pillars to guard the believers if I couldn't do basic things like make a snow elephant the way Wanda could with a Patrol staff?

"Don't force it. It'll come when it needs to." Zane appeared from the trees, and I wondered where he'd been all morning. He began digging a picture into the ground with his Patrol staff as he watched me catch my breath. I tipped back to lay flat, flinging an arm over my forehead like a damsel in distress.

"You'll have to carry me out of here. I need my knight to rescue me from exhaustion. And maybe to find me a snack," I joked.

But Zane chewed on the inside of his cheek as he drifted over. "Helen, there's—"

"There they are!" Apple's voice lifted through the snow fort houses, and I tilted my head to see her leading the Medicinier in our direction.

The man raked a hand down his butter-gold beard as he approached us. "I've been th-th-thinking about what you asked yestermorning about where you might hide," he said to Zane, twirling one of his beard locks. "Th-Th-The city of Harpwood is just past this forest. It's patrolled by the Ruby Legion, but there's a bank there, and the owner is one of us, though she'd hate it if she knew I t-t-told a soul. The treasury building w-w-was newly renovated this quarter past. The offices upstairs aren't yet occupied, and it's all hidden away quite nicely. I r-r-reached out to her on your behalf, and I received a letter back this morning. She's sending bankers clothes for you. That way you can come and go from the building as you need to without raising suspicion. Though...she doesn't expect you to lodge for free, of course. She needs workers."

"We'll do it," I said, pulling myself up from the snow. "We'll be bankers—there's no one who will work harder for her than the Patrol."

"Isn't it brilliant?! Thank you, Mr. Tubby!" Apple threw a hug around him.

"Well, you'd best s-s-set off right away, then! Mrs. Millsa is waiting for you at this location." The Medicinier pulled a slip of paper from his pocket with the address and Apple took it.

I moved to follow when they left, but Zane's hand

caught mine.

"Helen." This time he said my name sternly. "We need to talk." His gaze flickered to where Apple shouted the news to the whole ice village. "But not here."

My Patrolman tugged me into the forest.

I glanced back to where the dwarves were racing to pack. "Aren't you relieved about the bank?" I asked, but he didn't reply.

Zane pulled me along until I was out of breath. We crossed a creek on ice steppingstones and came to a windy cove between a set of hills. A tall black tree with smashed branches stretched into the sky. He let go of my arm but kept his back to me.

"What in the world is going on with you?" I asked.

"I'm not your knight, Helen."

I blinked. "I was just joking—"

"We need to face the truths." He turned, and I faltered to find his eyes brimming with tears. "You and I are scotchy for each other."

He stalked closer, his watery, deep navy gaze tracing my features, and I took a step backward, wishing he'd snap out of it.

"Trite, I warned you that there were things about me I never wanted you to find out. I didn't want you to see this side of me."

"What side?"

"This is the real me." He stopped an inch away, his mouth tipped into a frown. The warmth of his body was flushed away by the wind slipping between us.

"What are you talking about? Obviously I know you—"

"No, you don't. You never have, and that's the problem.

You think I'm something that I'm not. You think I'm your knight, and I'm *not*." He took my wrist, and I tried to pull away as a jerk reaction. "Trust me, if there's one thing I learned living among the Trites these quarters past, it's that I don't belong with them, with their itchy clothes and boring lives," his voice cracked on the last word.

My lashes fluttered. "But—"

"When our bond was severed, I saw things clearly. I saw what this bond has done to me. How it's muddled my focus, and how far I've fallen from my purpose as a Winter guardian. I can't be your Patrolman anymore. I tried. I really bloody tried. But honestly, Helen, I don't even *want* to be."

I tore my wrist away.

"I'm going to pretend you didn't just say that." I swallowed. My eyes stung. "There's something wrong with you. Your mind is being manipulated or something."

"I'm not mindswept. This is who I am. I'm an ashworm who's been pretending to be a raven. It's why I never let you learn the whole truth about my past. And I've been forced to hide myself for four bloody seasons to give you what you needed."

"Zane, I never asked you for anything—"

"Trite! You asked me for *everything*!" he shouted, and my back slammed against the tree. The tears he was holding slipped down his cheek and he swatted them away with his glove. "Don't you see that?" he rasped.

He took my arms and tugged them around the narrow tree trunk. I tried to register what he was doing, but he slipped a knot around my wrists so fast I didn't even see him do it.

"Don't follow me, and don't try to stop me from leaving.

This is where we say goodbye, Helen Bell. I really hope you live through all of this," he said. "I wish you a long and merry life." He yanked his pointed hood up to hide his pecan hair and glistening eyes.

I tugged at the binds on my wrists, and it dawned on me as he started backing toward the hills, Patrol staff in hand.

"Wait…" I warned. "You can't leave me, Zane Cohen! You promised you'd always keep us together!" The moisture in my eyes chilled in the wind.

He kept walking.

My lip quivered as he passed over the first hill and then the second. "Zane, *please*, wait!" I begged. My tears tumbled down in thick beads, dripping off my chin and hitting the snow.

But Zane didn't look back.

This isn't real.

He wouldn't do this.

I lifted my bound hands, splaying my fingers toward the snow. Flakes wrenched up into a blast of white. I pushed the flurry toward him. I'd knock him out if I had to, but I couldn't let him leave.

In the distance, Zane stilled like he heard it coming. He spun, his Patrol staff swinging out to dissipate the blast. I sent a fresh wave, trying to work around the binding of my wrists, but Zane slammed it back too, striking every thrust I conjured until I crumpled to my knees.

In the distance, he lifted his staff, and a giant swell of ice and snowflakes rose from the ground. It roared over the hills and blasted against my flesh, forcing my eyes closed and howling against my temples. When it stopped, my lashes were frozen shut. I rubbed my nose on my sleeve and shook the snow from my face.

But when I pried my eyes open and looked to where he'd been, Zane was gone.

THE FIRST DAY AFTER HE LEFT

CHAPTER, THE TENTH

My fingers trembled, losing their colour with the dropping temperature. A snowstorm moved in. I tried to fabricate a shield from the snow, but it only half-formed and tipped sideways. It smashed on the ground a foot away.

I tugged at the knot around my wrists. I tried to tear the rope free of the tree trunk with my teeth, but Zane had knotted it to stay put.

When the storm came, I slid down to tuck myself into a ball, shielding my face.

CHAPTER, THE ELEVENTH

The evening was as dark and empty as my slow-beating heart. Inhuman growls lifted from the forest. The stars didn't glow in the sky. The moon hid its face, and a fresh storm rumbled in the distance.

Apple would have led the others into the city to meet the banker by now, and I imagined the Patrols were nestled into their rooms. They would assume Zane was bringing me.

No one was going to find me here.

Silent tears slid down my cheeks until the dizziness of dehydration set in.

CHAPTER, THE TWELFTH

I heard footsteps crunch over the snow. I forgot where I was until my eyes peeled open and took in the grey, hazy morning sky overhead. The crunching drew closer, and a frail beat of hope rose through me.

"You came back…" The whisper was hardly a sound.

The footsteps stopped.

"I've found her! She's here!" And then, "Help! Help! There's something wrong with her!"

My eyelids slid closed again.

It was Ginger's voice.

Minutes later, I caught a glimpse of Lucas's topaz eyes as he carried me in a hurry.

PART 1

AN INTERRUPTION

Three Quarters Plus Eight Eves Ago…

The morn' Driar stepped into the ice palace, he had been certain that coming to Polar Territory was the right choice. Sunlight glistened through the silvery walls, and every hall was adorned with the chill of frost. When he inhaled, his insides filled with refreshing cold and absolute freedom.

"Where are the libraries?" he asked the palace attendant who had led him in.

"This way, Your Highness." The lady elf was cloaked in a gold and deep blue fur-lined coat with crystal buttons.

Driar followed the attendant down a glassy spiral staircase, trying to suppress his boyish grin. How blessed he was, to be able to study alongside the great Polar King who was revered for his scientific breakthroughs.

But as the young Red Prince entered the libraries—if they could be called such a thing—he stopped in the doorway.

"Where are all the books?" he asked, and the attendant patted a table strewn with papers and charts.

"We do not need books. Our libraries are full of knowledge based on our own research."

"Ah, I see." Driar looked 'round at the baskets upon baskets of sorted loose papers, and the high shelves of a thousand papers more.

"I do hope you enjoy your stay in Polar Territory, Prince." The attendant dipped into a shallow bow and left. On her way out, she said, "The midday feast will be served in the dining chapel in a pinch."

Driar inched into the room and lifted a page from the nearest desk. Upon it was a chart containing different dosage levels for medicinal purposes. But 'twas the title at the top that caught his eye:

Experiment Twenty Plus Five
Upon the She-Trite, The Eighth

Driar held the sheet a pinch closer, certain he must be reading incorrectly.

"Experiment?" he murmured to himself. He dropped the page and lifted another, but discovered it was also a tracking chart for a Trite. He left the page where he found it and stepped back from the table.

"Kingsblood," he whispered as he turned to leave, realizing he did not want to be in the library after all. He hadn't a clue where the attendant had gone, so he ventured back the way he *thought* he had come.

After a twist and a turn, Driar heard voices. He headed toward the sound, but when the young Prince rounded the corner, he stopped in his tracks. For, there in prisons of ice were dozens and dozens of pale-eyed Trites.

Elves carried trays of needles down the centre aisle, and a healer in a long navy robe with star constellations stopped before a particular she-Trite with a large, round belly. The healer lifted one of the needles from the tray, and the she-Trite glared as her arm was taken.

Driar turned away. He hadn't the stomach for needly things. He aimed for the spiral staircase he had descended before, scrubbing his eyes as he trotted back up to the glistening hallways, thinking all the while about how the Polar King was not simply *studying* Trite sciences at all. He had no books, no professors, and no instruction.

Even so, Driar would not waste this opportunity at freedom. He would simply stay away from the lower level of the ice palace, and try not to think about—

He halted at the end of the main hallway. For, someone stood in the lobby who did not belong in Polar Territory at all.

Bowing before the Polar King was a folk in a jangly hat of bells, with a long red and black coat, and kohl-stained silvery eyes. A folk who had perhaps followed him here or been sent to spy on him. A folk he did not trust a pinch.

The young prince ground his teeth as he realized he would not be free in this place after all.

Presently...

Driar paused in front of his mirror before putting on a shirt. In the glass's reflection, he saw the bookshelves that lined his chamber walls, along with a few maps and an oil painting of a forest without snow.

A folk with his face looked back at him. Rarely had he stood in front of this mirror in his early seasons; he had not taken the time to memorize his height, nor his pearl-white hair that was similar to his mother's, nor his oval lips that resembled Cane's and Quinten's. But that was where his similarities to Cane and Quinten ended.

He pulled on his shirt and adjusted it to cover his shoulders, his biceps, his stronger chest. He was still a sputtlepun lacking muscular definition, but he had grown. And as he dragged a loose robe overtop to disguise himself, Driar thought of his training.

Look a folk in the eyes when you speak to him, especially if you have to lie.

Driar shoved his feet into his palace slippers and grabbed a book on his way out the door. He marched to the meeting room, dreading another long court assembly. He hoped the palace attendants would serve warm toast with jam.

The drapes had been yanked shut when he arrived, leaving the meeting room in the dim, musty dark with only flickering candlelight to see by. He blinked to adjust his eyes as he took a seat and flipped his book open to a random page. His eyes did not absorb the words, however; his lavender gaze peered over the book-top, taking inventory of the court members present.

Whispers rose through the room. Driar could hardly keep his breathing quiet when Scarlet Strange was led in and seated among the Crimson Court. She kept her honey eyes ahead and her shoulders square. Driar felt a pinch jealous at how well she could pretend when he now understood the difficulties.

Sullen Sprit-Spellborrow drifted to the dais, reporting on the latest news from the streets. After him came Finance Minister Rosh Cinders, and then Commander Devious of the Ruby Legion to explain the position of the war on Green. None of them once mentioned a thing of the dark happenings in the Scarlet City.

Vapours of sweet toffee and brown sugar filled the room, and noblewomen giggled through red-painted lips. Bubbling drinks were poured and passed, and silver trays of sponge cake and sour buds were carried 'round by attendants. They did not appear bothered by the shadows in the room's corners, or the black-eyed creatures sitting among them.

At the end of the meeting, Forrester addressed the Crimson Court with slow, articulate words. "I'm investigating the disappearance of Cane Endovan Crimson-Augustus. I'll personally question the Green prisoners in the lobby and the Legionnaires who were on duty this eve past."

Driar's blood cooled. He forced his eyes down to his book. He even flipped a page with a shaky hand.

"I'm commissioning this court to pay whomever you

must. Hire any assassin you wish in the kingdom. I'll reward the folk who brings the disowned former prince to me, whether that traitor is alive or is returned to me as a heap of snow. And when I find out who helped him escape…"

The room went silent; even the elves had stopped filling glasses.

"…They will be placed in the arena next to Cane Endovan Crimson-Augustus if he lives that long."

Driar watched Scarlet for a reaction, but the young lady did not flinch.

The moment Forrester finished, Driar leapt from his seat and slid 'round the nobles. He bit his nails as he ducked into the shadows, book in hand. He made it all the way to the library before anyone caught up with him, and he whirled when he realized he was not alone.

There stood Lady Scarlet Strange.

"Miss Strange," Driar fumbled over the words.

"That is not my name." Her expression didn't shift a pinch.

"Right…Miss Kissing," he apologized.

"That is not my name, either." Scarlet moved into the library and shut the door behind her. "My name is *Mrs.* Crimson-Augustus. And thanks to you, my *real* husband will get himself killed because of what you said to him in those letters. What is your plan, Driar?"

Driar shook his head. He could not tell another soul—especially this woman who was spending all her mornings and afternoons with Forrester. What if she slipped up and Forrester found out?

"There's a good measure to explain."

"So then explain it."

Driar hardened his jaw. This could be the end of him.

The library door swung open.

"Ah, there you are."

Driar's flesh crawled at the deep thing Forrester's voice had become this quarter past.

When the heir strolled in as quietly as death itself, Driar stifled his nerves and turned toward the bookshelf to find a book.

"What are you doing in here, my love?" Forrester asked Scarlet.

"I was going to read." Scarlet's voice was smooth. Driar exhaled a breath of relief as he wandered further into the shelves and spied on where Forrester stood over her. When Forrester's purple eyes shot up to him, Driar snatched a book and dragged it out. He flipped it open, running a finger down the page until Forrester got bored of watching.

"I've prepared the midday meal for us. I'll point you in the *right* direction," Forrester said, though he stole another glance at Driar.

"Here it is, Miss Kissing," Driar piped up, carrying over a thick tome. He slapped it shut and handed it over. "You said you wanted to read a fairy tale. There's none better that I've read than this."

Scarlet reached for the tome and nodded her thanks.

Driar watched until they disappeared 'round the hall. He turned back to his books, placing a hand o'er his heart to feel it thud.

"A little bird told me the strangest thing yestereve, Brother."

Driar stilled. He slid his hands into his pockets to hide how tightly he gripped them. "Oh? And what is that?"

Forrester sauntered 'round, and a memory played through Driar's mind:

"Don't be a schemer, be an actor. Be a prince with not a thing to hide. Ragnashuck, you really think you'll fool anyone with that pale, gangly thing you call a face? Come now, Driar. You'll not get a pinch past your first eve with a stricken expression."

Driar stood a little taller and settled a bored lavender gaze upon his oldest living brother, shifting into a prince with not a thing to hide.

But a slow smile curled across Forrester's features. "You have grown up a good measure, haven't you, Driar?"

Driar glanced over to flick a loose thread from his shoulder. "I suppose we've all been forced to after watching our siblings fall. We were abandoned by Cane, then our mother went missing, and then Quinten tried to destroy us, and then..." he swallowed, buckling beneath Forrester's gaze for the first time, "...Tegan."

Forrester's gaze sharpened. "What of Tegan?"

"Hmm?"

The library became as quiet as a graveyard.

Forrester tilted his head. "Do you want to know what the little bird told me yestereve?"

Driar crushed the bookmark in his hand. "Certainly."

"Someone saw you leaving the lobby. If you were in the lobby, Brother, you must have seen Cane? Or...*helped* him even?"

The colours drained from Driar's chest. "Cane was still there when I left. I..." he glanced toward the library door. "I simply went to ask him about his interactions with the fairies. It's part of my study—"

"So, you *were* there."

Driar realized his mistake.

"Do be careful, Brother. I'd hate to get the wrong idea." A calm, deadly glower followed.

"Don't be a spinbug. Go chase the real culprit," Driar said, nodding toward the door. "You know I don't care to get involved in your quarrels."

Forrester nodded slowly. As he glided off and left Driar alone in the dim library, Driar's ears rang.

"Do not fail me, Brother."

THE
SECOND,
THIRD,
FOURTH,
AND FIFTH
DAYS
AFTER HE LEFT

CHAPTER, THE THIRTEENTH

I had no dreams.

I caught the aroma of old paper and metal. My fingers brushed the hem of a soft bedlinen, and my lashes fluttered. My body was telling me it was time to wake up. But I didn't want to wake up.

The air warmed and then cooled again. My eyes slid open to see stars through a window where the ever-present grey haze muddied the sky. The scent of tea drifted from my bedside table, but I wasn't thirsty. I squeezed my eyelids shut again.

The room was absent of peppermint and pine trees. It was the first thing I noticed when my thoughts sharpened, and my eyes opened to dim, muddy light falling over the sheets. My hand drifted up to rub my eyes, and I glanced over at an empty chair beside the bed. I stared at it. I was still staring at it when there was a soft knock on the door, and I heard boots lightly tapping on the floor.

I closed my eyes, not ready for them.

"She's still asleep," I heard Kaley whisper from the doorway.

"Well. Frostbite. She needs to tell us who kidnapped Cohen. Who in all of Winter would *take* him and *leave* her? It doesn't make a pinch of sense."

My eyes drifted back open, and I felt the ache return to my stomach.

"We don't have any time left," Kaley said. "The fairies aren't going to hold the island still for long. But I can't leave her like this."

"Yes. Well. We can agree on that at least, darling."

A long pause followed.

The door was softly closed.

In between restless patches of sleep an old memory crept in—one I'd buried deep of a man I'd once called *Father* seeing me at the foot of our staircase and still deciding to leave on a cold November night. The sound of our front door slamming rang in my ears.

Memories of all the things Zane had said to me over the

years fired through my heart:

"There's a certain bond that pulls a Patrolman toward their Carrier..."

"The truth is that you've tangled into my chest in ways a Carrier should never mix up with a Patrolman."

"I'm bloody desperate to keep you here with me in Winter. And I've been trying to find a way to convince you to stay."

"I told you one day I would explain the bond between a Patrol and a Carrier, but our entanglement has become a great measure more complex than that."

Had I misunderstood what he meant?

Was Zane's life better before I'd found him? I'd dragged him before Mara Rouge in the Quarrel of Sword and Bone—the very witch who'd killed his best friend. He'd been free of a Carrier bond for a long time before he met me. Had my bond tormented him? Our bond stretching across the intersects had nearly driven me crazy.

Suddenly all those things he'd said to me over the years sounded different in my head. They didn't sound like words of affection; they sounded like him admitting his frustrations and agony.

"I'm sorry..." I whispered, certain I was still waiting back in the snow between the hills, and he was going to return to untie me from the black tree.

My closed eyelids tightened. Opening my eyes would mean I'd see I wasn't still there in the blizzard waiting. It would mean admitting that Zane hadn't come back.

"Abandoning is in his nature."

I dragged the sheets over my head like it would block out the purring voice of the pale-eyed prophetess.

"He abandoned me first. Then he abandoned Mikal Migraithe seasons later after he suffered his first great loss. Now, it seems, he's abandoned you as well."

"It's foolish to put your hope in someone who acts in a pattern. That is the greatest insight I can give you now."

The prophetess's words drifted away as a new voice—masculine, but high and melodic just like hers—filled my head in its place:

"This is the real me."

The afternoon sun was shadowed by a blizzard. I decided to pull myself up and sit against the headboard. I took the blessed teapot from the nightstand and poured a cup, but I didn't drink it. I held the tea close to myself for a while.

The door opened, and Kaley stopped when she saw me awake. Lucas shoved her the rest of the way in and followed.

"Are you all right?" Kaley asked, shaking off her surprise and sitting on the edge of the bed.

I stared out the window. A pang of guilt rose through me for ignoring my sister, so I took a sip of tea to seem less inhuman.

"What happened to Cohen, Trite? Who took him?" Lucas tried.

I swallowed and the hot liquid burned my dry throat. "He left," I said.

"He w…" Lucas raised a brow. "He *what*?"

"He tied me to a tree so I wouldn't follow him, and he left." My heavy, pointed stare dragged over to him so he wouldn't make me say it a third time.

Lucas tightened his grip on the bedframe. "Your mind must be muddled, Trite. Cohen wouldn't leave you like a peg out of its shell to freeze to death—"

"He *left*!" I shouted it this time, and tea splattered onto the bedspread. "He left, Lucas! How many more times do I need to say it?!"

Lucas bit his lips together. "Then I'll beat his scotcher into the snow."

I dropped my head back on the bedrail. "Don't make jokes right now."

Lucas unpeeled his fingers from the bed and huffed. "I'll leave you two to your pebble talk then. My jests will only bring bad tidings to this situation and therefore, I have nothing more to offer." He made it to the doorway, but he paused again. "But you don't need him anyway, Trite. Not if what all the Patrols are saying you can do is true."

The warm buzz had left my fingers. I wasn't sure I still had the strength to summon the snow. I didn't feel like admitting to them that trying to stop Zane from leaving had almost made me pass out.

Lucas's boots thudded down the hall.

"Everyone needs to get to the island. It's not safe for the believers to still be here," I said to Kaley. My sister hadn't stopped staring at me with her heavy puppy eyes since she came in.

"Helen…"

"I'm fine, Kaley. I'll be fine. Go to the island, please." I fiddled with the teacup. "I'll feel better if you go. I need to know everyone is safe."

My sister looked at me for a long time before finally rising from the bed. "You should come. You can't do anything for us like this."

But I released a dull laugh. "I can. And I will," I said. "And you'll be safe. That's one less thing for me to worry about."

My sister stooped to hug me. After a while of it, I nudged her off toward the door. "You're going to miss your chance."

"You're not alone, Helen. Remember that."

After she left, I looked back at the empty chair beside the bed.

It was the middle of the night when I heard cries outside my room. Starlight shimmered over the floor in a pool of white. Quiet voices lifted in the hall.

"It's another nightmare," someone said.

The cool night air met my legs when I slid them over the bedside. Candlelight peeked beneath the door.

I crept to spy as another shriek lifted. When I opened the door, Apple stood across the hall with a knit clutched around her shoulders. The door across from mine was open, and inside I saw Wanda and Timblewon sitting on the edge of Kilen's bed. Kilen's face was in his hands as he sobbed.

"I thought it was real," the boy rasped. "I thought I was back with the feastbeggars and they were chopping off my hair. And *he* still speaks to me even when I'm awake!"

Kilen's cheeks were splotchy, his lashes drenched with tears. Suddenly he thrashed, and Timblewon grabbed the boy's shoulders. "Don't give in! Ignore his voice, Kilen!"

The hinges of my door squeaked, and Apple glanced over. She didn't make a fuss that I was up. She just cast me a bleak smile that didn't reach her eyes.

"Nightflesh calls to them," she whispered, looking back into Kilen's room where Wanda brushed a hand over Kilen's hair.

"No matter what he offers, do not give in to him!" Wanda said through teary eyes. "Or he'll use you to destroy us all."

Apple drifted over to stand beside me. "They're all fighting their own demons now," she whispered. "The Beast offers them what they most desire."

My throat was thick as I watched Kilen grip the sides of his head and rock back and forth.

Without another word, I crept back into my room. I took the blessed teapot and carried it back out to Apple. She put a hand over her heart when she saw it.

"He needs it more than I do," I whispered.

Apple took the pot.

I went back to bed after that.

A GREEN-ISH INTERRUPTION

In the full measure of his timestring, Cane had not once set foot across the Green Kingdom border. In fact, before he abandoned his birthright, he had scarcely even left the Scarlet City.

Tattered emerald banners lined the forest, flapping in the cold wind and charting a path through the twists of a thousand decaying trees. 'Twas a relief the banners were there—Cane was certain he would not have found his way through the dark woods otherwise.

When he rounded a veil of pine garland and came to a city of boardwalks and abandoned houses, he saw nothing of the lively woodsman cities he had heard about as a sputtlepun boy. Ashes littered the boardwalks, and branches were broken at every turn. Not a single candle was lit, but he thought he saw a thing or three move in the shadows.

He inhaled before taking a step in, his red cloak warm on his flesh.

"Season's greetings?" he called to the motionless street, but even with his princely charm, Cane was not given the chance to make a speech. He jumped when his shoulders were grabbed, and he was forced to his knees. Six burly Evergreen Host soldiers dressed in black hooded cloaks held silver-tipped axes toward his throat.

Cane raised his hands. "Kingsblood, I did not come to fight!" he promised, certain these men had crept through the woods like silent ghosts. "I seek an audience with your queen."

It seemed the Host soldiers were deaf. They ignored his words and tore at the sleeves of his robe to rip it off; Cane twisted so they would not break his arms away with the fabric. A soldier in wooden armour marched to the nearest stone fire and lit it with a match. He tossed the bright red cloak into it.

"If you'll just listen, I wish to speak to—"

The heel of an axe thumped against his mouth, and Cane tumbled off balance, hitting the boardwalk with a clamour. He was torn back to his feet by his clothes and hoisted into a sleigh hidden behind the dark houses. Cane froze at the sound of low growls, slowly drawing his eyes to look upon the white bears ahead. "Red ashworm," a bear murmured through barred teeth.

Cane stared at the creatures in horror until he was thumped o'er the head again, and everything 'round him faded to black.

'Twas a pinch later he stirred and realized he lay flat on a wooden floor. Scents of smoking firewood and gingerbread lingered in the air, along with sweet cider and the foul stench of death. The once-prince lifted a hand to his head and moaned. When he opened his eyes, he shrieked.

Standing over him was a young woman with the most piercing grey eyes. Her long, dark hair reached her waist now, loose 'round her shoulders, unlike the complex braids she had worn for the Renewal. A new wreath rested atop her head.

"Get him up." Her words were cold and dark, and Cane wondered if he had made a dreadful mistake coming here. Host soldiers grabbed his arms and hoisted him up on his wobbling legs.

"Your Majesty." Cane dipped into a low bow.

Her stare was like a cold blade slicing hog meat, and the former Red Prince clasped his hands together, puffing out his chest. "I imagine you have a question or three about why I've come." He stole glances at the dimming stone fireplaces, the multi-hued wooden walls full of punctures, and the half-shattered glass windows hosting views of thick forests beyond, and he knew this was the legendary Timber Castle Edward had often spoken of.

"My spies tell me you announced your opposition to the Crimson heir. I know why you're here." The Queen of the Pines nodded to an elf, and the elf shewed the Evergreen Host soldiers away. "But I will not aid you in your Red quarrel. I hardly have the means to keep my kingdom my own, let alone get involved in Crimson politics."

Cane's spirit lifted. "I am not here to ask you to charge into the Scarlet City for me. I simply came to fight for you at the border."

Her grey eyes slid back to him. Cane swallowed at the realization of how deeply she resembled her brother—'twas all in the chin and mouth. He dropped his gaze to the floor.

"Why should I believe you, Prince?" She sounded like Edward too.

A laugh escaped him. "Only you would still call me a prince, Queen. I am not considered that by any folk elsewhere," he said. "And I wish you would believe me because…I know we were not on the same side in the past. But in the end, I think we were both on *his* side."

The Queen's eyes shaded. "I was not as beloved to my brother as you were."

"You were, even if you did not know it."

Truly, Cane could not tell if she was moved or glaring now. But another elf arrived and handed her a long wood scepter. "I have people to govern and a war to survive. I gave you one chance, Red, because of what your own people did to you at the Renewal. But that chance has been used up and you're out of time. Leave my kingdom and do not return, or you'll be arrested and tried for trespassing like any other Red."

Cane's fingers flashed out to grab her arm as she turned away, and ten plus two pairs of hands snatched him, dragging him back from the queen. Ever Green turned back to him with widened eyes.

"Pinespittle! How *dare* you…" she whispered.

"*Please*. I have a strategy. I cannot tell the fullness of it without putting my beloveds in danger, however, you should know that I intend to overtoss my brother, Crown Prince Forrester, and put someone on the throne who will not be interested in taking your kingdom away from you."

Every folk in the lobby was quiet. Some leaned in. Those who held Cane even lightened their grip.

Cane tugged himself away and stepped toward the Queen of the Pines. "I want to go fight for you at the border to anger my brother, so that Forrester will not see what's coming for him."

CHAPTER, THE FOURTEENTH

When the floorboards rattled, I sprang out of bed in alarm. Loud footsteps boomed down the hallway and I stared at the closed door of my room, jumping again when three strong knocks shook the door.

My chest tightened as I went and slowly turned the knob. I didn't finish turning before the visitor shoved the door open, nearly throwing me back.

"Carrier." Porethius marched in on shiny sabatons. Her tattoos were bright on her flesh, her wings fluttering in impatience. "I was told you've been *hiding* in here."

"I'm not hiding—"

"It's time to come out," she said.

My shoulders dropped.

"Porethius…I'm not as strong as they all think."

But Porethius folded her muscled arms. "None of us are anything on our own. But we have the Truth in our veins."

I hugged myself and glanced out the window. After a

beat of silence, I asked, "Is he here, Porethius? Is Elowin with us? Why hasn't anyone seen him? Why has he stayed away and done nothing?"

She hesitated, and I looked back. I wasn't sure I wanted the answers.

"Don't you see what you've become, Carrier?" she asked.

"See what?"

"Winter has made you into what it needs to survive its darkest hour. What the Night Beast feeds on is hopelessness, and you bring *hope*. But I think you already figured that out."

Heat brushed my hands, and I lifted them. The columns glittered and I tugged my brows together as fear tingled my stomach. What if I left this room and couldn't do what needed to be done?

"Apple has made you an office down the hall," Porethius said, cutting into my worries. "It's time to get to work. And it's time for you to see the bank too before I leave."

"You're leaving again?" I dropped my hands. "Porethius," I rasped, shaking my head. "I can't do this alone. Kaley and Lucas left."

Zane left.

"Then it's a good thing you have a speedster at your disposal who is eager to help." She cast me a look and my mouth drifted closed.

Ginger appeared in the doorway leaking water from his boots. "At your service, Carrier." He bowed.

"Now, come." The fairy led the way down the hall. I hesitated, fighting the temptation to take one last look at that empty chair beside the bed. But I inhaled and kept my gaze forward.

The bank hallway was lined with mirrors and paintings like a museum. I followed Porethius down a wide, winding staircase, and the sounds of chatter, clanking rings, and tinkling service bells washed over me.

I paused on the stairs, realizing I recognized the closest boy standing behind a teller's desk; one of many narrow desks sectioned off throughout the grand space. Kilen was strapped in a black and gold imperial coat with buttons down the front and a short collar at his neck. Gold embellished words said: "RING-A-LING HARPWOOD TREASUREY" in a circular logo on his back. He flashed a smile to the elf passing him a bag of rings. I watched as he printed a ticket and got the elf to sign it. A moment later, he pushed a button to open a register and slipped the ticket inside. He was everything the opposite of the terrified, shuddering boy I'd seen in the night.

Past him, Wanda leaned against the wall of her booth, chewing on the end of a stick. She snorted a laugh as someone approached, made a face, and then carefully backed away and scooted over to Kilen's booth instead.

Across an open foyer were more booths. Timblewon's bright hair peeked from beneath a gold-roped cap that he tipped at a Rime man leaving with his rings. Apple's laughter flittered from behind a cart she pushed down the centre aisle. She wished a young man "good tidings," and sent him on his way. There was so much going on, I didn't know where to look.

Suddenly I felt foolish for thinking everything had stopped when Zane left. None of my friends had marks on their skin to summon the snow, yet each one of them worked faithfully.

An elf woman with frizzy, olive-green hair and large, round spectacles directed people to the booths as they came in, and I guessed she was Mrs. Millsa—the bank owner.

My chest filled and I let the air out slowly.

I'd start by introducing myself to Mrs. Millsa.

"Ginger," I said as he appeared at my side. "Get me some Winter maps, some pens, and a banker's coat."

His fiery curls bounced with a nod, and he grinned. "Yes, ma'am."

"I hope you're ready to work," I said.

AN INTERRUPTION

Two Quarters Plus Five Eves Ago…

"He's experimenting on them!" Driar shouted in the study. "The king has a band of ten plus three Yule Lads he sends across the intersect to snatch Trites in their sleep! This is not a clean study of science, Jolly, it's an abuse of magic!"

The silvery-eyed jester sighed. "Not. My. Problem."

"Have you no conscience at all?" Driar slammed his journal on the desktop. "This whole measure of time, the Polar King has been secretly conducting tests! Even the Crimson King doesn't condone Rime Folk crossing into the dead world."

But Jolly chuckled. "Your father could care less about Trite souls. Come now, Driar, is this the report you want me to deliver to the Crimson King? That you've been sitting around throwing a fancy little fit?"

Driar folded his arms and exhaled. "You are the only one here strong enough to do a thing about this," he said, nodding toward the closed study door. Beyond it, a dozen Trites slept, trapped in freezing prisons.

"Oh, for the love of..." Jolly pulled off his hat and whipped it at the young prince. Driar did not move out of the way fast enough, and it smacked his cheek. "What about me would make you think I'd be willing to risk everything I've worked so hard for? I dare say, you're as dumb as a spinbug, even with all your obsessive reading."

"Then teach me, and I'll do it!" Driar said, opening his arms wide. "Teach me to hold a sword, and I will put an end to what is going on here."

Jolly's wild laughter rang through the study. "Overtossing a king has little to do with holding a sword or a staff, you fool. It's about playing a game and deceiving your foes. You are not made for that."

The Court jester sauntered toward the door to leave, but Driar said one thing more. "You know, I've read a book or three about the ancient Truth that is so despised in our kingdom."

Jolly stopped walking. He looked back with a startlingly venomous face.

"The books were hidden below the palace library, but I found them," the young prince said. "It was just a heap of riddlesome stories, but there's been such a push to silence every word of the sacred truths in the Red Kingdom that I began to wonder what the Crimson Court has been trying so hard to hide."

"Careful." Jolly turned back, his wild eyes daring the prince to keep talking.

"Don't you feel it, Jolly? Can't you feel a war in the air around us? Doesn't it feel like we're missing what's happening?" Driar sank into the seat behind his desk. "You studied the Volumes of Wisdom in your early seasons as a Patrolman. Why did you turn your back on the knowledge given to you?"

Jolly's staff cracked down hard upon the desk, and Driar's lavender eyes shot up to him.

"I said *be careful*. You and I are far from being friends, Prince."

Jolly snatched his hat from the desk and left with a loud bang of the door.

Two Quarters Plus Four Eves Ago…

Once, Driar had been interested in science. Now, he was not so sure.

He walked the hallways of the palace, their glittering ice walls giving him an incredible view of the kingdom—hazy versions of the Polar snowhouses could be seen for miles in all directions. Filtered light prismed the hallway, casting it in soggy colours from an angry, distant sun.

When he reached the hall of Trite spectacles, Driar slowed his steps. Shallow voices lifted from 'round the corner, and the prince listened.

"And why do you think your problems involve me, hmm?" Driar heard a theatrical voice say.

A soft, female Trite voice returned. "Because I won't survive childbirth in my condition, and I think the reason you can barely look at me is because you have a soft spot for children. Don't ask me how I know; it's just a feeling," she said.

There was a dead, cold silence that followed, and Driar thought to go interrupt before Jolly said a cruel thing to the pregnant Trite woman. But what Jolly said was, "I have no reason to help you. You have nothing to trade, I'm afraid."

"Please, help me escape back to my world so my baby doesn't have to grow up here like this." The woman's voice shook like she was crying.

Driar leaned in closer, a drip of hope sinking through him. But the response was as clear as a bell. "No."

Driar folded his arms and leaned against the wall. He had never felt more helpless.

He jumped when Jolly rounded the corner. The young prince was grabbed by the shoulders and shoved back against the wall.

"Eavesdropping, Your Highness?" Jolly asked, silvery gaze wild.

"Was that Trite woman right about you? Do you have a soft spot for children?" Driar dared to ask.

"Not at all." Jolly smiled cruelly, showing a set of straight, remarkably white teeth. But the corner of his eye twitched through the black paint on his lids.

Driar scrambled to catch himself when Jolly released him. He watched Jolly saunter off.

"Cheat," he called, and to his surprise, Jolly waited. "I need you. Do a good thing, for once in your cursed time-string. Teach me how to do this, and then run off if you must.

I'll never tell a soul it was you. Do it for that Trite woman's baby."

But Jolly whirled. "Do you know why I'll never trust a folk like you to follow through with anything, Prince? Do you know why you would be positively impossible to train?"

Driar closed his mouth.

"Because you're nothing like your ruthless father, and you're just like your flimsy mother."

"My mother? What do you know of my mother, Court clown!?" Driar challenged.

Jolly's skin seemed to tighten. "She came here too, a season or three ago. The Polar King helped her to escape into the dead world. She's never coming back, despite what the Crimson Court says in their Pebble Papers."

Driar's eyes were wide and unblinking. He whirled and marched 'round the bend to where the fair Trite woman paced in her prison, running a delicate hand along her belly.

"He may be too much of a coward to help you, Trite. But I'm not. I will get you out," the young prince promised.

Presently...

A knock on Driar's bedchamber door brought his attention up from his book. He slapped it shut and rose to answer.

"Yes?" he asked as he whipped open the door, guessing it to be Ember or Hamsa up to no good. He blinked at the pair of hollow-hooded Timepieces filling his doorway with smoke and the scent of ash.

One flicked its sleeve, and a gold-edged note appeared. It fluttered into the air, floating past Driar and landing on the floor in his room.

"You have been summoned by the Crimson Court," the first Timepiece said in a slow, airy voice.

"We must ensure you arrive on time." The other's voice was no better.

Driar glanced at the faceup note upon which was scripted in bloodred ink:

Official Summons of the Crimson Court
For:
Prince Driar Sollo Crimson-Norsebin
To defend yourself at the trial
In light of the evidence brought against you

Driar paled. The book slipped from his fingers and clattered to the floor as twenty plus five sessions of training turned to flames in his mind. No strike or parry would be sufficient against Masters of Time.

Obediently, Driar swished from his bedchambers, flanked by the creatures of air and smoke in fluttering black hoods. Excuses flipped through his mind as he tried to piece together a plausible explanation for his behaviour these last weeks.

The courtroom buzzed with tension when he arrived. Upon the dais, Forrester stood tall with hollow, poisonous purple eyes. The silver coronet seemed to have grown taller on his head.

"Order," Forrester said, and the room hushed apart from

the soft clinking of glasses. His gaze slid to where Driar was ushered in. "You are all witnesses to the trial of the second Red Prince, Driar Sollo Crimson-Norsebin, who has just arrived."

Driar's knees grew weak. He looked 'round the room at the faces of those he had grown up alongside, those he had received council from, those he had studied with. None cast him a sympathetic look. His hands tightened at his sides, and he fought the desire to shove away those closest so he might run for the servants' tunnels.

"A witness has brought forth testimony that the second Red Prince was seen leaving the lobby during the eve when the traitor, Cane Endovan Crimson-Augustus, escaped." Forrester did not look up from the page he read from, even as he offered the room his evidence.

Driar tried, "Forrester—"

But Forrester continued reading. "It is for this reason I wish to have the second Red Prince—the one you see before you in the custody of our Timepieces—put into the arena in place of the traitor he aided."

The breath left Driar's lungs. "Forrester, I did no such thing!" His voice wavered; his trainer would have been repulsed by how poorly he delivered the lie.

"Someone must pay for the crimes of our disowned brother." Forrester's eyes lifted to Driar finally, and in them Driar saw no chance of turning this around. The young prince's jaw hardened as he recalled that evening he had spied on the argument between Forrester and Tegan in Tegan's chambers. Tegan had been pronounced dead the following morning.

If Forrester would bring forth a witness of Driar's

wrongdoings, Driar could bring forth a testimony of Forrester's crimes too. The young prince opened his mouth to shout the horrid truth of their future king to the whole Court when a loud crash shook the room, and the dais filled with thick, pure white smoke.

Members of the Crimson Court marvelled as a slender figure in all white stepped from the fog and took a bow. "I'm back," he sang, pulling off his mask. "And...oh, what do we have here? A trial? How tasty." Jolly Cheat's silvery eyes gleamed like nickels as he absorbed the faces in the room.

Applause started quietly from the corner. It became deafening as the rest of the Court joined in, a folk or three cheering. Jolly took another bow, but he flinched when Forrester grabbed his shoulder.

"Welcome back. But do let us continue with our important work," the prince said, and Jolly lifted his hands in apology.

"Of course, Your Highness. I wouldn't *dream* of getting involved." But those nickel eyes darted over to Driar, and Driar closed his mouth, forgetting to oust Forrester before the Court.

The crowd hushed when Forrester lifted his ring-adorned right hand. "Shall we take a vote? All in favour of casting the guilty Red Prince into—"

"It was not the second Red Prince who freed the traitor in the lobby," a young woman with a honey-gold braid stood from her seat and yelled.

Members of the Crimson Court shuffled in their chairs, whispering as Forrester's fiancé walked toward the front of the room. Forrester gaped down at Lady Holly Kissing. Driar tried to lock eyes with her to ask what she was doing, but

Scarlet ignored him and faced the Court.

"I can prove it," she said, and Forrester dropped the paper in his hands to the podium.

"And *how* would you do that, Lady Kissing?" he challenged through his teeth. "Perhaps this is a thing we should discuss in private—"

"Alas, you must be heartwrenched," Jolly Cheat cut in, nudging Forrester as Scarlet turned to face the dais.

"Try to marry me, Prince," she invited Forrester.

Forrester's mouth hung open, and the gossiping whispers of the Court rose in volume.

"You won't be able to do it. Winter will not seal the marriage of someone already wed."

Driar had never seen Scarlet speak so much at once, nor this loudly. But she continued, "I am wedded to Cane Endovan Crimson-Augustus. That is why you and I will never be married while he lives." Her words cut like knives. "That is the only reason I came back to this palace of ring-hungries who care nothing of true matters. When I learned my husband had been taken, I came here to free him from *you*. I helped Cane escape. No one else."

Folk stood, shouted, and pointed. Forrester closed his mouth, staring down at Scarlet with all the hatred within him. "I knew you were lying about who you were, *Scarlet*," he said, and fresh gasps filled the courtroom.

Driar's heart hammered against his chest as it sunk in that Scarlet was taking his place. Cane would never forgive him for this. Cane would lose his wife. Cane would…

"Ready her for the arena," Forrester decided, and only then did Scarlet's expression waver a pinch. "As I said, someone must pay for Cane's treacherous crimes."

AN INTERRUPTION, YET AGAIN

O'er the plains of snow, a mere dip away…

Upon a shore of ice, a young Patrolman stared o'er the snowseas with a wisp of grey in his chest. The measure of time he had stood there was lost to the Winter wind, and when the dark seas rippled with movement and memories, he tugged down his pointed hood to reveal his pecan hair.

Zane Cohen-Margus-Bowswither unzipped his raven-black jacket and tugged himself out of it. He tossed it to the snow alongside his Patrol staff and unlaced his curled-toe boots as well.

His heart was as cold as the seas as he stood there a moment more, surveying the silver cliffs in the distance, estimating the depths of the waters.

"Elowin," he whispered against the wind ruffling his

hair. "I spent these last quarters at her side wishing she would remember me. Now I only want her to forget me."

The breeze across the open waters howled in return.

The young Patrolman glanced at the creamy pink and grey of the Winter sky, wondering if he would ever see them again. He plunged into the frigid water and was consumed by a blanket of darkness.

Bubbles and weeds muddied his vision, and the cool kiss of water slipped into his clothes. Zane blinked against the murk, searching the dimness for anything that moved. He paddled deeper toward the black-sponged sea floor when a thing shifted in the corner of his eye.

Shades of red inked into the faint blues of his chest as a slow, slithering tentacle moved along the rock and weeds. And from the water's shadows, a sinister voice said,

"You're back."

Zane did not have time to reply before a slippery coil latched itself 'round his ankle and dragged him into the pit of the snowseas.

The young Patrolman was propelled from the water into darkness. He landed upon hard metals and rolled once before he caught himself against a cave wall. He coughed. Around him gloomed stale cavernous air devoid of even the meekest light.

"Am I one of your prizes? You had to spit me in here with your gold?" Zane asked the sea monster through his thoughts alone.

"Not all treasures sparkle," the creature replied.

Tentacles slithered by in the water, and Zane drew his legs up to himself.

"I thought Octosirens only liked things that sparkle." He spoke aloud.

"Gold and blood. Our currencies are easy to remember. And your sweet blood is the most valuable of all my treasures."

Zane looked 'round as his eyes adjusted, discovering heaps of gold, gems, and pearls this monster had accumulated during its timestring.

"Well, you bloody have me. Just get the next bit over with." He swallowed, eyes travelling back to the dark and restless waters.

"Your blood smells different," the Octosiren mused, and Zane huffed a laugh.

"I certainly hope so. It's been a good measure of seasons since I've killed for savagery and eaten seaweed for a midday meal. I imagine I smell like books and cake now." His hands drifted to a pile of gold rings, and he slid one onto his finger.

"You carry the aroma of heartbreak. How interesting."

Zane's hands slowed on the rings. "I had a difficult choice to make. But it was the right one."

"Perhaps not. You smell of other things too. You smell of something silver in your belt." Zane's shoulders tensed. *"And something else that's potent."* The Octosiren hushed as the colours turned bleak in Zane's chest. He did not move a muscle, especially when the creature growled,

"You smell of love for someone you cannot have."

Zane's blue eyes fired up to the water's surface where the low rumble of the Octosiren's laugh emerged. A tentacle burst up through the dark and slammed Zane into the cave wall by his chest, pinning him there and snapping over his fingers. The ring he had taken fell off and rolled into the water.

Zane gasped when the Octosiren released him; his fingers curled into cold, loose dirt.

"Do not touch my treasure. If you touch a single thing while I am gone, I will feel it."

Zane remained there, heaving as the monster lowered into the water and disappeared within the darkness below. The Patrolman looked at the modest patch of dirt beneath his hands and knees and the heaps of treasure surrounding it in a perfect circle.

CHAPTER, THE FIFTEENTH

Apple barged into my office, sobbing. "I have dreadful news, friend!"

She slapped a Pebble Paper down on my desk. I went to read it, but she stopped me.

"Wait," she swallowed, tears glistening on her cheeks. "It's the Medicinier. I'm afraid Mr. Tubby has been found out for helping us. He was dragged from his office by the Ruby Legion. He's been…"

I stood slowly from my chair when she couldn't find the words to tell me. I marched around my desk to go tell the Patrol that we were leaving before the same thing happened to Mrs. Millsa, but Apple caught my arm.

"Helen," she wept. "It's not just Mr. Tubby. The whole town where we hid was raided. It's been left empty and desolate like the others—another black mark on the map. The Ruby Legion may come here next. It's not safe to leave the bank anymore, especially at night."

I gripped my hair and slumped back against the desk. "Why didn't you go to the island, Apple? You should have left with the others."

But Apple shook her head. "I'll stay with you, friend. No matter what that means." She sniffed. "I cannot leave Ginger anyway after what happened to his parents, and he insists on staying with you."

I looked up in surprise. "What happened to his parents?"

Apple pulled a handkerchief from her pocket and dabbed her eyes. "Well, they were attacked in their home. It's why Ginger ran to the factory. And…well…my father was with them too when it happened."

It felt like a rock sank to the pit of my stomach.

"Good grief, Apple! Why didn't you tell me?!" I lifted from the desk and hugged her.

Fred.

With everything going on, I hadn't even noticed he was missing. I wanted to kick myself.

But Apple shuffled out of my hug. "Oh, it's all right, friend. He's in a better place now." But her eyes reddened and filled with tears again. "I'll see him again when… when…" She bit on her trembling lips. "Don't worry about me, Helen. There's a good measure of other things we must worry about now." It came out a croak. "I'll fetch Ginger for you." She fanned her face as she left, and I slumped down into the desk chair.

THE PEBBLE PAPER

SEASON'S GREETINGS! THE INVESTIGATION INTO THE DISAPPEARANCE OF PRISONER CANE ENDOVAN CRIMSON-AUGUSTUS HAS COME TO AN END.

THE CRIMSON COURT HAS FOUND LADY HOLLY KISSING TO BE GUILTY OF AIDING AN ENEMY TO THE RED KINGDOM. FOR HER CRIMES, SHE HAS BEEN SENTENCED TO THE ARENA AT DAWN. OUR SECOND RED PRINCE HAS BEEN CLEARED OF ALL SUSPICION.

LADY KISSING'S ENGAGEMENT TO PRINCE FORRESTER HAS BEEN CALLED OFF.
DO SEND YOUR WARMEST THOUGHTS TO OUR BELOVED HEIR.

IN OTHER NEWS, THE PALACE MAGICIAN CRASHED THE TRIAL WITH A MARVELOUS BANG, HAVING RETURNED TO BRING CHEER TO THE ROYAL FAMILY DURING THIS DIFFICULT TIME OF THE CRIMSON KING'S FINAL QUARTERS—

I laid the paper on my desk when Ginger arrived to deliver a cup of cocoa. The maps on the walls shuffled as he rushed in and skidded to a halt. He held the mug out toward me, and I winced at the splash marks around the mug's mouth.

"Thank you," I said. I studied Ginger with a new level of compassion, wondering what it might have been like to grow up with ginger bakers as parents.

"I've also got a fresh pot over the fire downstairs for the gathering you requested." Ginger bowed and I waved to remind him to stop doing that.

"Good. Tell the others we're meeting as soon as the bank closes in three hours. I have a hundred questions about these maps."

He nodded. Then, for the millionth time, he bowed.

"Ginger," I said, tapping a finger over Cane's letters. My hand drifted over to Prince Forrester's summons I'd taken from the village.

"Hmm?" He dipped his finger into my cocoa and licked it off.

I stifled a reaction then slid the mug over for him to finish. "How long would it take you to run to the Three Kingdoms of the East?"

Ginger scratched his fiery hair. "I don't really know; I've never been there. But the entrance is just past the wasp fields. Their Glory Feast is coming up soon, I think. That's what Apple said."

I began tapping my pen on the desk. "Their Glory Feast?"

"The Three Kings come together to eat—King Li, King Ha-yoon, and King Ren—and the best entertainers travel across the snow for a chance to make them laugh—"

"Did you say *all three* kings will be together?" I dropped the pen.

"Uh...did I say that?"

I stood and lifted Cane's letters, thinking back to when Eliot Gray spoke of the Three Kings of the East and their armies.

"I don't know why you're asking me all of this." Ginger folded his arms, showing the first signs of suspicion. "We're not allowed to go there. You won't get a snowball's throw from the kings without being arrested. I heard someone say so."

"I need to get Apple and the Patrol out of here. The villages are being destroyed, and we have no allies, and I still don't have orbs for Kaley and Lucas so Nightflesh is going to keep crushing hope and transforming himself," I said without taking a breath. "But we do have evidence that suggests Forrester is trying to mount an attack against the East."

Ginger made a sour face.

"We'll need an entertainer to get us into the Glory Feast, right? And if we bring someone who's been close to Forrester, they can confirm what Cane's letters say about his plan to attack the Three Kingdoms." My nails tapped the wood incessantly. "*And* we need to do something about Scarlet before tomorrow."

Suddenly Ginger started laughing. His high, uncontrollable giggles filled the office and bounded down the hall. "You're going to make me take you to the East, Carrier?" He buckled forward and rolled onto the floor, arms flung wide. "I heard you were crazy, but this is fun!"

I shot him a look as I walked to the hooks by the door and grabbed my bankers coat. I slid my arms into the sleeves. "Not yet. We're going to take a little jog first. There's one more person I need at tonight's meeting."

Ginger propped himself on his elbows. "But Apple said no one should leave the bank."

"I know. But we'll be careful."

☾

Four years ago, I would have screamed during the run in Ginger's arms.

We were a blur of colour, an extension of the wind, until we came to a screeching halt in the snow. I nearly flew off Ginger's back, but he caught my flailing arms before I face-planted into the clearing.

"If you need to tummyspew, I'll turn around," Ginger offered in a loud whisper.

I held my stomach and stood straight. "I'm fine."

The orchard was shadowed by a giant, swirling cloud of blackness hovering directly above the Scarlet City. I peered at it as I inhaled the fruity scent of crisp apples muddied by a lingering aroma of smoke.

"What is that?" Ginger asked, pointing to the sky.

"I have no idea," I muttered as I headed for a tree. I pulled the bankers hat out of my pocket and fastened it on to hide my hair. Ginger did the same. After staring at the pale white apples, I reached for one dangling from a branch.

"How can you be thinking of eating at a time like this?" Ginger glanced warily at the tall, magnificent palace past the trees. "What if someone sees us here?"

"Just act normal and they'll think we're Reds. Its not like we're wearing green or something." I put a hand on the boy's shoulder. "Listen, I need you to run around. If you have any trouble, scream for me, and I'll come get you."

"What am I looking for?" He stole another worried look at the palace.

"Not what. *Who*," I corrected. "I need you to find the Court magician. He might be in the Scarlet City or moseying around the palace courtyard."

Ginger exhaled a heavy breath. "When Porethius asked me to be your assistant, I thought I'd just be bringing you cocoa," he muttered. But he turned and disappeared in a wisp of colour, kicking up snow as he left.

Minutes passed and I shifted on my feet. I glanced over my shoulder, then tucked myself behind an apple tree. It started to snow, and I made a face at the blotted-out sun above, wishing I'd borrowed Apple's pocket watch.

It was another few minutes before I poked my head around the tree's trunk again, fidgeting with my collar. I tiptoed out from my hiding place to spy on the palace in case an orange-haired boy was being dragged in.

I looked at the sky again, trying to determine how much time had passed and how worried I should be—

Snow sprayed over my face, and Ginger *flew*—rolling over the clearing and eating a mouthful of snowflakes. But I whirled when a voice appeared close to my ear.

"Care for a quarrel, Trite?"

Jolly Cheat nudged his hooked staff against my shoulder.

"Ow! That hurt!" Ginger complained as he lifted from the snow, and I spotted a welt on his forehead.

"You hit him?!" I shot at Jolly.

"You bet your scotcher I did," he bragged. "Twice." He stood over me, silvery eyes twinkling amidst the rings of black kohl. "Now, do tell me what in all of Winter you're doing *here*."

"I'll get you for that, you frostbitten ashworm!" Ginger threatened, rubbing his swelling jaw. Jolly's gaze flickered to him, but my hand braced against the madman's chest.

"Touch him, and I'll bury you in snow," I warned. Jolly looked back down at me.

"Whatever you say, sweetheart. And I thought I was the crazy folk." He muttered the last part.

"You're not crazy," I said, rolling my eyes.

Jolly's expression changed. "Hmm?" It sounded like a warning.

"You're just pretending to be crazy so you have an excuse for your behaviour. It's one of many natural instincts."

He was glaring now. "I'm. *Not*. Natural."

"You're also not a madman," I snapped, and for a split second, I thought he was going to strike me into the snow beside Ginger. I moved on. "I need you to do something for me—"

"Are you obsessed with me, common-blood?" he interrupted.

"What? No—"

"You just study me like a book?"

Good grief. I rubbed my temples.

"And what about me would make you think I would *do* something for you?"

"You said you want me to face Nightflesh. And I can't do that if Holly Kissing goes into the arena," I began, and Jolly burst out laughing, high and crazed. "And I've lost my Pat…"

His laughter fizzled out when I didn't finish my sentence. He waited, and I opened my mouth to speak again, tongue twisting.

"I've lost…"

It crashed into my gut.

Zane left me.

"I don't have as much help as I did before." I glanced off at the orchard as warmth spread up my neck.

"Hmm. A mish, a mush, a kiss, a fuss; I think someone's cheeks are flushed," Jolly sang and poked my cheek, and my gaze fired back.

"Get Holly Kissing out of the palace, *please*. And I'll set you free from Nightflesh."

"Well now I'm convinced," he said, and my hope climbed. "You're right. I must not be mad after all. I suppose I didn't know what true madness looked like until I watched you spew that ridiculous, spinbug idea into the wind."

"Nightflesh doesn't trust you. You left," I reminded him.

Jolly's tongue slid over his lips as his silvery eyes narrowed. "That's a lot of pebble talk for a non-Winter-dwelling Trite. I should freeze your mouth shut." His grip tightened on his weapon, and I flinched when it twitched forward.

"I need you for this," I said again.

"Oh, for the love of Winter. Everyone needs me these days." He stretched with a yawn like this conversation was boring him.

I straightened myself. "If you want to be free of Nightflesh, then I need you to help me do this *one* thing—"

"Two things," Ginger mumbled.

"—these *two* things," I finished.

"Ragnashuck, there's a thing more?!" Jolly glared at Ginger again.

"I'll get to that." I shot Ginger a look too, and the boy shrugged. "For now, I need Holly Kissing. Without her, you might as well buckle in to serve Nightflesh for the rest of your life."

Jolly's jaw shifted. He looked back and forth between

my eyes.

"It'll cost me a good measure too much to do such a thing, and there are other games in motion, I'm afraid. You're asking me to put another thing at risk. Let her be turned to snow, Trite. That insipid Lady of the Court should be no concern of yours; she *shouted* her guilt to the Crimson Court."

I pulled out the pure white apple from my bankers coat pocket. Jolly's bright gaze dropped to it as I held it between us. His eyes flared; his chest filled. "Get Holly Kissing out of the palace, and my friend here will make sure we get far away after it's done. Nightflesh won't find you where we're going."

Jolly eyed Ginger and snorted. "I doubt he'll do the trick." But he snatched the apple from my hand. With a growl, he hurtled it into the orchard so far, I didn't see where it landed.

"Ragnashuck," he cursed. "Rag. Na. *Shuck.*" He whirled toward the palace, growling as he marched away, "Frostbitten, common-blooded Trite!"

I released the breath I'd been holding and leaned forward to rest my shaking palms on my knees. "Honestly, I didn't think that would work," I mumbled to Ginger.

"What do we do now?" the boy whispered back.

I slumped to sit in the snow, folding my shuddering hands on my lap. "We wait to see if he turns us in to the Crimson Court or comes back with Scarlet."

AN INTERRUPTION

Driar leaned his forehead against his chamber door. He had thought of going to seek out Scarlet to ask why, why, *why* she would do such a thing.

For most of his life, Driar had thought only of himself—'Twas a curse of being a Red Prince. But his colours had shifted these quarters past. And of all the folk he had dreamt about during his time away studying the sciences, the one person he had thought of most was Cane.

Driar tugged at his pearl-white hair, inhaling every pinch of breath he could before swinging wide his door and stepping into the hall to face the nobles. He marched o'er the hallway's ruby carpets, past the rose stained-glass windows, and he arrived at the dinner table where his brothers and esteemed nobles of the Court awaited their meal. Forrester swept in and took his place beside the king's empty chair. His purple stare cut to Driar for a pinch, his thin mouth twisting.

Driar waited behind his seat, staring at the chipped engravings in the wood as he always did, when a screech sounded across the table. The Court magician clamoured as he yanked his chair out of the way. When the silver-eyed juggler looked up, he locked gazes with Driar, and Driar was not sure whether to cower or question the put-off fellow.

Letting his gaze drop to the table, the magician waited in silence.

The dining room doors burst open and in marched a Ruby Legion commander with fresh blood and snow painted o'er his arms. Driar's younger brothers shuffled 'round the table to get a closer look.

"Your Highness," the commander said to Forrester. "The disowned prince is at the border with the Queen of the Pines. He's shouting for you to come meet him."

Stillness came over the table.

"He *what*?" Forrester seethed. "That ashworm wishes for me to go meet him in war?" But suddenly he laughed, and a measure of nobles 'round the table laughed with him.

Not Driar though, nor the moody magician.

"Has he forgotten who I am? Kingsblood, I should have faced him in the arena myself." Forrester tugged off his rings one by one and tossed them onto his plate with a clatter.

"I shall meet him at dawn. After I watch his wife perish in the arena." Forrester smiled, and Driar's hands tightened on the chair's back. Across the table, the magician scowled and looked off.

"Someone must inform the king," the commander said, glancing toward the empty chair at the head of the table.

"I will do it," Driar blurted, and a measure of heads

turned his way.

An awkward pause followed during which no one objected, so Driar left his seat and rushed for the hallway. He had made it less than ten paces when a light set of footsteps echoed his.

"Daring a visit to the king, hmm?" Jolly Cheat kept his merry voice low. It was the first time either of them had spoken to each other since Jolly had made his grand entrance at the trial.

"Keep away from me or I'll have you drowned in paint. And I'll enjoy it after you abandoned me the way you did," Driar shot back.

A fluttering laugh escaped the magician. "Torture is not your thing, Prince. Ragnashuck, how about you stick to what you're good at, and I'll stick to what I'm good at."

"And what are you good at, exactly, apart from leaving at the worst of times?" Driar paused to glance 'round the turn. He whisked into the empty hall that would take him to his father's chambers.

"I told you I had a thing to take care of when I left Polar Territory," Jolly answered as he flicked dust off his shoulder. "And I bring the same news now, I'm afraid."

Driar halted his walking and turned back to the magician. "You're leaving? But you just got here."

Jolly folded his arms, stretching his all-white jacket. "Your father is a clever folk. Not as clever as me, of course, but clever enough to see through you as I did. Don't go see him, Prince. It'll muddle things up."

The air in the hall felt thin. Driar tugged at the collar of his shirt and looked toward his father's bedchambers.

Jolly began to saunter off as a thought crossed Driar's

mind. "Wait a minute…" he whirled to where Jolly was vanishing around another bend. "What thing do you have to do?"

But Jolly had already disappeared.

Driar looked back toward where his father lay in a dark room surrounded by the stench of mortality. He wanted to see for himself how much longer it might be before the man passed on. According to the latest reports, the Evergreen Host was on the verge of extinction. Cane had days, maybe hours, before Forrester would find him at the border.

A turn and a stair away, a notorious cheater flitted down the hall. He reached the dungeon and tapped his staff against the stone arch to catch the attention of the nattering guards in ruby capes. The majority of the guards ignored him.

"Excuse me, daft spinbugs," Jolly sang.

The guards stopped their chatter. Twenty plus one bodies turned toward where Jolly lounged against the arched frame, but his silvery eyes landed on a guard at the back. "Ragnashuck, didn't anyone teach you how to shave? What a gangly thing you are."

The guard rose and flexed his thick arms as he crossed the room. "You should show some respect, clown." He came nearly against Jolly, and Jolly shrugged.

"You're probably right." Jolly studied his fingers and rubbed at a pinch of dirt left there from his scuttle with the redhead in the orchard. The rest of the guards stood 'round the room, and a crook of a smile dented Jolly's face as they drew in close.

"How fun. Now, I'll take these if you don't mind." His staff punched forward, slamming the nearest brute in the gut, and toppling him into the others. Jolly held up a dangling ring of keys and winked as he slammed the door shut, locking them in.

He rushed to the adjacent hall with a scowl, and a slew of unsavoury words rolled off his tongue, "Button-muddling, common-blooded *Trite-slug*!" His jaw tightened as he rounded the corner toward the darkest cells where not a flicker of torchlight warmed the space.

When Jolly had stomped to the end of the row where the gloomiest cell of all sat tightly fastened behind a thick lock, he shook the keys in a way one might call forth a snow pup with a treat.

"Yoo-hoooo?" he hollered into the darkness. "I've brought good tidings, my lady. Let's jingle all the way! There's no time to waste!" He shook the keys harder.

A set of cautious honey-brass eyes emerged from the shadows. The lady did not come to meet him at the cell bars, but he did not have time to exchange pleasantries or convince her.

Jolly stuffed the keys one by one into the lock until he found the one that fit. He swung the door open with an angry clatter and reached in to grab her by the arm.

AN INTERRUPTION FROM THE SNOWSEAS

The air had cooled a time or three and the Octosiren had not returned. Zane never slept; he kept his eyes on the troubled waters, waiting for the monster.

The darkness of the cave seemed to shift over time. It began as a deep black-orange and then settled into a sickly black-blue. The Patrolman could not tell if the cave's insides were changing with his mood or if it was simply his eyes adjusting to the endless string of dark as he paced 'round his modest circle.

Finally, the dark waters stirred. Zane could feel the monster's restlessness even before one of its tentacles brushed along the surface.

When the thing rose from the water and peered with a yellow eye, the young Patrolman sat in the dirt and crossed his legs. A low grumble lifted as the Octosiren's eye darted 'round his troves.

"What did you touch?! Something has been meddled with."

The monster paced, filling the cave's waters like an army of eels. Zane folded his hands and rested his arms on his knees as he watched. He did not offer a response.

"I will spill your blood into the snowseas..." the monster threatened.

"Get it over with then," Zane finally said, breaking his silence.

The creature roared and the treasures in the cave rattled.

"I've traded away your life already, but if you've touched a thing, I'm certain I will lose control and you shall meet your fate in my lair."

"Interesting." Zane tapped a knee with his finger. "Ragnashuck, I thought that woman might try a thing of that sort. Thank you for confirming my suspicion." He moved his hand toward a bowl of copper rings resting beside his dirt circle, and the Octosiren bristled as Zane's fingers flitted over them, never quite touching the jewellery.

"You do not fear death." 'Twas a question, and Zane folded his hands, resting them back where they belonged.

"I'm the son of a sea witch who wished to snuff me out a good measure of seasons ago. I was never supposed to be given a pinch of good cheer in my timestring, yet, I had it. Dying alone seems..." he glanced off at a thick treasure box spilling with emeralds, "fitting."

The dark, cold laughter of the Octosiren rumbled through the cave.

"Be careful what you wish for."

"Be careful what you bargain for," Zane returned, blue

eyes firing.

The monster stilled in the water, and Zane stood slowly. He felt a flit of laughter threaten his chest when the Octosiren twitched. "Do you have another question for me?" he taunted.

The monster lifted its head from the water to reveal long fangs covered with strings of seaweed. Zane slid back a pinch as the creature set its glowing eyes upon him.

"What. Did. You. Touch?!" The creature demanded, and Zane's own steady gaze narrowed.

"Everything."

Zane kicked gold trinkets across the cave and sprang for the water's surface, diving clean and sailing into the cold underseas.

The Octosiren lashed out, snatching the Patrolman by his ankle. Bubbles exploded between them as Zane tore a silver dagger from his boot and plunged it into the beast's tentacle.

The water filled with a piercing screech, and the Patrolman rolled away.

Weeds and pitch darkness brushed his cheeks as he paddled. He slipped 'round the turns of the cave until he saw the faint glittering of light ahead. But black tentacles spilled from the cave's mouth, filling the snowseas floor and spreading over him to block out the sunlight like a leak of ink.

Zane arched down into the weeds, feeling his colours burn without air. Slimy plant life stuck to his elbows as he lowered into the marsh. The monster would smell him, even amidst the seafloor sponges. He studied the water's surface, waiting for a space to appear between the Octosiren's tentacles, but his eye caught on something that sparkled, floating down through the water. He caught it between his fingers, brows tugging together.

A feather.

Fingers brushed his leg. He spun, gasping cold water into his body as he stifled a curse. He blinked wildly at the figure before him.

For, floating in the water was Helen Bell.

He reeled back, pressing his eyes shut. His colours heated in his chest as he convinced himself she was not truly there. But those same fingers brushed along his jaw and his eyes flashed open a time again, taking in the sight of the Trite with long hair and smooth, cream skin. A sweet song tickled his ears, and he felt his knees weaken as she tugged him gently toward the depthless weeds below. Her glittering gold hair floated amidst the sponges, and he squeezed the feather in his hand; a sudden smile tempting him when he noticed her glowing topaz eyes.

"Your sirens are doing a scotchy job at imitating a Trite," Zane told the Octosiren through the folds of the sea. He spun the dagger in his hand and stabbed the siren's arm that held him. A bubbling scream erupted from the animal who faded back into a seal-fleshed terror of the seas.

Zane kicked upward, stroking against the shifting water toward the only slit of light above. The sea's belly filled with the crawling seal-skinned sirens creeping out from the weeds. They paddled up after him, singing, screaming, tempting him to return.

He pushed the Octosiren's tentacle aside and rushed for the surface. His hand drove into his pocket as the Octosiren swerved toward him, its fangs opening wide as Zane burst from the sea with his arm bent back.

He hurtled a golden box into the sky.

The last thing Zane saw was a flock of silver winged birds rushing in to catch it.

The Patrolman was torn back into the snowseas by black limbs and webbed siren fingers.

He did not come up again.

CHAPTER, THE SIXTEENTH

Ginger drifted off to sleep with his head on my shoulder. I kept my eyes focused straight ahead on the palace doors. The coiling black clouds darkened above, and a handful of times I'd considered leaving the orchard. But Ruby Legionnaires hadn't flooded in to arrest us, so I clung to the hope that somewhere inside the palace, Jolly Cheat was doing what I'd asked.

An apple fell from a branch to my left, and I jumped. Ginger snorted awake. He rubbed his eyes and looked around like he was trying to remember where he was.

Suddenly, the palace doors burst open, and Jolly came out *dragging* Scarlet behind him. She protested as she tumbled down the stairs in his grip. I rushed to grab her.

"No time for reunions, *common-blood*," Jolly snapped. "I didn't come alone."

Shouts and the loud boom of armoured footsteps filled the palace stairs. Ruby capes speckled the woods so fast that I shoved Scarlet toward Ginger. But my flesh tightened at the sight of the Ruby Legion.

Their eyes…

Their skin.

"What's wrong with them?" I asked, but in the same breath I said to Ginger, "Get us out of here!"

"What?! I can't carry three of you! Carrying one grownup folk is barely possible with my size!"

My wide eyes slid over to him. "Seriously?"

"Oh, for the *love of Winter*!" Jolly growled as he yanked me to him. He slammed the heel of his staff into the snow, and we took off with Ruby Legion arrows spitting over the orchard. A puff of snow and a smear of colours passed as Ginger sped off with Scarlet.

Legionnaires sped over the snow like grey phantoms with wide mouths, dark eyes, and leaking smoke. I stared until Jolly cleared the orchard and slipped between two city buildings. We flung around shops, lantern posts, and gold sleighs, and my gaze caught on Mara Rouge's pale statue by the Red Kingdom gate laying in pieces: a severed head, crumbled shards of stone, and crushed flowers at its base.

The iron gates swept by us, and we entered the rolls of smooth white snow beyond.

I didn't think I was holding on too tight until Jolly peeled me off and flung me into a heap of snow. I rolled, blinking at the shock of cold. A thump sounded beside me, and I glanced over to see Jolly laying flat, chest pumping.

"*You*," he heaved, staring up at the sky, "nearly strangled me to death."

I dragged my knees beneath me to sit. "Sorry."

"Frostbitten Trite." He flicked a handful of snow at me and got me right in the eyes. "I dare say, it's deliciously tempting to drag you back there and be rewarded for it." He lifted a lazy hand and pointed in the general direction of the kingdom gates hidden by hills of snow.

A wave of snow splattered a metre away and Ginger appeared, cheeks flushed. He trotted toward me, but I pointed to Jolly.

"Take him first," I said.

Jolly unpeeled his staff from the snow. He flicked another pelt of snowflakes at my face, and I bit my lips in annoyance.

"Pesky, *pesky* common-blood. Stop trying to make me like you. It won't work." But Ginger swept him away before he could offer another catty remark.

I caught my breath as I waited.

Ginger came moments later and scooped me up off the ground. I heard his strained breathing as he ran, and I realized I'd worked him too hard. After seconds of racing through a tunnel of smeared colours, he slid to a halt and the town of Harpwood appeared around us.

Ten Patrolmen in bankers coats held their Patrol staffs levelled at Jolly's throat. Jolly was on his knees, and Wanda was poised over him with her staff's ice pressing against his jugular.

"Ah…there you are…" Jolly managed, and Wanda glanced up at me.

Shadows peeked at us from the windows of empty houses down the street, and Rime Folk in red garments pointed.

I swooped in. "I need his help," I said, and all ten Patrolmen exchanged looks. Timblewon's ice slid out further from his staff in a long, sharp icicle that pricked Jolly's jaw.

"I can't frostbitten let him live, Trite," Wanda said in her raspy voice. "He and I go way back, you see."

"Give him one chance—"

"Nope." Timblewon shook his head. "Can't do that, Trite."

Jolly coughed and dared the climb to his feet. He grabbed my shoulders and yanked me in front of him like a shield. "You didn't tell me I'd have to see *them*!" he whispered.

"Don't give me a reason to let them finish what you started," I muttered over my shoulder.

Wailing came from the bank entrance, and Apple ran out. I didn't realize Scarlet stood on the stairs until Apple's arms were fastened around her. "Thank Elowin!" she cried. Scarlet's face remained composed, but a tear slipped down her cheek and she hugged Apple back.

"I'll have you all know that I was the one who rescued Lady Kissing from the palace," Jolly announced over my head. "I am your hero this evening."

I rolled my eyes.

"I'd never ask you to trust Jolly Cheat," I said to the Patrolmen. "But right now, we need to get out of the streets. Let's have a meeting inside."

I pulled Jolly toward the doors of the bank; he kept me positioned between himself and Wanda as her large eyes followed him. He looked around when we came inside, taking in the tellers and the safes and the piles of rings on every desk.

"Ragnashuck. What are you thinking bringing me in here?" he finally blurted. "Do you *want* me to steal all this merry treasure?"

"Quiet, Jolly." I brought him through the bank and

smiled at the hot cocoa bubbling in the stone oven in the meeting room. I picked up the ladle.

"Is that…"

I glanced back. Jolly's black-ringed, silver irises were fastened on the blessed teapot on the table inside a crescent of delicate teacups.

"Help yourself," I said, reaching to stir the cocoa.

"…tea…?" He whispered the word to himself. The teacups clanked and I heard liquid pouring from the pot a second later.

Everyone trickled in—the Patrols, Apple, Ginger, and Scarlet. "Where's Porethius?" I asked, and Apple shook her head as if to say she hadn't come back.

I sighed and sipped my cocoa. Apple filled the rest of the mugs and passed them around before taking a seat at the table in front of where Wanda stood. Not a single Patrolman had stopped glaring at Jolly.

"I've decided to visit the Three Kings of the East," I said. "Ginger will take me there."

Wanda released a choke-snort on her tea, and a drip fell into Apple's hair. Apple inhaled the longest, quietest, most repulsed gasp of all time.

"Just Ginger?" Mirkra asked from where he leaned against the wall. I waited for him to point out that I had no Patrolman. Mirkra had offered himself as my Patrol after I'd appeared downstairs in the bank. I'd politely declined.

"No, not just Ginger. To get into the Glory Feast, I'll need an entertainer. And once there, I'm going to tell the kings that the heir of the Red Kingdom plans to attack them. I'll show them Cane's letters as evidence."

"So, you'll take Timblewon, right?" Mirkra folded his

thick arms, glancing warily at Jolly.

"No. I'm bringing the Crimson Court's own magician to confirm my story."

This time it was Jolly who fumbled his tea. "What?!" He pointed at Timblewon. "Take pink-hair! I'll not sacrifice myself to the Three Kings for you, Trite! Haven't you already asked enough of me?"

Timblewon objected too. "I can't entertain kings, Mirkra. I was a white lion trainer. What would I do without lions? And besides…" Timblewon tugged off his bankers hat and scratched his fuchsia hair, "I'm a scotchy fighter. That's why I hosted Patrol competitions and never entered them. You know that."

"Oh, come on, Timbie. That's not true!" Kilen gasped.

"And you think *Jolly Cheat* will save you if you're in trouble?" Mirkra challenged me. "He won't help you survive the wrath of kings!"

"Ragnashuck, if only you knew how recently I taught a prince to do just that," Jolly muttered, lifting his tea again. He slurped it loudly, locking eyes with Mirkra across the room.

I rubbed my temples. "I know this should be a group decision, but we don't have time to argue," I said. "The Three Kings have the only armies in Winter that Nightflesh hasn't conquered yet. If we can get the kings to turn against the Ruby Legion, it'll keep Nightflesh's armies occupied, and if we can get orbs to Kaley and Lucas and start spreading hope, we'll slow Nightflesh's transformation. This is our only chance."

"By the sharpest wind," Apple huffed. "Is this what we've resorted to? Begging foreign kings for help?"

"It's that or the frost giants," I said. "That was the only other idea I had."

Grunts lifted around the room.

"You can all sleep on it," I decided. "Tell me what you think in the morning. But remember that we're running out of time."

I swished through the group and past Mirkra's skeptical glance. I kept moving until I escaped the building, tugging on my bankers hat as I did. The cold bit at my warm cheeks as I looked both ways down the road.

The streets crawled with shadows; shrieks lifted from distant alleys. I pulled my coat tighter as I headed off the road into the forest, inhaling the cold scent of ice, evergreens, and decay. I trudged until I came to an icy cliffside. The dark town curved below the cliff, and I watched Rime Folk drift between the shadowy buildings. I felt their hopelessness like an illness in my stomach.

I dropped to crouch, rubbing my eyes, and I pulled off my hat to toss it into the snow.

"Elowin," I whispered. "I thought you promised these people an army. I'm not an army."

The breeze turned thick against my skin, and I suddenly felt lost in the endless abyss of silence. I rose to my feet, sliding my trembling hands into my coat pockets.

Something fell from the sky and hit the ground in front of me.

I blinked at a gilded box sitting in my upturned bankers hat, and my gaze fired to a flock of birds overhead.

I reached for the golden case. The scent of swamp and fish leaked out as I shook it, creating a sound like bumping nails. I turned it over and unclicked the latch with my thumb.

Four rusty, pointed pieces were strewn inside. I dumped the metal into the snow and wondered if it was a puzzle.

Not a puzzle. I sprang to my feet when I realized what was before me.

The iron pieces would form a four-pointed star.

My eyes shot back to the birds as a spring erupted in my chest.

"Zane…" I breathed. I moved to chase the birds, but an arm reached across me and grabbed my shoulder.

"Let them fly off." The aroma of sage flooded my senses. "We have a preposterous task to complete, and a Night Beast to evade."

My mouth parted as the birds scattered into the dark clouds.

Jolly's stern, silvery gaze appeared before me.

"I heard a rumour or three," he flicked a hand back toward the bank, "that you're wandering Winter without a guardian. And if there's a thing I know about that pretty, blue-eyed snow pirate, it's that if he doesn't want to be found, he won't leave a trail."

"You don't know him like I do," I said, but Jolly raised a brow.

"Ragnashuck, shake off your blinders, you fool. I've known him a good measure longer than you have. Forget Cohen and focus on the Night Beast haunting my every sleeping hour," he said, then added, "You should be filled with cheer that I've changed my merry mind. I think I'll come to the East with you after all. Seems a bit stuffy in the bank with those Patrolmen."

The iron star gave off a dull sheen from where it rested in the snow as every last bird disappeared from sight.

PART IV

AN INTERRUPTION

A blessing is how this story began.

'Twas a single fleck of gold, no heavier than a feather, floating along the Winter skies, searching and searching for a shoulder to land on. The whistling calling wickets were not amused at the sight of it bobbing along, taking its time, twirling upon the gales, and waving to the galloping prayers in the clouds as it passed.

The blessing landed on the wooden pauldron of an infamous once-prince whose eyes blazed burgundy; his mahogany hair stained with Rime blood and frost. Feeling the tiny weight touch his shoulder, the prince paused his slashing to listen.

Cane wiped the grime from his chin, the drips from his cheeks, and the snow from his emerald cape. "Do not be afraid," he whispered to himself.

He hardened his jaw and stared across the battlefield. The Queen of the Pines was tossed from her polar bear, her iron blade skidding o'er the snow. Cane scooped it up and hurled it back. Ever Green caught it with pale fingers, narrowly blocking the blade descending for her throat. Cane charged the Legionnaire, tossing him to where the queen's iron sword turned him to a puff of snow.

Cane offered her a nod. "Hang on a little longer," he pleaded. And, as the blessing had whispered, the once-prince added, "Do not be afraid."

But when a fresh blast of trumpets came singing o'er the hills, Cane's burgundy stare lifted to the screeching reindeer in the sky. The coronet atop its rider's ivory hair glistened in the dull sunlight, his long crimson cape a flag at his back.

With so few Greens left, Cane knew Forrester would spot him and send every Legionnaire his way.

A copper sword struck his arm and Cane growled, ducking just as an iron blade slid out before him and blocked the Legionnaire sword before it struck again. The Queen of the Pines dropped to a knee and sliced, turning the Legionnaire back into snow. She rose, her grey eyes falling on the reindeer descending into the hoard of ruby fabric and copper armour.

"It seems we've lost, Red." The queen wiped snow from her arms.

Cane looked 'round at the empty emerald capes covering the snow and the folk or three left firing arrows. It had ended so quickly. This was not the distraction he had hoped for. He closed his eyes, inhaling the message of the blessing.

"My wife and brother will not survive another evening if this is over." His throat tightened, but a coarse laugh drew his eyes open again.

The Queen of the Pines looked ahead, her sword turning in her hand. "My kingdom is lost. My army is doomed. But I am not dead yet, Red," she said, and her stone-grey eyes settled on Cane. "Get me inside your palace, and I will move the pace along to help your brother." She wiped blood from her mouth. "The Crimson King has been mine to deal with since the eve of my birth."

Cane stared at the queen with Edward's chin and sloped cheeks, wondering how one Green sibling could spend their timestring hiding in fear, and the other could be so dreadfully fearless.

The once-prince inhaled and muttered to the air, "Elowin, I need one thing more from Porethius, if she is still willing."

The words had barely escaped his lips when a thunderous crash rumbled o'er the plain where a violet-winged fairy drew a dual-bladed sword. Ruby Legionnaires scooted to a halt at Porethius's feet, one or two scrambling backward. She glowed like the Winter stars, her symbols a testimony, and Cane felt the blessing lift from his shoulder, for it seemed he did not need it anymore.

The Queen of the Pines dropped her sword into the scarlet-speckled snow and pulled out a dagger instead. "Tell your fairy to deliver me quickly so she may come back and keep you from getting snuffed out," she said. The queen tightened the leather belt at her chest and gave the once-prince one last nod. "I wish you good tidings, Red. I hope you win."

And so, the blessing bowed to the Red and Green royals and flittered off with a, "*Farewell!*"

From there, the blessing rose into the sky before burning across it in a flash of light, where it followed the sound of a train whistle, spiralling back in time to a moment where a certain train conductor was pouring his morning tea with a steady hand. The blessing slipped in through a crack in the arched window's glass.

"Oh, hello," Cornelius said. "You've arrived just in time. My teapot has gone cold."

And into the teapot the blessing went.

CHAPTER, THE SEVENTEENTH

The iron star clattered in my pocket as Ginger and I reached the factory. Again, I took in the deep gashes scarring the metal and the burn marks up the walls, trying not to think about my friends hiding inside while that had happened. The snow tunnel at the back of the factory had collapsed—or maybe the dwarves had crushed it on purpose when we'd left. It was a heaping pile impossible to dig through.

"Wait out here for a minute," I said, and Ginger slumped into the snow and crossed his legs.

I crept around the walls until I found a window low enough to bash in, and after tossing my backpack through, I slipped inside and landed on my feet in a room of copper pipes. I imagined the sounds of bubbles and rushing liquid filling the room and the scents of hazelnuts and dark chocolate seeping from the cracks. I imagined white butterflies fluttering at the ceiling and golden paintings on the walls.

The quietness shouted at me as I crossed the chamber and scooted down the hall to the main room where damaged walkways and balconies hung from threads, threatening to detach and crush me. Blots of old smoke fogged the skylights and glass obscured the floor.

I turned once to take it all in, coughing up dust. I let my backpack fall to the dirty floor and heard the wreath and drum clap together inside. My hand pressed lightly over the star in my pocket.

Only half a year ago, Kaley and I had set out to hunt down these items across Winter. I'd imagined everyone would be with me when we finally brought the pieces of the Triad of Signs together. Cane had found the drum, and I'd carried the wreath out of the Green Kingdom myself. Though he'd left, Zane had managed to bring us the iron star. I'd pictured him at my side for this, at least.

I took in a deep breath, feeling the hollowness of the broken space. Then I asked the factory, "Where would I find a room that only a Carrier can find?"

Not a thing stirred. Decorative bows hung limp, and wooden spindles littered the floor like snapped bones. I folded my arms.

I'd never exactly *spoken* to the library back when I was there, but a book had sent me to find a door, and a door had sent me down a passage where I'd met Porethius Plum for the first time.

"I know you've been badly hurt," I tried, sure Ginger would think I was crazy for talking to a vacant space if he was spying. "But I need your help to find the orbs. I know the spirit of the library came here with the Patrol." I did another slow turn, eyeing the hallways. "Where are you hiding them?"

Dead silence responded.

I sighed and looked up at the ruins of the factory one last time. "It was worth a shot," I mumbled, yanking the backpack off the floor. "I'm the last Carrier of Truth, you know. You could at least answer me—"

The floor opened beneath me like a hatch door, and I screamed.

It was pitch dark when I slammed into a cushy pile of *something*. Dust particles puffed into my mouth, and I wheezed. My orb warmed against my chest, and I tugged it free to illuminate the room, fanning the chalky clouds of powder away to read the title on the bags below my knees: FLOUR.

I coughed again and climbed to my feet, holding my Revelation Orb in front of me to get a better view of the room. I was in a pantry.

"You sneaky little building," I whispered as I turned and found that the room stretched on for another twenty feet. Shelves lined the walls from top to bottom holding baking tools and sacks of old sugar. But my eyes misted with gratitude when I beheld the pantry's true treasures tucked in around the mixing spoons and dry ingredients: glassy, dusty, empty Revelation Orbs.

I scooted off the flour bags, releasing a powdery puff, and I shivered as chill leaked in through the rips in my bankers coat.

"You wouldn't happen to have a better jacket too, would you?" I tried pushing my luck. My fingers ran over the glass orbs, picking up flour and dust. I pulled my bag open to load it when a low click filled the quiet room, and a door popped open to my right.

White coats on copper hangers glimmered in the closet, all with the same fine gold threading. I tugged one out with my powder-covered hand and laughed. It looked like a marching band jacket with its golden buttons and short collar.

I shrugged it on and got to work filling my backpack.

Minutes later, I hauled it up a narrow staircase and pushed through a false wall back into the main room. Ginger was spinning in circles, kicking up dust.

"There you are!" he scolded. "You never came back!"

"I was busy." I held up the backpack.

Ginger's chubby cheeks rounded as I took an orb from the bag. I extended it to him.

"Thank you for being here with me for this, Ginger," I said.

He looked at me in question, but he slowly took it. "Is this for me?"

I nodded. "You're no longer my assistant, Ginger Dough. You're my apprentice."

Ginger and I were rubbing our eyes when we returned to the bank, and my shoulder ached from the weight of the backpack. I was still blinking after nearly being blinded by the bright light that had erupted from the Triad of Signs. Ginger had squealed and clapped when it lit, and then he'd gotten to work placing each orb into the contraption at rapid speed.

“What happened to you, friend?” Apple asked, and I looked at the mess of flour down my white coat. I patted it off my shoulders.

“I got into a fight with a bag of flour,” I said, marching to the meeting room. Patrolmen fell into step behind me with curious eyes on my backpack.

“Where did you get that coat?” Mirkra appeared from the hall and cut me off. “I haven’t seen one of those in…Do you know what that coat is?”

“Warm?” I guessed.

“It’s a Carrier coat. Mikal put them in storage after the collapse.”

“Oh…” I realized all the Patrols were staring at me. But Mirkra flashed a smile, and I pulled the bag tighter over my shoulder.

In the meeting room, I turned my bag upside down and dozens of glass balls spilled out, rolling across the table. Patrols shuffled to catch them before they tipped off the edge, and Kilen gasped when he held one up and ivory and gold swished inside like a greeting.

“Yesterday, I had no idea how we were going to slow down Nightflesh’s transformation. But today I have hope—” Something snapped within me, and I whirled away from the group. I didn’t know why exactly. My lip quivered.

Kaley was going to train new Carriers.

My plan had worked.

My plan…

I closed my eyes.

He wasn’t here.

Zane wasn’t here for this.

Everyone was looking at me.

Hopebringer.

A thumb smooshed over my cheek, and my watery eyes opened to Jolly making a repulsed face as he wiped my tear on his new bankers jacket. The kohl was gone from his eyelids. "You smell like salt," he informed me.

"You smell like sage," I said, and he perked up.

"Do I?" His straight teeth showed with his smile. "Delightful."

I wiped my tears away and inhaled a lungful of air. Jolly's wrists were tied with rope.

"They still don't trust me." He lifted his bound hands when he saw me looking.

I let out a slow breath then turned back to the others and raised my chin as I tugged Apple's pocket watch from my coat. "Ginger, we'll leave for the East as soon as you get back from making your delivery."

AN INTERRUPTION

A Quarter or Three Ago

Kaley stood outside the crumbling Trite house for thirty minutes before she had the boldness to step toward it. Paint slapped its chipping walls in a variety of vandalised images, where horrid curses were written, and not a single window was left un-smashed.

Her running shoes dragged o'er the sidewalk as she crossed it and crushed the uncut weeds that had taken over where grass was meant to be.

When she knocked, a large man opened the door with hateful eyes and a stench on his skin. He looked prepared to snap little Kaley in half, but she spoke anyway.

"I'm here to see Winston Bell," she said quietly, and the man came out. The door slammed shut behind him.

"What?" His voice was as dark as dusk.

Kaley cleared her throat and tried a time again. “I’m here to see Winston.”

The man did not blink, nor did he move out of the way so she might pass. “Are you a cop?” his husky tone demanded.

“Do I look old enough to be a cop to you?” As soon as Kaley said it, she shut her mouth.

The man frowned. But to her surprise, he swept aside and shoved the door open for her to enter. “If you don’t leave in the next five minutes, you’re not leaving at all.”

The warning crawled o’er Kaley’s skin as she entered the house. She was hit with the whiff of old vomit, spilled substances, and lost dreams. Slowly she crept across the unswept floor, stealing glances at people slumped there. Some moaned, others snored. Some did not move at all.

“W…Winston?” Kaley’s tongue felt a pinch like lead.

After glancing in several rooms, she reached a staircase that was rotted in its middle. At the top was only one room more. So, she climbed, keeping to the edges and holding tight to the rail.

When Kaley entered the last room, she gasped.

“Winston!” She rushed to him and dropped to a knee.

Her brother’s eyes were closed, his hair matted, and he slouched against the wall. He did not appear to be breathing.

“Winston!” she called again, shaking his shoulders.

A low sound escaped his lips, and Kaley blinked back moisture. “What happened to you?” she whispered, asking herself, truly. Asking why she had waited so long to come find him.

Winston’s pale lashes fluttered. Kaley might not have recognized him if it weren’t for his light hair and the black tattoo wrapping his throat.

"Winston, wake up! We're going home." She reached beneath his arms, but his hand flung up to push her off.

"I don't have a home," he rasped.

"Yes, you do. I'm your home. Helen is your home. Come home, Winston."

Winston peeled his eyes open, and his lips cracked in a sad, dull smile. "If I try to leave, these people will come find me; I'll be left dead in a ditch anyway." Kaley started when his bone-thin hand slid out and folded over hers. "Get out of here before they decide to keep you here too."

"Winston!" Kaley grabbed his hand and squeezed. "You need serious medical help. If you don't come with me right now, you're going to die!"

With the way he looked at her, Kaley was sure he already knew that. The tears in her eyes grew fat, threatening to plunge down her cheeks.

"You're my brother," she croaked. "Come home."

"Get out. And don't let them see your face," Winston said, his eyes sliding shut again.

Kaley stared at him for a measure, her heart twisting and tangling.

But she rose.

"I know you made bad choices. But I loved you anyway," she whispered.

He did not respond.

When Kaley left the house, the man at the door watched her until she passed the sidewalk and rushed down the street, ten plus ten more tears soaking her fair cheeks. She should have crumpled to her knees like her body wanted, but she kept walking, even as her tears blinded her, her legs wobbled, and her mind cried out. A hand flew up to clutch the glass orb necklace tucked beneath her sweater.

She could not tell Helen. Not yet. Not when Helen did not remember.

As Winston Bell's eyelids grew heavy as gravestones, and his living soul became too much a burden to carry, he shed a single tear, and he whispered, "Help…" His last word fell into the afternoon hush.

He died in a quiet, unmerry, lonely way.

His prayer took off soaring.

A dip and a Trite street away, a fellow lifted his head as a sound plunged into his ear. When a beam of sunlight slipped against his eyes, an explosion of colours prismed o'er the inside of his hood.

He turned back toward a store he had passed.

Ticks and tocks and watches and clocks left rhythms of noise in the air. The young fellow went to a wall of old, broken desk clocks and selected one in a case of wood with a glossy finish. The clock was dead—or, mostly dead at least—but he turned the thing 'round and wound up the back. With a new tick and a matching tock, the fellow whispered something very secret into the clock's ear, and he nudged the minute hand back ten plus five minutes.

The clouds outside the window moved backward.

Trites in the street walked backward.

The wind blew backward.

All in all, it was a good measure of things heading backward.

After thanking the clock for its service, the fellow returned the ticking thing to the shelf and left the store.

When he arrived at the house, he spotted little Kaley Bell leaving it. He watched the Trite girl disappear into the park, and 'twas then he moved for the front door.

A stocky Trite man stepped to block him. "You can't come in here," the man said.

But the fellow lifted his hooded head, and the Trite man's face changed. Without another word, the man stepped aside, his brows tugging.

The fellow moved inside like a swift river; a breath of life in a valley of bones. His cloak rippled, brushing ankles and toes as he passed, and souls stirred or sat up or opened their eyes and blinked.

Winston Bell was a lifeless being, alone and growing cold. The fellow pulled away his hood when he reached him. And he said, "Open your eyes, boy."

Winston's eyes opened obediently. His heart began to beat, his lungs began to breathe.

The fellow reached beneath and lifted him from the miry floor, carrying the boy down the stairs, through the hall, and out the front door where the Trite guard scrambled far out of the way.

Indeed, time tends to be a funny, funny thing.

Presently...
(Well, sort of)

Snow did not exist on the island. When Kaley Bell and Lucas Leutenski met the fairy guarding the long glass bridge across a turquoise sea to a golden sand beach, Kaley believed she was dreaming. Only a moment ago, they had been sailing o'er dark, icy waters with black clouds on the horizon and shadows lurking below the snowseas. The scene had completely transformed the moment they had stepped onto the glass bridge.

"There's no way we're still in Winter," Kaley whispered to the youthful Patrolman at her right.

"Darling, there are places in Winter where green grass grows, gardens thrive, and buildings are made of stained glass and copper." Lucas pulled his pointed hood down and scuffed his dark hair.

Kaley sneaked a glance at him as she followed the fairy guide onto the shore of sparkling sand. Hoots and cheers came from the grasslands beyond the beach where fifty plus eight woven stick structures dotted the green. The breeze was warm—a fresh kiss off the sea.

"You wondered why you were never brought here by the fairies," Kaley said, tightening the backpack on her shoulders. "But it sounds like you ended up in a place just like it."

Lucas paused. "Well, ragnashuck, Trite. You seem so certain I was never meant to end up here, yet you brought me here yourself."

Kaley felt his hand slide into hers. She glanced down at it as the fairy guide turned to face them.

"Our time pocket was crafted by a powerful Master of Time. You'll experience a greater length of time here than those outside it," she said. "But our pocket doesn't live completely outside of time. Winter's magic only gives the children a chance to grow up and become strong enough to face the wintersphere on their own."

A bell rang and a flock of children raced from the nearest building. Laughter tore across the grasses and Kaley felt a spark of warmth rush through her chest.

"Welcome to the island. Don't eat the sog fruit, and make sure you wash the sand from your feet before climbing into bed!" the fairy said.

TWO FULL QUARTERS LATER
(AND YET, ALMOST NO TIME LATER AT ALL)

A loud knocking sound released ripples across the sky. Kaley dropped her papers to her desk and stood, watching the glimmering veins spread o'er the time pocket's shell. She looked across the yard to where Lucas spoon fed a chubby cheeked, two-seasons-old boy freshly ground wheat from the field mixed with cream.

Lucas set the wheat down and handed the boy a soft syrup candy instead. He trotted across the grass, his white top flapping in the breeze. "What the frostbitten rung-nut was that?" he asked Kaley.

"Watch your language, Lucas. Yesterday in class, Sorwen called Chakyak a '*Frostbitten thief*' for borrowing his ink," Kaley scolded.

Lucas threw his head back and howled a laugh. “That whipsteaming sputtlepun is my favourite.”

Kaley stifled a smile and tucked her pen into her dress pocket. “Anyway, what do you think that’s about?” She pointed to where the glittering veins were fading from the sky.

“You’ve received a package, Miss Bell,” the Post Fairy said as she landed in the field, shaking the ground and stirring the grasses.

“Me?”

“Ah. So that’s what all the knocking ruckus was for.” Lucas leaned in, snooping at the large velvet sack in the fairy’s hands tied neatly with a silver rope.

Kaley lifted the note card. On it was Apple Dough’s unmistakeable, embellished script:

For Kaley Bell
The Supplies You Requested

Kaley made a face, and when she did not open it quickly enough, Lucas took the silver rope and yanked it free.

A hundred lively glass balls tumbled out into the grass.

CHAPTER, THE EIGHTEENTH

A storm sprinkled the wasp fields where Ginger dropped me off. In the distance, a tower-like mineral archway peeked over the field's hills: the entrance to the Three Kingdoms of the East.

Ginger left to get Jolly before I could ask about the wasps.

Blue insects busied themselves through the snowflakes, congregating at clear glass hives. Cool cobalt liquid funnelled to the bottoms of the hives, dripping out a tiny hole at the base and leaving an inky stain in the snow. I wandered to one and stuck my finger under it. A cobalt drip splattered on my fingertip, and I stuck it in my mouth.

Tangy sweetness tickled my tongue. "Mmm. If only Apple could try this," I mumbled.

Every wasp in the hive turned its head toward me like they'd heard what I said. They began crawling out the top, and I backed away, the hairs on my arms raising as they buzzed around me.

"You're friendly bugs, right?" I asked, and they released a quiet, melodic tune. I lifted my hand, and one landed on my forefinger, so I brought it closer, studying its blue-armour shell. But a needle came out of its mouth, and it stung my face.

"*Ow*!" I shrieked, rubbing my nose.

"Are you frostbitten mad?!" A Patrol staff whisked by and suddenly every wasp within an inch of me was trapped in a twist of ice. Jolly grabbed my arm and swung me around. "*Please* tell me it didn't stab you with dizzy venom," he said, and I opened my mouth, but my tongue felt fat. Jolly sighed, and Ginger's face paled.

"Ragnashuck."

It was the last thing I heard before my knees went weak and my head started spinning. Everything was fantastical swirls and liquid colours after that.

My legs were jelly, and my head was lead. I rode on Jolly's back with my forehead slumped on his shoulder while bright, vibrant colours bled past. I heard Jolly make wild promises to strangers.

After a while, he tossed me into a pile of snow.

"Ugh…" I moaned. My hand came out to search for a flat surface as my surroundings began to tip. "Why'd you do that?"

"You didn't think to warn her about the wasps?" Jolly said, and I caught a glimpse of Ginger's fiery orange hair.

"I thought she knew! Everybody knows not to touch a

wasp!" Ginger's high voice rang like shrill bells in my ears, and I rolled onto my side, plugging my ears with my fingers to block out their noise.

Later, I heard Jolly say, "Well, at least her pathetic wobble-toes got us in. It was more believable to say we came for the healers than to try and convince the entrance guards that I was an entertainer in this hideous jacket."

"Hey..." I pointed a finger at him, or at the sky—I couldn't tell. "Apple made that jacket. It's...beautiful." My head dropped back into the snow.

The sound of squeaking hinges pained my ears, and I heard Jolly chatting with someone as I stared at the sky.

I hummed to myself.

Jolly and Ginger carried me to a room smelling of cake and pastries, and I was tossed into a chair. Ginger asked me a few questions. I tried answering, but after a while he gave up.

"She's a total spinbug," Ginger said.

"All we can do is feed her and put her to bed, I'm afraid." Jolly appeared before me with something in his hand that smelled delicious. He broke a piece off the end and waved it around my mouth. "Say *ahh*," he coached.

My mouth popped open, and he stuffed it in. I tasted lemons.

"It's just like feeding a baby," Jolly explained to Ginger. But he shoved the rest into my mouth in a big handful and I coughed, spitting half of it onto the floor.

"Ah. Yes, well, not all babies like to eat their food when told. Bad girl." Jolly shook a finger at me. He hauled me from the chair and half-dragged me down a hallway. A moment later I was flipped onto a flat surface. My mind shut down.

"Well, that settles it. I'll take it from here, you flimsy common-blood." Jolly turned to go, and I raised a hand to stop him, but beyond the burst of colours that erupted in front of my eyes I saw his navy coat disappear out a doorway.

It was evening when my head stopped spinning enough for me to sit up. Ginger was snoring on the floor beside my wood-slab bed. I winced and rubbed my bruised shoulder muscles, looking around at the dimming lantern in the corner, the plain desk, the empty bookshelves.

Ginger snorted when I nudged him with my toe. "Where are we?" I said, and he sat up, rubbing his eyes.

"We're…"

Cheers erupted from outside. I teetered with a rush of vertigo, pushing aside the curtain. But the sleepiness rushed out of me when I saw the notorious Red Kingdom magician across the street.

Jolly stood on a balcony in a new, glittering sapphire coat and a feathery hat. Rime Folk crowded the street below, all pushing each other aside for a better view.

I nearly choked when the blades Jolly juggled burst into live flames.

"Huh. I wonder how he did that," Ginger said from beside me, and I pushed past him, guessing my way around the hall.

When I came out of the building, I was met with scents of wild spices and sugar. The streets were narrow with townhouse-like structures of deep scarlet, azure, and jade with curved roofs that looked like bamboo. Balconies filled with people in red and purple robes protruded into the street. But what struck me most about the city was the sky: clear and blue. Real evening light touched my face, the sunset gilding the folks' flat, woven, square hats.

The crowd was so loud, I couldn't have shouted to Jolly if I'd wanted to. He pulled out two more knives to juggle ten at once, tossing them high into the sky like flaming birds. Blue and green sparks flew off, and Jolly hopped onto the rail of the balcony, not missing a beat.

All the knives disappeared like vapour, and the crowd hushed.

"Huh…" Jolly turned and put his hands on his hips. "How strange." A twinkle lit his silvery eyes.

People shrieked and pointed, and I staggered off balance as ten knives appeared above the crowd, plummeting toward us, blades glistening. The flames whipped back to life as the knives fell, and Jolly sprang from the balcony like an eagle taking flight. Mothers screamed and pulled their children close, and I grabbed Ginger's jacket to shove him out of the way, but a hand appeared over my face and snatched the blades out of the air, one by one as they fell.

"Feeling better, sweetheart?" Jolly asked as his hands worked. But he didn't wait for my answer; he tossed the knives back into a juggle, and the crowd erupted with cheers.

At the end of his performance, Jolly bowed from the streetside, and when people approached him with parchment and opened books, he whipped out a fluffy feather pen and autographed everything in sight.

I sighed and folded my arms to wait. Ginger clapped wildly beside me like everybody else. When a blushing Rime girl passed, I caught a glimpse of the autographed paper she clutched:

NICHOLAS BICKOLAS

"Nicholas Bickolas?" I burst out laughing.

My arm was tugged from its fold, and I realized Jolly was beside me. He scribbled his autograph across my palm before I could yank my hand back. He grinned and took my shoulders to turn me toward our building. "Alas, I must bid you all farewell and head back inside this lovely establishment where I am staying." He knocked a knuckle off the building's sign that said: FUNNELBEAR'S TEA AND TARTS.

"Are you *trying* to get your fans to flock this place?" I asked, and he smooshed a finger over my mouth.

"Shhhh," he said. He shoved me and Ginger in ahead of him and slammed the door shut. "Ragnashuck, can you smell those tarts?" He took in a long, drawn-out sniff. "I think it's time for an evening snack."

We entered a long room with drawn rosy curtains and pedestal-covered tables of coloured tarts; sugary pink, blossom orange, shimmering emerald. Berries, leaves, sugar crystals, and nuts sprinkled the tops. My stomach growled on cue, and Jolly poked it as he passed. "You seem ready for one."

"Jolly—"

"Didn't you hear my beloved admirers hollering in the street? My name is *Nicholas*," he corrected. "I'll never be Jolly Cheat again. It was a scotchy name anyway."

"And you think Nicholas Bickolas is better?" I stifled

another laugh, but he didn't smile so I wiped the grin from my face. "Nicholas," I tried, even though it felt weird.

"Hmm?" Jolly whipped around and the hem of his sapphire coat fluttered. "Do tell me what's on your mind. Are you dying to know how I made the blades come down from the sky?"

"I can live without knowing that," I assured. "I want to know where we are—"

"Ah. Just a moment." He held up a finger in front of my face. A beat of silence passed, and he squinted. Then he put another finger up. "Two moments, then."

When another second passed, I pushed his hand away from me. "What in the world is going on? I don't remember anything since the—"

A knock sounded against the door. "Ah!" Jolly scooted past me to go answer it. "Right on time."

A rush of cold air swept in as the door was thrown wide, and Jolly removed the ridiculous feather hat from his head as he bowed. "You must be the assistants to King Ha-yoon. How riddlesome and unexpected!" He glanced back at me with a gloat. "What can I do for you folk? Hmm? Spin a poem? Recite a tale? Perform some magic, perhaps?"

A flutter of feathers filled the doorway, and a sleek red bird landed on the doorstep in front of the men. A card was in its beak.

Jolly reached for the card and dipped his head in thanks. The bird flapped off, and the men bowed in return before leaving. Jolly shut the door and held up the card for me to read:

Official Summons from the Palace Entertainment Association
For: Nicholas Bickolas
To perform at the Glory Feast of the Kings
On Tomorrow's Moonlit Eve
For one hour plus one half

"Good grief, that was fast!" I tugged the card to myself.

"Not really. I've been entertaining that street crowd for *two days*. I'm a pinch insulted the fools didn't come sooner." Jolly unbuttoned his jacket and tossed it over the back of a chair. He whistled, and an elf poked her head out from a back room. "Nimby, sweetheart, can I bother you for some tea?"

The elf blushed. "Not a bother at all, Mr. Bickolas. I'll bring it right away!" She disappeared around a door.

"Oh, for goodness' sake, Cheat, did you have to charm the poor elf lady too?" I said, and Jolly flinched. He didn't look up though; he reached for the nearest tart and bit into it. I sighed. "Sorry. I meant…*Nicholas*."

I dropped into the chair across from him. "What does it matter anyway what I call you?"

Jolly—Nicholas—took a second tart and flicked the cup off the bottom.

"It matters to me. And that's all that matters in the grand scheme of matters that matter." His silver eyes met mine. "A name is everything. A name is life or death or weakness or power. That's why we don't say the names of those we fear, and we keep our real names hidden from our enemies when we must stand and perform in their presence."

He bit into the tart.

"Oh." I glanced at Ginger, who shrugged. I changed the

subject. "Well, anyway, I guess I owe you a thank you."

"For what?" Nicholas asked. "For freezing the wasps before you were stung to death? For getting you into the Three Kingdoms? For finding you a place to sleep off the venom? For getting us an invitation to the Glory Feast?" He took a napkin from the pile and dabbed his mouth with it. "What ever could you have to thank *me* for, useless Trite?"

I bit my lips together. "You might be able to charm a crowd, *Nicholas*, but your sarcasm sure isn't cute," I said, and he eyed me doubtfully.

"You're obsessed with me," he said. "You think everything I do is cute."

Ginger snorted a laugh.

"Whatever. Think what you want." I took a tart for myself and slouched back into a chair as the elf arrived with a steaming pot of tea. It smelled like turkey and stuffing.

"Oh, I *do* think what I want. I think I'd like to rub it in Cohen's face how you feel about me. I think I'd like to watch his pretty blue eyes turn green with jealousy or grey with rejection."

This time when I looked up, I was glaring.

Nicholas was smiling.

"I think you're heartwrenched, and it's given you blinders. I think you don't need him, and you can't see that. I think *he* saw it though."

My chair screeched when I stood. I set the tart down before I could throw it across the table at him. "Well, *I think* you're a liar who likes messing with people for absolutely no reason," I said.

"Oh, I do like messing with a folk, yes, but I'm not a liar. What would my daughter think of me if I was?" Nicholas drew his teacup to his lips and sipped.

My mouth tumbled over my response. “Wait…You have a daughter?”

“A sweet bundle of cheer, I dare say. And she’s mine. A little Trite thing too with such unimpressive eyes. But she’ll be remarkable; I’ll make sure of it.”

I blinked. “A Trite…”

“A common-blooded, non-colourful *Trite*. Didn’t I tell you I was taken? My heart is hers, I’m afraid. Every last pinch of it.”

A chuckle slipped from my mouth. “I’m no mathematician, but I don’t see how that’s possible. You were only in the Trite world for a few months.” I dropped back into my seat.

“That I was.” He sipped his tea again and didn’t explain further.

My eyes fell to the uneaten tart I’d set on the table. “Zane told me he didn’t want to be my Patrolman anymore.”

“Ooooh,” Nicholas cringed. “Ouch. How scotchy. But it seems like it did the trick.”

“It wasn’t a trick.”

“Wasn’t it? You didn’t follow him, did you? It appears that was what he wanted. Don’t be daft, common-blood. I can spot a trick a village away.”

I chewed on my lip. “Why would he want to keep me from following him?”

“How should I know? Maybe he didn’t want you to see something.”

“Would you like some more tea, Mr. Bickolas?” The elf swept in with the teapot again, but Nicholas sighed and pushed his cup away.

"No thank you, Nimby. I've drunk all I need to drink and said all I need to say." Nicholas rose from his seat, took his coat along with the card from the red bird, and swept out of the tart room. "Time to come up with a performance worthy of kings," he sang from the hall.

But I stared at the pedestal of pink tarts.

Nicholas's words rang through my head long after everyone left and Nimby the elf turned off the lights in the dining room.

Maybe he didn't want you to see something.

AN INTERRUPTION

'Twas a painful blast of cold when the young Patrolman was spat ashore. His colours were nearly snuffed out, his timestring close to snapping, his song too quiet to hear.

Winter snow lay beneath Zane's cheek, and a conversation lifted above his head.

"He's bloody dead," a woman growled. Dark dreams and bad memories accompanied her tone, and Zane tried to open his eyes.

"He did not come easily." A deep voice lifted from the seas. *"Our deal is complete. Should you ever step into the snowseas again, you are mine to devour, sea witch. I will not spare you a second time."*

"You had better *hope* we don't meet again," she purred in agreement.

The ground rumbled with an undersea growl. Water sloshed up the snow to where the Patrolman lay as the great creature disappeared below the surface like a black cloud.

A boot struck Zane's shoulder. He tumbled over to his back like a fish drying in the sun. Between his slit eyelids, he saw the brightness of the pale sky, felt the icy air turning the water on his lashes to frost.

"What shall we do with him, Prophetess?" a folk asked.

"He will die a dreadful death as my gift to the Night Beast. The death he deserves."

Red polluted the dim hues in the Patrolman's chest, and in the blur above him, Zane was sure he could see a cherry-coloured smile.

The darkness was potent and suffocating. The Patrolman did not remember being carried in, but he remembered falling.

Zane awoke on a stone floor. Heavy pain weighed upon his eyes when he tried to open them. Flashes of a terrible fight filled his mind:

The Octosiren's fang catching his thigh.

The tip of his dagger slicing inside the monster's mouth.

The struggle for air.

The thrashing of black tentacles.

The stabbing of screaming sirens…

Zane lifted a hand to his swollen throat as though the Octosiren's tentacle was still wrapped there. He coughed and moaned as his neck prickled.

A low thudding sounded in his ears.

Thump...thump...thump...

'Twas like a knocking against his mind.

"I thought they'd snuffed you out," someone said. "I was waiting for you to puff into a pile of snow."

Zane winced as he rolled his head to the side. He spied a man in the cell beside him with a dirty white beard, droopy eyes, and golden irises. He knew he had seen the man before, but he was not in any condition to remember.

Thump...thump...thump...

Zane rubbed his temples.

"You hear it too, boy?" The man grunted and stroked his beard, revealing hands bound with heavy manacles. "Don't listen to it. You'll become like those possessed creatures. Whatever comes knocking from here on in, don't answer."

Memories of a circus came back in pieces—ones of music, and colourful powder, and a checkerboard tent.

"Obb." Sound was lost from Zane's hoarse voice. But the aged man nodded.

"Don't ask me to make you a door, boy. Can't you see I'm out of commission?" Obb raised his bound hands. "And even if I could, I wouldn't make another door for all the rings in Winter."

When the man looked off, Zane spotted snowy-blue bruises along the fellow's fingers.

The Patrolman pulled himself up to sit with a grimace. "I'm alive," he muttered, his colours beginning to warm in his chest. "I'm bloody alive..." He looked 'round at the cells fashioned with iron and ice, studying the gaps in those bars and wondering if he might fit through. He surveyed the tunnels beyond. His gaze landed across the hall at a shelf of metal gears and trinkets.

"Those were all my things," Obb said. "Everything from my pockets. They'd be lucky if they knew how to use them."

Zane swallowed and inched backward to lean against the wall.

"The fools didn't take everything though. Luckily, I still have this spool of invisible string. That's the trick of invisible string, you know. You move it when no one is looking, and they'll never know it was moved."

Zane dragged his gaze over to the man. "You have a spool of string?"

"I do. And I'd like to make a trade," Obb said, blinking his droopy eyes.

An unexpected laugh filled the Patrolman's weak chest. "I don't want your string."

Obb huffed. "Don't be a fool, boy. Don't you know the value of invisible string?"

"What do you want me to trade?"

Obb leaned in closer to whisper through the bars. "I want to be turned into snow."

Zane lifted his head from the wall.

"I want to finish my fight before I can be used to bring more bad tidings. I am doing no good here."

But Zane shook his head. "I won't do that. Your mind is muddled if you think I'll—"

"I just need those." Obb pointed toward the shelf with his nose. Zane's gaze slid to the trinkets and snagged on a set of silver medallions resting atop a dusty box.

"How am I supposed to get those?"

But Obb smacked the bars. "Do you know how many doors and peepholes they've forced me to make, boy?" His cheeks grew red. "Six hundred and thirty plus five!" he shouted, and it echoed down the hall. "That is how many abomination doors are conflicting with the intersects! I tried to hide as many as I could by tucking them under a bed where they would not be noticed or locking them inside a Trite jewelry box. But a good measure were left in places a Trite could stumble through, you know! Don't you know what a problem that is?"

Zane felt the plea press against his bones. It had been a measure since he had thought about the tears between worlds, but now that a Guard of Doors was right before him, he could not unthink the news. "How—"

"Can't you see I will be forced to keep making them? Do me this, boy. Do me this one favour, and I shall give you my invisible thread." Obb's bound hands went into his pocket. He drew them out again and laid them flat, but nothing could be seen on his palm. "I heard them nattering. They'll bring you out in a pinch. That is your chance to grab the coins," Obb added.

"Ragnashuck," Zane rasped, eyeing the man. "You don't really have any string, do you?"

Obb released a grunt, finally dropping his hands to his lap. "Fine. You're correct. I haven't any invisible string. But get me my things back, and we can set a thing right."

Zane sighed and scrubbed a hand through his damp hair. "I'm alive," he whispered to himself a time again. His bright gaze flickered back up to the bars trapping him in, a bud of hope blossoming in his chest. "You said they would bring me out in a pinch?" he asked the old man.

"I'm certain of it."

"Then make me a door," Zane said. "Make me a door out of here, and I'll do whatever you ask."

For a moment or three, Obb's golden eyes did not blink. "Even if I could," he clasped his bound hands, "I wouldn't."

Zane leaned his head back against the wall. "Then we have no deal. You have only a pinch to change your mind before they come for me."

CHAPTER, THE NINETEENTH

"Look at me in this coat." Nicholas turned back and forth. "I'm *gorgeous*."

After declaring Ginger and I were his servants, Nicholas had boarded the Palace Entertainment Association's sleigh, and we'd been pulled along by a flock of tall-legged birds.

"I wouldn't get carried away," I returned as I followed him through the courtyard of ice, crystal, and snowy flowers. The ground floor of the palace was made entirely of glass, revealing nobles in indigo blossom-dresses and imperial coats with dragon-like masks.

Every folk we passed bowed and greeted us in another language.

"What are they saying?" I whispered to Nicholas.

"I haven't a clue, sweetheart." He pulled a canister from his pocket and began dabbing black kohl around his eyes.

Red birds carried cards in their beaks overhead like the one that had delivered our invitation to the tarts and tea building. Glistening golden gates surrounded the yard with sky-high spindles and chiffon banners revealing the moon-light through transparent fabric.

Nicholas entered the palace with a spin.

Nobles sat at tables piled with twisted bread sticks and fluorescent bottles. Upon a dais, three thrones were decorated with sea green ribbons and gold beads. Stringed music accompanied a choir of boys ringing hand bells, and I looked up at the sparkling, pear-shaped chandeliers. I bumped into someone's back.

"Sorry." I caught myself on a table.

A man in a brass mask turned. He said nothing, but he stared at me through the thin slats of his face covering. I glanced around for Ginger.

The lights went out and everything turned black.

Questions rose through the room. Bodies bumped me, and my hand was grabbed. I pulled it away as bright symbols flared over my knuckles, and I crossed my arms to blot out my lights, putting everything back in darkness.

"Season's greetings. Welcome to my show."

The music piqued.

The lights came on.

The man in the mask was gone.

Nicholas bowed on the stage. Everyone clapped, but I spun, looking for Ginger. I stuffed my glowing hands into my pockets, and my heels squeaked as I marched for the nearest chair and climbed on to get Nicholas's attention.

Nicholas didn't see me, but everyone else did.

My waist was grabbed, and I was dragged off the chair

by elves in palace uniforms.

"There's been a huge misunderstanding," I said when I realized. "I'm not trying to ruin the show!"

I was pulled behind a curtain into a candlelit room and shoved into a chair.

"Don't move until this eve's entertainment has ended," an elf instructed, drawing out two inches of a gilded dagger. I shut my mouth.

I could hear Nicholas spinning riddles and flirting with the ladies. People awed and cheered.

Finally, after what felt like *hours*, applause erupted from the main area.

"Oh, for the love of…"

Nicholas stood in the doorway pinching the bridge of his nose. "Is this how Cohen felt trying to keep track of you?" he asked, folding his arms.

I sighed. "Probably." I stood.

"We have a meeting with King Ha-yoon in a pinch, useless Trite," he said, reaching in to yank me the rest of the way from the room before the elves could object. He had me through the curtain in a heartbeat and danced us through the crowd toward an arched opening.

King Ha-yoon's private room was made up of frost-kissed windows with a view of a colourful city beyond where flags and banners waved in the sky. King Ha-yoon himself was a thick, muscular man. His black hair shimmered with a blueish hue, and his slanted eyes hosted bright silver irises like Nicholas's. He seemed pleasant enough—he dragged a knit blanket over his lap when we sat down.

After pouring us hot drinks, the elves swished back to stand along the wall. I said nothing as Nicholas began to talk. And talk. And *talk*.

He had the king laughing in no time.

I watched people out the window carrying baskets and cloth bags before the backdrop of a lush, pink sunset. Paper lanterns flickered on down the street, and torches were lit as the last of the sunlight glided away in a serene escape. I'd forgotten Winter could look this beautiful.

"Your skies are still clear." I cut into the conversation and Nicholas fumbled the cup of cocoa in his hands. An elf approached silently to clean it up. "The rest of Winter has grey skies now. It's that way everywhere, except here."

King Ha-yoon blinked his silver eyes.

"Ha! This Trite woman with me is crazy." Nicholas smooshed a hand over my face as though it would stop me from talking, but I pushed him off.

"My friend is just being nice, but we've really come here for help. I'm sure you've heard of what's been going on across the rest of the snowglobe."

Nicholas tossed his napkin onto the table in surrender. But King Ha-yoon offered a small laugh and nodded to the nearest elf to bring more cocoa.

"And this entertainer beside me is no ordinary magician. He's Jolly Cheat, the infamous magician of the Crimson Court," I added.

King Ha-yoon looked up in surprise.

I pulled Cane's letters from my pocket, along with Forrester's summons for Ruby Legion recruits. I laid both flat on the table. "We've come to warn you. The heir to the Red

Kingdom throne plans to attack the Kingdoms of the East."

King Ha-yoon glanced at the papers. A crease formed between his brows, but he lifted his cocoa and sipped, then nudged the letters back toward me.

"Why would you bring this to me, even if it were true?" His gaze slid to Nicholas. "You say you're Red and a member of the Crimson Court?" he asked. "Your allegiance is to the Crimson King."

Nicholas was glaring at me, leaning his cheek against his fist. When I looked to him for help, he flung a hand as if to say, *"You've gotten yourself into this one."*

I took in a deep breath. "We brought these letters between the second Red Prince, Prince Driar, and the former Red Prince, Prince Cane, as evidence so you'd believe our story. It's also why I brought the Crimson Court's own entertainer; so he can confirm that all of this is true."

King Ha-yoon put his cup down on the low table between us. "In my experience, folk don't share information unless they're looking for a trade."

"Not a trade," I said. "We just need allies. The believers have been disappearing and there are so few of us left."

"So, you wish for asylum?" The king chuckled. "The Dead King is not spoken of much here anymore, so I have no reason to help the believers." But he eyed the letters on the table.

"We're not only here for asylum. We also want your armies to defend themselves from this new threat. The armies of the East are the only ones that haven't been conquered. But based on these," I tapped the letters, "they're going to be coming for you."

King Ha-yoon glanced over at Nicholas again, and

Nicholas reluctantly nodded. "She speaks truthfully, I'm afraid," he mumbled.

Elves moved in with more trays, but King Ha-yoon lifted his hand to stop them.

"I cannot discuss this any further tonight. Perhaps tomorrow, though, if you can return here for the midday meal. We will speak more of this then."

Without warning, the king rose. Nicholas sprang to his feet and pulled me up with him. With a low bow, Nicholas said, "Of course. Thank you for such a delightful sip of cocoa."

I bowed too as the king turned to leave.

We stayed like that until the sound of King Ha-yoon's footsteps left the room.

"Ragnashuck," Nicholas whispered and reached over to smack my hand. "Why didn't you let me do the talking?"

A moment later, cold air nipped at my face as we left the palace and crossed the courtyard to where Ginger waited, slumped against the golden rail. Nicholas's brows were tugged together; he fiddled with the buttons of his coat.

All of a sudden, a foghorn-like sound blasted from the palace. I slapped my hands over my ears along with everyone else outside until it stopped. The echo rumbled over the kingdom, seeming to sail in every direction.

"What...was...*that*?!" Nicholas scowled up at the palace. "Is that really their curfew bell?"

I blinked back a rush of strained moisture. "That was the worst," I said, lightly touching my ears. People around the palace complained and pointed.

"The wretched sound is still moving." Nicholas turned an ear to the wind with a peculiar face, but I didn't hear it anymore.

I looked back at the palace where candles were being blown out and lanterns dimmed as people were ushered out of the lobby.

"Let's just get out of here," I said. "I don't think that chat with the king went well."

Nicholas's jaw shifted back and forth as he marched for the sleigh. "No, Trite. I dare say, it did not."

I was looking forward to sleep. My muscles ached from the wooden slab bed, but we'd only just arrived back at *Funnelbear's Tea and Tarts* when a loud, pecking knock rattled the door.

Nicholas lit a paper lantern, illuminating the pedestals of tarts in the kitchen as Ginger sped to open the door.

Cold blew in, along with a bright red feather that tumbled over the floorboards. The bird was already flapping into the sky. A card was left on the doorstep.

"What a mysterious little red chicken," Nicholas murmured. He whistled as he brushed around me to reach for the card. But when he flipped it over, the song paused in his rounded lips. The message glowed on the page:

You're not safe here.
Run.

AN INTERRUPTION

In a room with no candles, nor any window light, the Crimson King fought the phantom iron nails pressing into his head. When the palace attendants whispered at his bedside every eve, he ignored it. When his eldest living son came in to complain, he ignored it. When a shuffle sounded at the door, he ignored it.

Anger was his medicine. For, he was not finished being King. He offered a deal to the darkness to allow him to rise again and finish his conquest of the Green Kingdom so he might become a legend whispered about 'round hot fires. On his timestring, he swore he would watch every Green turn back into the snow from—

"Season's greetings, Your Majesty."

The king's eyes slid open at the sound of a voice he could not immediately place. 'Twas a voice that brought prickles to his skin like a brush of pine needles. In the dim room, a folk rested in the bedside chair with dark hair, sharp grey eyes, wooden armour, and an emerald cape at her shoulders.

"We have a fight to finish, you and I," she said.

The Queen of the Pines rose to her feet.

Somewhere deep and dark below, a young Patrolman awoke to the sound of thumping boots against the stone floors. Obb opened his golden eyes, and in the aged man's gaze, Zane saw a final plea.

"Ragnashuck," Zane mumbled. There was no magic door or peephole in his cell.

The scent of sour flesh filled the air as Zane's cell gate rattled. The Patrolman climbed to his feet, eyeing the gnomes in their rusted red armour. He walked to them with his arms out, and the gnomes bound his wrists roughly.

On the floor, Obb squeezed his eyes shut. The aged man's chest rose and fell, and Zane sighed at the fellow's scotchy acting.

Nevertheless, when the gnomes pulled Zane from the cell, the Patrolman whipped his hands out and snatched two silver medallions off the shelf. He dropped the coins to the floor and kicked them away.

Obb opened his golden eyes as the medallions rolled to a stop before his face.

Growls filled the hall as the gnomes fumbled with the lock of the aged man's cell, and Obb released a howling laugh. He offered a nod of thanks to the young Patrolman as he pulled himself up to sit. Zane nodded back.

The Patrolman was struck in the jaw and tossed off his feet, but he craned his neck to watch as Obb's laughter grew, the folk's cheer turning into a song. "Go tell it on the mountain!" Obb bellowed. "Elowin is the *True* King of Winter! Glory to him!"

A moment later, the aged man's cell burst into a flurry of snow.

The gnomes stopped their rustling.

Silence filled the hallway.

After a significant pause, Zane was torn back up to his feet.

He stared at where the aged man had once been until he was yanked 'round the bend. And when he turned, he came face-to-face with his past.

The Prophetess's eyes were eyes no more. For once, Zane stared into them, wondering what sort of soul was left behind them. Guessing there was not one at all.

She lifted a handful of bread toward Zane's face, but he turned his head away.

"Eat," she instructed and tried to shove it in his mouth. Zane bit his lips shut until the gnomes pried them open. When the woman shoved the bread in, he refused to eat it.

A gnome slammed a fist into his stomach, and Zane buckled forward, nearly tripping o'er the creature's boots.

"Chew," the woman said again.

Glaring, Zane swallowed the thing whole.

The Prophetess's cruel smile returned. "If you faint before I give you away, I'll toss you back to the Octosiren. Think of that in the seconds to come, Steelheart."

Zane said nothing.

The Prophetess's pecan hair swished as she turned to a staircase.

"I will bloody enjoy this," she admitted. "You think yourself more noble than me. But you're far worse," she said, snorting a laugh.

Zane climbed the stairs in silence, fighting a dizzy spell.

"I knew you'd eventually abandon *her* like you abandoned the rest of us."

Electricity sparked in his eyes when he looked at the woman's back, but Zane chewed on his lips so he would not ask.

The Prophetess turned to face him at the top of the stairs. "You left her to freeze to death in a place where no one could find her." She tipped her head to the side, showing off her ashworm tattoo. "I didn't know you were still so heartless."

Zane's lips moved, but he bit them shut. The Prophetess waited.

"But they did find her," he said, his mouth betraying him. "Right?" Zane studied her pale eyes as dull colours began to swim inside of him, then heat, inflamed burgundy, and deep panicked purple during the seconds the woman did not tell him what she knew.

"*Right*?" He took a step toward her.

"Steelheart," she said. "You should know by now that I don't give insights for free."

The gnomes pulled open a large stone door. Sharp laughter and clanging bells spilled out, but Zane kept his eyes on his mother as her cherry lips split into a wide smile.

"Now you'll be turned to snow not knowing if you murdered the last Carrier of Truth all by yourself."

The Prophetess shoved his chest, and Zane staggered

backward through the door. The stone was heaved shut and the woman was sealed away with her knowledge.

"Witch!" Zane shouted.

But the room behind him quieted. The scent of smoke and burned flesh crawled into his nose. He turned slowly.

In every crack and corner of a long cave with a dais of black, ivy-covered thrones, a thousand creatures of darkness waited, watching him. Hisses lifted from the shadows. Whispered falsehoods rushed in on a phantom breeze making his hairs stand on end.

Smoke and black mist rolled off a shadowed balcony in coils, creeping o'er the floor toward his feet. A being rose in the darkness.

The creatures erupted in screaming laughter and chants. The noise echoed off the walls as a helmet appeared in the cloud of blackness. A faceless being emerged, sending ripples of wind through the cave. Patches of black flesh moved with him.

"Elowin is alive." Zane forced the whisper o'er his thick tongue, and all the noise died. "He's going to come back. Maybe not now; maybe not before I'm gone. But *Elowin will come—*" His truths were sliced by black smoke bursting from the being and spiralling into his chest.

Zane found himself on his back, crying out as fire and hate and emptiness devoured his colours and his hope.

The smoke vanished, and the quiet sound of footsteps met his ear. The Patrolman opened his watery eyes.

Eliot Gray stood over him with a face patched with red, his curly hair in knots, and in a robe stained with ash. A long dagger was in his hand.

Zane released a tear-filled laugh. "Eliot…Of course it

would be bloody you."

His shirt was grabbed—Eliot tore him to his feet, and Zane flinched as the dagger was raised in silver-stained fingers.

"They told me I have to," Eliot whispered.

"Just bloody do it."

Zane cringed, squeezed his eyes shut, and waited. His last thought was of Helen Bell; the Trite who had tangled into his chest since the day she had waved to him through a window. But as all the creatures of darkness began to chant for death, Eliot whispered one thing more: "But you know I've always been scotchy at following orders."

Zane's eyes flashed open to the black robe hanging from Eliot's front. 'Twas unzipped, and when Eliot tugged the robe aside…Zane's eyes widened.

His hands plunged into the robe and freed one of two Patrol staffs hooked to Eliot's shoulders as Eliot tore the dagger down, slicing at the ropes on Zane's wrists. Eliot grabbed his staff and spun as ice speared out. In a heartbeat, the two were back-to-back.

"Ragnashuck," both boys breathed at once.

The creatures rushed. They flooded in like hungry dogs crawling o'er the ground and cloaked ghosts descending from the air. Zane and Eliot struck, and dark blood warmed the floor.

"Get to the stairs!" Eliot shouted o'er the growls.

But a blast of noise shook the cave, and Zane slammed his hands o'er his ears as the creatures screeched and toppled over. 'Twas like a shrill, bone-shuddering horn of the snowseas.

"What was—" A tentacle of black smoke blasted

through the hoard and Eliot screamed.

Zane spun toward Nightflesh with shaking hands, but the shadowed balcony was empty, and a single, lit candle sat upon the largest throne. He reached for Eliot's jacket instead.

Eliot's breathing was liquid as Zane pulled him toward the stairs, slashing gnomes and smoke creatures. When he looked back, he could not spot a Beast in any shadow.

"He's letting us leave," Zane said, shoving Eliot into the stairwell.

Eliot coughed, spitting out blood and snow. "No, he'll never let me leave."

Creatures lunged for the stairs as the boys stumbled up the steps.

"He'll chase us down unless something more important caught his attention with that horn," Eliot rasped.

Chomping teeth and hisses filled the stairs, but Eliot stopped at a window in the stairwell.

"We can't fit through that!" Zane turned to face the hoard.

"We don't need to frostbitten fit through it." Eliot raised his staff and a blizzard of snow rushed in through the opening. "I'm not going to make it," he said. He turned the stairs to slick ice with a burst of flurries.

"I can get you out," Zane said, eyeing Eliot's gushing side where snow spurted and a trickle of scarlet blood ran down, but Eliot shook his head.

"You'll be lucky to escape even if I block them, Cohen."

Creatures raced 'round the corner and scrambled up the ice, slipping and falling.

Zane gripped his Patrol staff. "Ragnashuck, Gray, I can't just—"

"Yes, you frostbitten can." Eliot glanced over with a sharp look. "Will you tell her?" he asked, his hard eyes glossing over. "Will you tell her I was on her side in the end?"

Zane closed his mouth. The smell of sour flesh filled the air as gnomes shoved the smaller creatures out of their way.

"Please, Cohen, we were brothers once. Please tell her." Eliot yanked a twist of icicles through the window and held it steady, aiming it toward the gnomes. Red liquid pooled at his boots.

"I will tell her," Zane said. Flakes brushed his warm neck as Eliot Gray thrust the icicles down the stairs. He added, "Give my greetings to Thomas."

Zane's colours tugged this way and that as he turned away and raced up the stairs. He did not stop; he could not look back until he heard Eliot yell, "Glory to Elowin!"

The Patrolman staggered to a stop in the stair's heights, a fist pressed against the wall, those last words driving into his soul.

As the feet of darkness trampled Eliot Gray, his Patrol staff tight in his hand, he felt his snow leaving him to pass on. But growls broke into wailing above him. The feet trampling his flesh tumbled off, and two hands grabbed his arms.

Zane Cohen's melodic voice filled his ears, "Tell her yourself."

Eliot was flung over a shoulder.

The once-Patrolman could not keep his eyes open. When sharp cold touched his face, he felt himself speeding o'er the snow.

His lashes fluttered when the sky above filled with darkness.

A serpent of smoke and snow descended from the clouds in an arc, widening its mouth and snapping. Zane slid to a halt and dropped Eliot who reached for his Patrol staff with a shaking, pale hand.

Zane fought with ice and a steadfast heart, smothering the serpent with flakes. The creature burst from the drifts and snapped its fangs.

"You need to go, Gray!" Zane shouted. "Go make sure she's okay!"

Eliot tried to stand, but he stumbled back to a knee, gripping his staff with bloody knuckles.

"Not me." Eliot's whisper was overshadowed by the snaps, blasts, and roars. "I don't deserve it."

Zane's weapon flashed toward Eliot, and a thrust of snow forced Eliot into a roll. "I'll be right behind you." Zane's voice faded as Eliot rolled, and rolled, and *rolled* with the wave.

The once-Patrolman found himself in the trees.

"No…not me…it shouldn't be *me*…" Eliot wobbled as he stood, but a wall of ice sprang up before him, cutting him off from the serpent and the Patrolman fighting in the snow.

The last thing Eliot saw through the ice was the shadow of the snake arching its back and the Patrolman leaping into the sky and disappearing into the smoke.

CHAPTER, THE TWENTIETH

It poured through the night. The rain melted the snow and revealed glassy turquoise streets that had been hidden since we'd arrived. Nicholas sat at the end of the kitchen table with a tea pinched between his fingers. Ginger hadn't said a word all morning. None of us had eaten anything since dawn, despite the mountains of tarts.

I pulled on my white Carrier jacket. All night I'd lain awake, listening to the rain and practicing my speech, sorting my arguments into categories based on reservations I thought the king might bring up.

"If I die in the street on my way to this meeting," Nicholas's silvery eyes flashed up, "I'll destroy you." He whispered the last part.

"It's too late to go back now."

Nicholas's jaw shifted. He dropped his glare to the table.

"Forget that note. We need this meeting. But I can meet with King Ha-yoon alone," I decided. "There's no need for you two to come along."

They both grunted and rolled their eyes.

"Apple's boot would hoof my rear," Ginger muttered.

Nicholas shoved the teacup away from himself. "*You* should stay behind. You can't hide bright, gangly hair like *that*," he said to Ginger.

"Agreed," I said before Ginger could object. The boy's orange curls bounced as he slumped back against his chair with a pout.

I pulled Apple's pocket watch from my coat pocket. "Let's go," I said to Nicholas as rain began to smack against the windows again.

My boots were drenched, and I shivered as my wet hair cooled my shoulders. We were a sopping mess when we finally sat across from the King of the East.

Food was served on cushions, and drinks were carried to us in bottles. Light music drifted into the room as King Ha-yoon entered. He waved the elves away and sat with no food before him. He stared at us without blinking.

I cleared my throat. "Thank you for inviting us."

"I don't care to waste time on pleasant greetings," the king said. The music stopped, and the elves quietly shuffled out of the room. Nicholas's gaze slid over to them.

King Ha-yoon stared at me until I reached for a creamy fruit.

"You won't get the armies of the other two kings. Nor mine," King Ha-yoon said.

I looked up in surprise, and I noticed bloodshot veining

into the king's eyes. My hand brushed the orb warming beneath my shirt.

"You have lost, Carrier," the king said. "We have already been turned."

Nicholas and I sprang to our feet.

The king's pink eyes moistened. "I warned you. Why didn't you run?"

The note.

The hallway lights blacked out. Nicholas grabbed my arm.

Mist leaked in from the darkness, and I realized the large windows were covered by thick curtains.

"Sleep." A beastly voice sailed into the room, and King Ha-yoon fell over, eyes closed.

"No, no, no, no, *no*…" Nicholas staggered back. He dropped to the floor and covered his face as someone—or *something*—emerged from the shadows.

Black mist rippled off a monster in scratched armour with dragging, damaged obsidian wings. A helmet shadowed a face without eyes, half-patched with dark flesh, and I steeled myself so I wouldn't scream.

Nightflesh stopped silently before us.

I dashed for the window, ripping aside the curtain to smash the glass and summon snow from outside, but I blanched. Beyond the solid pane, buildings were engulfed in flames. Rime Folk raced through the streets, and black mist toiled overhead, diving down to slither around buildings like smoky serpents with ice fangs, devouring everyone in its path.

I turned back, trembling, staring at his hollow helmet.

"Stop—"

Darkness blasted toward me, plunging into my mouth and down my throat. I tried to yell as my body was lifted into a swarm of black mist. I shook as voices barked at me from the dark; my father's voice, telling me I was the reason he left. Winston's voice, telling me I never cared. Grandma's voice, telling me I never bothered to say goodbye. They slashed me like knives.

And then his growl,

"*Unworthy*!"

Tears ran down my neck as the blackness tightened, cutting off my air and spreading across my vision like ink. Depthless darkness slowed my heartbeat until a wisp of fresh wind touched my shoulder.

There was a flash of orange curls, and two timid hands grabbed my waist.

The blackness tore from my throat, from my eyes, and from my mind, like a dagger sliding out of flesh.

PART V

AN INTERRUPTION

The young Patrolman's dry lips were cracked. 'Twas the first thing he noticed when he moved them, and they stung. A damp chill hung in the air alongside the scents of moist rock and mould.

Knock, knock, knock.

The flesh beneath his earlobe was bruised; he reached to touch it.

Zane Cohen sat up, trembling with shivers and chills, and he saw darkness. He looked 'round the silent cave of ice spindles and stone floors. He released a quiet sob when he recognized it, for the cells in the tunnel were empty.

"Why did you bring me here?" he asked the quiet. "Why *here*!?" His shout echoed down the hallway. Nothing stirred in return, and he placed a trembling hand o'er his mouth, biting back a cry as he saw his chance of returning to Helen dissolve in these cold tunnels. "Ragnashuck."

"Knock, knock."

Zane sprang to his feet. He blinked, teetering, and wondered if perhaps he was hearing a thing. The woman he heard was dead.

She was dead.

She was…

He lifted a shaking hand to his temple, wet with blood and snow.

Knock, knock, knock...

"Stop!" the Patrolman growled at the cave, gripping fistfuls of pecan hair.

"Let me in," she whispered.

Zane paced, squeezing his eyes shut. His arms shook, his head was heavy, and his feet stumbled o'er loose rocks. When he turned, he jumped.

She stood outside his cage.

Mara Rouge's hollow eyes were liquid black and pale blue. She gripped an iron sword, her hair billowing in a nonexistent breeze, and her black-scaled armour glimmering in the lightless tunnel. "Did you really think you could take on another Carrier and I would not kill her the same way I killed your first?"

"Cohen! Wait! Come back!" a young voice from Zane's memories cried, and Zane spun. Growls sped by as though gnomes were there in the cell with him. *"Zane, I'm surrounded! Help!"*

The Patrolman shook his head and grabbed his ears, his nails cutting into flesh. "He never said those things."

"How would you know? You left little Thomas Borrows behind," she said, her cool, two-toned sound seeping through the ice bars.

"Zane, help!" Thomas sounded exactly how Zane remembered.

A thick tear rolled down the Patrolman's dirt-covered cheek. He sprang for the ice bars, his hand pushing through to grab the witch. But she smiled—a pinch too wide—and she vanished.

Zane's hand swung through air. He released a croak and grabbed the bars as his legs weakened.

"He didn't say that," he whispered. "He couldn't have." But one tear more tumbled to his chin. "I'm sorry. Ragnashuck, I'm sorry, Thomas." His knees buckled and he slid down to the soil, sobbing until he wished to faint and forget.

The air grew still and quiet again.

A roar blasted into his ears, and Zane toppled over. *"Your Carrier is mine!"*

Zane's fingers dug into the dirt, his lungs tightening until he could scarcely breathe.

"I will not answer to you!" he shouted at the voice of the Beast as he flung a handful of dirt through the bars.

"Zane..."

His heaving slowed. He shook his head, for he did not want to hear Helen's voice in this place.

"Zane?" she cried. *"You said you'd always keep us together."*

Fresh sobs slipped from the Patrolman's mouth; a tear fell into the dirt where his fingers splayed.

"I had to. I'm sorry!" he whispered. "I didn't want you to see me turn to snow..." In that moment, the Patrolman wished he had died in the snowseas after all. His frozen fingers lifted to rub his chest.

A breath of quiet fell over the tunnel, and Zane rolled back to sit. He leaned his head against the ice bars, letting the cold numb his temples.

He swallowed and stared at the wall. “What have I bloody done?”

“Let me in, and I will not touch her.”

Knock, knock, knock.

Once, he had been trapped in this very dungeon. And Helen Bell had sacrificed herself for him.

Knock, knock, knock.

“You want my soul,” Zane rasped.

“If you lose another Carrier to me, your soul will be no good anyway.”

Zane dragged his nails through the dirt, feeling a numb pain pulse up his fingers.

“I will not touch your Carrier as long as you are mine.”

A pinch above…

Driar stared at the WANTED poster on the pillar outside the palace. The sketch artist had even included dark paint on Jolly Cheat’s lids and the signature look of madness in his eyes. Rain muddied the sketch and filled the Scarlet City with fog.

Driar drew the bookmark from his pocket and flicked it as he ascended the palace stairs to the front entrance. He shook his wet coat as he passed the ballroom toward his chambers, but six Ruby Legionnaire Commanders marched down the hall after him. The Commanders passed by, and so Driar followed them instead.

He halted in his tracks when the door to the throne room was opened.

Forrester sat upon the Crimson King's throne, and a dark-haired woman was brought roughly before him. The woman's wooden armour clapped together as she was tossed to the carpet, and Driar nearly choked. He rushed in and tucked himself behind members of the Court, squeezing his bookmark until it cut into his palm.

The Queen of the Pines grinned through a punctured lip. "The war is over. At last, the Crimson King has fallen," she said, licking the blood and snow from her mouth. "It seems Green has won after all."

Forrester's purple eyes turned deadly. "Our war is far from over."

But she laughed, a speckle of snow falling from a cut in her shoulder. "Send me to be with my brother, Prince, before I chew through these ropes and come for you next!"

The sound of a blade being drawn echoed off the walls. Before anyone could protest, Forrester marched down the dais, sword raised, and Driar squeezed his eyes shut.

"Glory to the True King! The king of Edward Green, Prince of the Pines!" Her last shout filled the air.

When Driar found the courage to open his eyes, he saw snow sprinkling the bloodred carpet of the throne room. The Crimson Court was in an uproar:

"May the Crimson King rest in peace!"

"The bloodline of the Greens has been snuffed out at last!"

"We must paint every Green village *red* before any other

kingdom can claim them."

"Your Highness!" One of the Ruby Legionnaire Commanders shouted over the noise. Forrester raised a hand, and the Court hushed as the Legionnaire marched to the dais.

"I bring bad tidings. Despite our efforts, the Evergreen Host still lives," the Commander said.

Forrester blinked his piercing eyes. "How?"

"Well…a fairy fights for them at the border."

Forrester's ivory hair fell out of place as he dropped another step down the dais. "The same fairy, I presume, that you assured me would be vanquished in a pinch after you *insisted* I leave the battleground?"

"We used every means available to us." The folk's voice shook. "We tried to turn her to snow along with the former Red Prince…" the Commander hesitated as Forrester drew closer.

"What of my disowned brother?"

The room was so quiet, Driar worried someone might hear his thudding heart.

The Commander took in a deep breath. "Cane Endovan Crimson-Augustus lives." Murmurs lifted from the Court, and a beat of hope filled Driar's chest. "He's the last Green soldier on the battlefield. We tried to turn him to snow, but it seems the fairy is protecting him."

Forrester's jaw flexed. He hurled his sword to the throne room floor where it clattered, and ladies shrieked. One scrambled back and bumped into Driar's chest.

"I will destroy him and his beloveds and every folk who utters a word of the *Dead* King again!" Forrester kicked the pile of snow at his boots. "My father was a merciful king in comparison to *what I will be—*"

"Brother." Driar found himself standing in the middle of the throne room, though he did not remember pushing his way through the nobles to get there. He dropped his bookmark and tugged the seal from his finger. With a steady hand, he held it up, and gasps burst across the room.

Forrester stepped forward. "Driar, if you *dare*, I shall—"

"Brother, I wish to challenge you for the title of Crimson King in a Quarrel of Heirs. I wish to fight you rightfully; with the respect you did *not* offer to Tegan when you slayed him in his sleep. You *coward*!" Driar felt the power of his own shout, and he thrust the ring outward.

Forrester did not blink as he stared.

Warm beats passed through the frozen room.

The heir's purple eyes slid to the sword on the floor, but he turned away and marched from the throne room, leaving whispers and sharp inhales in his wake.

Crimson capes and scarlet dresses flooded in. Driar was surrounded with questions, flirtatious gestures, and fanning feathers. A scribe jotted down answers to shouted questions as though Driar had spoken, even when he had not.

The young Prince stared at the doors where Forrester had disappeared, knowing he could not sleep in his own bed tonight. Wondering if he would ever sleep again.

The remaining Red Princes stood on the dais in their crimson coats, staring at him in silence.

CHAPTER, THE TWENTY-FIRST

I heard screaming when I hit the snow. Ash stained my fingers, webbing over my knuckles and leaving scorch marks up my sleeves. My eyes settled on my bare hands flat on the snow. Then my gaze dragged down to my coat.

He'd destroyed my coat.

Nicholas.

The screaming.

I sprang to my knees.

Nicholas shook where he sat. Ginger lay on his side, gasping for breath.

I grabbed Nicholas's sleeve and turned him toward me. His hand flew to his cheek, to his neck, to his shoulder where his coat was burned right through.

"My face is ruined!" Nicholas shrieked. "My beautiful, frostbitten *face*!"

I tugged his hand away to see. A ribbon of black wound

up the side of his neck and cheek like a tattoo. The same black stain coated his shoulder where his jacket had been scorched off.

"What happened?" My voice was gone. I touched my throat and realized my hand was trembling.

"I attacked him, you *foolish Trite*!" Nicholas shoved my hand away and tugged my hair aside to look at my ear. He tapped a burn on it, and I winced. "I had no frostbitten choice!"

"You attacked Nightflesh?!" I rasped.

"Who *else*?!"

A croak escaped as I realized what I'd seen in that room.

"He's…he's flesh!" As soon as I said it, black ink crept across my vision like a hand. I fell back and scrubbed my eyes, blinking.

"Unworthy!"

It boomed through my soul, and I gasped.

"Fight him, Trite." My shoulders were grabbed in the darkness. "Don't you dare take the easy way and give in to him. There's no coming back from that!" Nicholas's words rang in my ears.

I breathed in and out. The ink trickled away, and I blinked against the view of white snow.

Nicholas still held my shoulders, but he glowered past me toward the way we'd come.

When Ginger crawled over to us, I saw his singed, fiery hair. He was otherwise unscathed.

We all sat in silence for a moment. The wind cooled the tender flesh on my ear and throat.

"What were you thinking coming in there, spinbug?" Nicholas snapped at Ginger.

"I followed you!" Ginger said. The boy looked like he was about to cry with puffy eyes and red cheeks. "I was scared something would happen. And, by the sharpest wind, it did! And I was scared to be alone with the tarts. And I was scared by…by…what I saw when I went in."

Quietness took us over again.

My mind filled with damaged, metal-plated wings, a hollow-eyed helmet, and obsidian flesh covering all but a few patches across his body. My spine twitched.

I glanced at Nicholas and Ginger and lifted my hands, feeling ash beneath my nails, and the tightness lingering around my throat. Something felt different.

"Don't you see, Carrier?" A beastly voice slammed against my ears.

I shrieked and spun on my knees, making Nicholas and Ginger jump. My wide eyes darted to the hills. "He followed us!" I shouted. I stood on my wobbling legs, and fragments of burned fabric fell from my coat.

Nicholas and Ginger stood too. "I hear nothing," Nicholas said as he looked around.

"Don't you see?"

The words filled my head with a thousand screaming voices. I fell back to my knees, moaning and pressing against my temples.

"This is about my duel with you."

"Helen…?!" Ginger said.

"Run," I said to him.

His brows tugged in. "What?"

"Run, Ginger! Take Nicholas with you." I fumbled for my orb as it heated.

"You're not coming?!" Nicholas's face was wild.

"Nightflesh knows where I am!" I scanned the hilltops, the dunes, the sky.

"I *dare say*, I just attacked the Night Beast for you, Trite!" Nicholas grabbed my shoulder. "If he finds you, I'll have lost my beauty for nothing—"

"Take him, Ginger!" I shouted to my apprentice. "Take him now! And don't come back!"

"But—"

"It's my last order! Do it!"

I took off on numb feet toward the desert of endless snow. Nicholas's last objection was cut off in a whisk of wind as they disappeared. My eyes blurred, my breaths heaved, but I stumbled in the opposite direction, knowing I could never let the Beast I'd just seen find my friends in the bank.

Knowing that he had turned to flesh.

Knowing that there was no more time.

Knowing that it was just me and Nightflesh now.

A TIME-TWISTY INTERRUPTION

Presently in the time pocket...
(AFTER TWO FULL SEASONS)

Sirens erupted over the island. Kaley fumbled her pen and watched it clatter to the floor where it rolled across the schoolhouse. The door flew open, and Lucas marched in with a dozen sputtlepuns on his heels.

"There's smoke everywhere," Lucas said.

A scream sounded outside.

"The pocket is breaking!" A fairy's shout tore o'er the fields; an alarm echoed by voices all 'round the land mass. "Defend the island!"

"Stay here!" Lucas instructed the children with a firm finger-shake.

In a pinch, Lucas and Kaley were out the door and down

the grassy hillside.

"Lucas!" Kaley shrieked, pointing.

A ship split through the pocket's wall at the beach. Thunderous cracks veined o'er the shell and darkness seeped in, breathing along the edges, surrounding the pocket and blocking out the light. A dark, serpent-like tentacle lifted slowly, and Lucas pushed Kaley back toward the children as it grew fangs of ice.

The serpent struck, and a fairy was knocked from the sky. The winged warrior plummeted into the sand, lifeless.

Kaley tore up to the schoolhouse as a hundred fairies rushed o'er the sky like hornets in golden armour and fluttering wings. Their sabatons pounded the sand as they landed, and half drew dual-bladed swords.

A deep-skinned, sapphire-eyed guardian stood at the forefront. "Take aim!" she cried, and golden bows were drawn by the rest.

"Go, Trite!" Lucas shouted. "Find your keys!" He ran in the direction opposite.

Kaley raced back into the schoolhouse where the children were pressed against the windows, some screaming, others crying. She clattered to her desk and ripped open the drawer, finding the brass keyring beneath a sheet. She stuffed the keys into her dress pocket.

"Miss Bell!" a child hollered, and Kaley rushed to the window to see a legion of grotesque creatures in torn burgundy cloaks rippling o'er the beach toward the fairies.

"Maya, Torin, Chestwither…" Kaley's hand trembled as she turned the doorknob. "Go find the rest of the children and the dwarves and bring them here. Make sure every child is accounted for."

The three eldest sputtlepuns nodded, and the glass ball 'round Torin's neck began to glow as ice grew from Maya's and Chestwither's Patrol staffs.

"Go now!" Kaley yanked the door open and the three took off from the schoolhouse. She slipped out and latched the door shut behind her, watching Lucas kick through ankle-deep seawater and thrust a burgundy-cloaked creature under the surface with his Patrol staff.

Fairies drove the creatures into the sand and sea. Cold wind rustled the grasses, leaking into the pocket and bringing a layer of frost o'er Kaley's flesh. Her knees shuddered as speckles of Winter snow littered her bare shoulders. The serpent of black mist and snow lifted, and she flinched when it struck another fairy who fell alongside the dozens already strewn across the beach.

The pocket's shell burst inward with an ear-piercing shatter. Smoke tufted in, and a tall being of mist and flesh in a hollow-eyed helmet stepped inside. Kaley backed up against the schoolhouse door.

Nightflesh lifted his gauntlet, and black mist emerged. Kaley screamed for Lucas as the mist raced for the youthful Patrolman, and Lucas went still as it swerved 'round where he stood.

A cry lifted from the field as twenty plus six children charged with staffs in hand, kicking up sand and grass.

The sputtlepuns swung at burgundy-cloaked creatures. Guardian fairy fought alongside child, and Lucas lifted his gaze to Kaley on the hilltop. Her stomach dropped as the mist lunged and devoured the Patrolman in smoke. Torin and Chestwither plunged in after him, vanishing into the cloud.

Old Jymm appeared at the sand's edge, pulling children

out of the fight, and the rest of the dwarves began racing away with whomever they could grab.

At the water's edge, Nightflesh remained still.

His head turned toward Kaley.

She spun to the schoolhouse and grabbed the doorknob but hesitated. A tear fell from her jaw. Her trembling fingers could not seem to turn the knob.

A hand grabbed her arm, and Lucas reached past her to open the door. "Find us a way out, Trite!" he said, leaving a bloody smear when he let go.

Kaley tore the keys from her pocket. Hundreds of children now huddled inside the schoolhouse as she rushed in, flipping through the keys and muttering, hoping, *praying* as she picked a random classroom door down the hall.

"What are we to do, Miss Bell?" Kimberlow asked in a high voice.

"Pray," she urged.

The children bowed their heads, held hands, and began to whisper as Kaley settled on a key. She noticed an inscription etched into it: ROOM FOUR HUNDRED PLUS SIX. She shoved the key into the lock of the classroom door and turned.

A roar came from the beach, shaking the schoolhouse. A rippling cloud of black swarmed o'er the island, rolling toward them with the sound of screams and booming thunder, and the schoolhouse door flew open. Dwarves raced in with children flung o'er their shoulders, and Lucas shoved the last of the sputtlepuns in ahead of him while carrying a motionless Torin. A deep gash leaked blood and snow from the boy's chest.

"Now, Trite! *Now*!" Lucas shouted as a mouth opened

from the cloud, fangs of ice forming as it rushed for the schoolhouse.

Kaley pushed the classroom door open and found an entirely different place on the other side: a long, wallpapered hallway.

Children raced through.

Lucas slammed the schoolhouse entrance shut as the snake's mouth encompassed the entire building. Young screams filled the hall as everything went dark.

Lucas ran and pushed Kaley through the classroom doorway as the schoolhouse windows shattered and the blackness came rushing in. But a hand stopped the door as Kaley tried to close it, and the sapphire eyes of a guardian fairy appeared, paling like a candle flickering out. The fairy stretched her arm, and a time pocket formed 'round the children, growing to encompass the hallway where they stood and whatever refuge lay beyond. Darkness rippled o'er the fairy until all that could be seen was the arm she held through the door.

The time pocket sealed with a brittle shell.

Her arm fell away into the blackness.

Tears sparkled in Kaley's eyes as she firmly pushed the door shut.

The roaring disappeared.

"Well…Frostbite…" Lucas's strained whisper filled the silence.

A figure appeared at the end of the hall: a woman with long greying hair, and sharp grey eyes. A middle-aged male folk crept 'round her, taking in the sight of those who had just entered.

"Who are you? And where are we?" Lucas asked, raising

his staff and inching in front of the children.

The man broke into a wide smile. "Pinespittle," he said. "I have not seen a weapon of Mikal's offspring in a merry measure."

Lucas lowered his staff, realization flickering in his topaz eyes as Kaley noticed a large painting on the wall with twelve Rime Folk in it—including the two who stood before them now.

The woman stepped forward and offered a gentle hand to the nearest child. "I am Cora Thimble, and this is Charlie Little. We are the founders of the underground cathedral." Her eyes dropped to Kaley's hand. "How in all of Winter did you find my keys?"

CHAPTER, THE TWENTY-SECOND

My eyes burned from the ink trying to claw its way in. I smacked the side of my head to keep myself alert. To keep myself from growing too faint to care and letting the ink steal my sight.

My ankle began to burn over the hours even though I hadn't had trouble with it for months.

I dragged my boots through the snow like I was wading through mud.

He never stopped.

"I offer you my first temptation."

It came in the voice of Asteroth Ryuu, and pain heated down my throat where the blackness had tried to strangle me. *"Surrender yourself to me, and you shall no longer feel pain."*

I blinked up at the blur of dark, smoky sky toiling restlessly. My lips were parched. I swallowed against my dry, blazing throat and brought my focus ahead. I kept walking.

Moments later he came back.

"If you have true Carrier power, turn this snow at your feet to water and drink it." I cringed, and black spots pooled in my vision. The voice had been Quinten's this time; the dark, gloating, princely voice he'd used after I'd realized what he was. I tasted poison on my tongue, and I coughed.

I clenched my fists. My boots dragged on.

"I shall offer you a deal."

To my left, I thought I saw the snow move. I blinked rapidly, sure dehydration was setting in.

"Simply kneel at my feet, and your beloveds shall be spared." It was Mara Rouge's voice.

Ink plunged across my vision, and I gasped, bringing my feet together. A new sight lit before me in the darkness; tentacles of black mist, curling smoke, and a burning island. I staggered backward.

Beings that looked like Porethius sprawled across a stretch of sand. Hundreds of them lay unmoving, their beautiful hair splayed, their wings broken, their swords scattered between them. Piles of snow lay on the beach amidst it all with empty shells of gold armour.

A croak escaped me—the first sound I'd made in hours. "Don't do this…" I begged. "Please; don't do that to them."

"It is done."

"No…" Hot tears spilled down my cheeks.

"And so shall all your beloveds fall unless you kneel in the snow this moment. I will even grant you rulership over everything you can see, up to half of Winter, for your beloved believers to dwell safely in."

Images of Winter filled my head: I saw the Red

Kingdom palace shadowed by black clouds, I saw the red-painted train, I saw the burned Blossom Fields, the rubble of Wentchester Cove, and every town I'd ever visited that was now hollow, dark streets and empty houses. Everything that had been destroyed. Everything I could save with one deal.

I walked, battling against the vision until daylight returned, and I panted and shook against the strain, wishing for just a little bit of water as he waited for my answer.

Kaley had been on the island.

I'd sent her there.

Tears squeezed from my eyes.

I dropped to my knees, running my thumbs along my fingertips. Glowing symbols lifted to the surface of my skin. And I said the only thing I could.

"Get frostbite, Nightflesh."

A low rumble lifted from my right, then my left.

The snow moved. Pale flesh rose over the hills on all fours, and I jumped back to my feet. The Greed's vicious violet eyes were on me as they crawled at rapid speed. Feast-beggars lifted from behind the hills, drifting over the snow, their whispers prickling my ears. Clashing metal sounded from my right, and I tasted a bitter laugh in my throat as an endless army of gnomes marched, banging their clubs against their chests. I recognized the smell of wet fur even before the witch's snow pups trotted over the hills.

"Don't you see, Carrier? I shall destroy you in the end."

My fingers twitched. Snow crept up and swirled around them.

"Is that all you've got?" I croaked, and a tear slid down my cheek.

I raised my hands and torrents of snow surged up from

the ground. An ice-plated sword pieced together in my grip, and a shield solidified on my arm. I turned and swung at the first glimpse of movement, but my sword halted an inch away from the creature of darkness standing before me.

"No. I have one temptation more."

The figure before me had the same pecan hair.

He had the same face.

But Zane's electric blue eyes were *black*. I lowered the sword.

His face was smothered in ash, smoke drifted off him, and a torn, obsidian robe fluttered in the cold wind around his shoulders.

The advancing creatures came to a stop, watching us from the hills.

"I shall offer you a trade. Serve me in his place."

"I…" My lips trembled. "I can't."

Zane's hand flashed for my throat, and I stumbled backward, narrowly escaping. He followed me, drawing a curved cutlass, and he swung it. I ducked and raised my sword, but he smashed it aside and grabbed my coat collar, squeezing it tight in his fist.

I pushed against his chest as he lifted the cutlass to my chin.

"I offer you one. Last. Chance."

I blasted snow against Zane's face, and when his grip loosened, I tore away and fell on my back. Zane's body punched through the snow, and he dropped over me, pinning my chest with his knee. I tried to blast him again, but he trapped my arm down with one hand and raised his cutlass with the other.

"Make your choice, Carrier!" Zane's two-toned growl

tore through me, and I released a sob.

But a mass of dark curls slammed into Zane, and Zane's body rolled through the snow. I blinked up, my own sobs muffled in my ears.

Eliot Gray extended a hand.

I took it.

As a roar erupted from the creatures of darkness, Eliot pulled me against him and took off over the hills. The hoard gave chase as we ducked around slopes and got lost in the maze of snowy mounds. But when we swerved around a cliff and came into a dense forest, I pushed off Eliot and turned back.

"I can't leave him!" I cried.

But the hook of Eliot's Patrol staff caught my waist and kept me there. The forest filled with my sobs as I slid to my knees, and Eliot's staff clattered to the ice. He slumped down beside me.

"He's gone, Helen."

My face was hot with tears, and I shook my head.

"I'm sorry." His hand slid into his curls, and he gripped his hair.

"He's not…he can't be…" I couldn't breathe.

The witch's pups howled from the hills, but Eliot didn't force me to run. My weeping died away, and I pulled my puffy gaze to him.

I realized his eyes were red, and the robe he wore was drenched with blood. He teetered. I blinked away the moisture.

"What happened to you?" It came out as another sob.

His lashes fluttered. "I can't even begin to frostbitten tell you."

When the howls sounded just beyond the cliff where we hid, I reached for Eliot's Patrol staff and slid my arm beneath his shoulders to lift him. Eliot didn't object or ask when I stuck the Patrol staff into the snow and began skating us through the woods.

THE PEBBLE PAPER

BREAKING:
IT HAS BEEN RECENTLY DISCOVERED THAT OUR CRIMSON QUEEN WAS VICIOUSLY MURDERED IN POLAR TERRITORY DURING HER VACATION.

WANTED POSTERS FILL OUR STREETS THIS EVE, MARKED WITH A PAINTED FACE OF THE CRIMSON COURT'S OWN MAGICIAN, PUBLICLY KNOWN AS JOLLY CHEAT, WHO HAS BEEN FOUND GUILTY OF MURDERING OUR BELOVED CRIMSON QUEEN.

THERE IS A GOOD MEASURE OF EVIDENCE IN THE COURT'S CARE TO SUPPORT OUR CONCLUSION OF THIS HEINOUS CRIME AGAINST THE RED KINGDOM.

IF YOU SEE JOLLY CHEAT, REPORT THE SIGHTING TO THE RUBY LEGION IMMEDIATELY. IF YOU CAPTURE HIM, YOU SHALL BE REWARDED.

KINGDOM-WIDE TRIBUTES AND VIGILS FOR OUR BELOVED QUEEN WILL BEGIN THIS EVE, IN CONJUNCTION WITH THE PLANNED SERVICE FOR OUR RECENTLY DECEASED CRIMSON KING. THE ROYAL FAMILY COVETS YOUR WARMEST WISHES AT THIS TIME.

CHAPTER, THE TWENTY-THIRD

The town was dark. Thunder and veins of snowy lightning sizzled across the smoky sky, and the rolling coils in the heavens were beginning to look more and more like a nest of snake bodies slithering over each other.

A sign hung on the bank doors that read: CLOSED UNTIL FURTHER NOTICE. I half-carried Eliot up the stairs with me and knocked on the door.

It cracked open, and Mirkra's pale, creased face peered out. His eyes widened when he saw us. "Ragnashuck, Trite, get inside before you're seen!" He waved us forward.

I glanced at the sign.

"Odin and Seth were caught by the Ruby Legion yestereve and turned to snow. The sputtlepuns didn't even get a chance to defend themselves," he explained, reaching for Eliot with a peculiar look.

I handed Eliot over without a word and leaned on his Patrol staff to catch my breath. Questions lifted from the rest of the Patrolmen creeping out from behind teller desks and tables as Eliot was carried in.

"Is she back?" Nicholas's voice rang from among the group. "Where is that frostbitten common-blood? I'm going to bury her in the…" Nicholas's form filled the doorway. His hands were bound in front of him, his burn marks were patched up, and he was dressed in clean clothes.

"Ragnashuck," he muttered as he looked me over. He swept out of the way. "I'll not ask what happened to you. I don't care," he promised, but his silvery eyes followed me as I came in.

"Wait…" Eliot tumbled out of Mirkra's arms and staggered back toward me. Fresh blood and snow leaked through his robe, and he left murky footprints. "I need to talk to Helen," he said. "Alone, please. If I can."

His request drew Nicholas to spin around in surprise like he just realized Eliot was there.

The Patrol exchanged glances, but as they took in the amount of blood on the floor and how Eliot's pale form trembled, the skepticism left their faces. They slinked away to the meeting room. Wanda nudged Nicholas ahead of her with her Patrol staff, and Nicholas craned his neck to stare at Eliot until they disappeared around the hall.

None of the lights were on in the bank. The fireplace in the corner was cold, and all the rings and banking slips had been put away.

Eliot limped toward me until I could see the matting in his curly hair. When he stared, I realized no green was left in his eyes, but they flickered in and out of focus.

"Eliot?" I waited, eyeing his blood loss.

"You were right about me." His voice was so quiet that

I leaned in to hear. "I was wishy-washy, never truly picking a side. And now I'm too frostbitten late to choose one."

"It's never too late, Eliot," I said, and the corner of his mouth lifted weakly.

When he swayed, I carefully wound my arms around him to give his body a rest. He leaned against me, and I felt his warm blood and cold snow gushing out.

His throat bobbed. "I won't make it to the end, Helen." It came out with a shudder and his breathing grew ragged. "I won't be there to help you."

"It's all right." I shifted as his full weight sank against me. "Harmony would be proud of what you did." He twitched, and I struggled to hold him, but I didn't let go.

"I hope so," he whispered.

Every memory I had with Eliot came creeping back. Most of them were laced with an objectionable underlining, but some of them…some of them were good. I swallowed as a heavy gush of snow puffed out from his side.

"She'll be the next one to hug you." I tilted my face so he wouldn't see my lip quiver.

"G…" Another tuft of snow brushed my jaw. "Goodbye, Hel…" Eliot's arms slid away, and his chest deflated against me. My arms fell through a brush of snow, and I let Eliot's Patrol staff clatter to the floor.

Snowflakes floated to my boots.

The bank was quiet.

It was minutes before I could move. And when I did, I marched to the meeting room and pushed through the door. I hardly heard those who spoke to me. I grabbed the blessed teapot from the end table, and I left. I clutched it to myself as I climbed the staircase in silence, walking to the end of the hall and around the bend until I reached a broom closet. The door squeaked when I opened it.

I stepped in. I shut the door. I sat down.

I pressed the warm teapot against my chest.

My eyes glossed over as the seconds ticked by.

"You haven't abandoned us, right?"

Nothing answered.

"I was wrong," I whispered. "I can't do this." No symbols appeared on my flesh, and I was left in the dark. "Why are you letting this happen to us?"

I awoke to screams.

The blessed teapot was tucked against my stomach where I was curled on the closet floor. I dragged the pot off so I could sit, and I blinked as I listened.

Another scream.

I jumped to my feet and pushed out of the closet, racing down the hall as shouts lifted and glass shattered on the main floor. I came to a sliding stop at the top of the stairs, and my heart faltered as cold wind rushed in from the open bank doors.

Zane stood in the lobby, staff in hand. Eyes black. Tattered robe ruffling around him.

Blades of ice smashed through the room, and Patrolmen ducked. Wanda sprang from behind a desk with her weapon raised, but Zane struck her back and she was swallowed into the current of snow and smoke rushing in from outside.

Kilen slid across the floor swinging at Zane's legs. Zane

stopped him with his boot, pinning the boy beneath his heel as wind and ice tore the room apart.

Ginger's fiery hair streaked through the smoke and Zane lurched backward as though he'd been struck. Ginger skidded to a stop, reaching for Kilen, but a wave of snow toppled over him, and Ginger tumbled into a teller's desk.

I ended up at the bottom of the stairs. My pulse pounded in my ears. I pushed through the smoke and wind as Timblewon rammed a wall of snow against Zane.

Zane blasted through it, staff swinging toward Timblewon. I swooped in and grabbed his hand around the weapon, and he stopped. Zane stared, black eyes taking me in.

"Get out of him," I said to the monster.

Zane's head tilted slightly. He swatted my fingers off and swung, but another hand caught his arm before his staff's ice met my stomach.

Nicholas's silvery eyes were wild, his shirt was flapping in the storm. "Not today, rogue," he told Zane.

I took Zane's cheeks and forced the Beast to look at me. "Don't take what isn't yours!" I shouted at him. "He still believes. He still belongs to the Truth!"

Zane growled and tore from mine and Nicholas's grips. "He chose this," a beastly voice said from his mouth.

"He didn't choose *this*." I leaned in and my symbols flared, lighting up the smoke. "Don't you know whose power flows in my veins?" I whispered through my teeth, and Zane blinked. A speck of blue appeared. But he blinked again, and it vanished.

He tried to take a step back, but I grabbed his collar the same way he'd grabbed mine in the hills, and flecks of colour appeared on his face like my eyes were casting rainbow lights.

Zane's expression warped, and he slapped a hand over his eyes. The storm raged around us; snow scathed my cheeks, and Nicholas threw an arm up to shield himself. But Zane's hoarse cry came through the wind. "Get away from me! Run!" he begged in his own voice. "Helen, *run*!"

But I said to him, "You made me a promise."

His hands flashed up and grabbed my wrists, and I braced for him to throw me off. But the snow fell to the bank floor, and the smoke dissolved like an exhaled breath.

Zane pulled my hands from his collar and peeled his eyes open.

His face was covered in ash.

His eyes were bloodshot.

But his irises…They were electric blue.

He stared at me.

I grappled for his robe, and I crushed him against me, clasping my hands behind his back like a lock as his staff clattered to the tiles.

Zane's arms wound around my shoulders. Tears wetted my cheek, but they weren't mine.

AN INTERRUPTION

Curses lingered in the air of the tunnel below the library where Driar found himself waiting. He'd sat upon a stack of books when his legs had grown too tired to stand, and he had—unfortunately—fallen asleep that way, leaving his back to creak and crack in protest when he awoke and moved.

He released a shriek as a teeny herd of mice scurried by his feet, followed by a chubby mouse-mother who seemed to frown at him as she passed. The mouse family disappeared into a hole in the stone wall.

Driar had heard no news while tucked into the palace's darkest corner. As soon as the Crimson Court had set the time for the Quarrel of Heirs, Driar had gone to his childhood hiding place with a basket of bread bits and settled in to spend the countdown alone.

It seemed the mice had helped themselves to his bread though. He scowled at the basket of crumbs.

Slow, cold footsteps moaned from the library above, and he held his breath until the footsteps disappeared.

When all grew quiet, Driar stood and stretched his back, but when he twisted left, he startled at the sight of a Red Prince in the tunnel.

Ember's steady eyes were like purple grapes—sour and sweet. Though he was a mere ten plus three seasons old, he was just as tall as Driar.

"How did you find me?" Driar's heart dipped cold.

"Hamsa saw you sneak down here once," the young Red Prince said. "Most of us know you hide here."

"Have you sold me out to Forrester then?" Driar's gaze flickered toward the tunnels.

"None of us have told Forrester where you are."

The words settled in like a warm touch of truthspire. "Why?"

'Twas then that Driar realized his brother held a tall, velvet satchel in his grip. Ember tugged the satchel's string and drew out a long, golden blade.

Driar staggered back.

"Hamsa stole this before our father's room could be cleared out. If you bring this into the quarrel, it will muddle Forrester's buttons and perhaps he will grow irate and irrational." Ember passed the blade over.

Driar took it, his hand fitting well 'round the handle. The familiar feeling of holding a weapon put a pinch of confidence into his wrist. "Why give this to me? Aren't you afraid Forrester will find out?"

But Ember's heart-shaped mouth twisted into a smile.

"You'll be snow soon, so I am not worried about you nattering to him about it. And if, by a Winter's miracle, you're *not* turned to snow…" Ember's grape gaze filled with sour and sweet again, "then the rest of us will be merrily ubbersnugged."

"Merrily?"

"Forrester has gone spinbug mad. How many more Red Princes must die until this family is satisfied?" Ember's mouth curled down now.

Driar's eyes fell to the blade of the Crimson King which had once slain a Green King, had fought battles during sunsets, and still carried the whispers of souls it had taken with little mercy. Then he glanced to where the family of mice had disappeared.

Ember released a heavy breath into the dark tunnel. "Kingsblood, you won't win, of course. But I wish you good tidings in your fight, nevertheless…for whatever it's worth," he said.

Driar stared at his brother. "We are too young to fight wars," he said. "Don't you think?"

After a cool moment of silence, Ember nodded. He shared no further comments as he turned to leave, apart from one: "If you can make it to the dining room before Forrester finds you, you can take the servants' tunnel all the way to the arena for the quarrel. He will try to stop you before you get there."

CHAPTER, THE TWENTY-FOURTH

Apple and Timblewon had to pry Zane and I away from each other, but when I was sitting in a steaming copper bath of snow blossoms and peppermint leaves, I realized how long it had been since I'd relaxed. I didn't know my muscles ached until Apple convinced me to submerge them in hot water.

In the flickering lantern light, I studied the paintings and pastel self-portraits of Mrs. Millsa lining the bathroom walls. Then I climbed out, dried off, and went back to my room.

My Carrier of Truth coat hung by the bed where Apple had left it after doing her best to clean it and stitch it up. The cuffs were singed, half the buttons were torn off, and it was covered in olive green yarn where the holes had been sewn shut. But it smelled like snow blossom soap and the same sugar scrub I'd bathed in.

I caught a glimpse of my glowing symbols in the floor-length mirror when I raised my hand to push my hair behind my ear, and my gaze hovered on my reflection. A crease was between my eyebrows, my mouth was tipped into a frown, and there were bags under my eyes. But a subtle glow lit my irises, flecks of gold speckling the dull hazel there. Along with the rippling symbols on my skin, I didn't look a thing like a Trite.

There was a knock on the door.

"Come in."

Zane's silhouette stood against the hall lights. He came in, closing the door behind him. I looked around for a lantern and realized I'd left mine in the bathroom.

"I can get a candle," I offered.

"I can see you just fine."

He moved through the dark, the hazy night glow flickering along his features as he passed the window. The scent of healing herbs and fresh pine soap followed him.

"Zane, I don't want an apology. I know why you left," I told him.

He blinked a few times, his bright blue eyes salting over with grey. Then he lowered to his knees and took both my hands. His throat bobbed, and I tried to pull him back to his feet, but he held me firm.

"You need to know how I really feel about you," he whispered.

"Zane." I shook my head. "You don't have to—"

"You must have known," his gaze darted up to mine, "that I never meant those things."

I bit my lips. "I know you didn't want me to see something. So, you said what you had to."

He stared. Then he stood, gripping my hands. He almost spoke, but words never came out.

"I said I didn't want an apology," I told him.

The corners of his mouth pulled. "Let me say a thing or

three, and then I'll be as quiet as you like." He inhaled deeply. "I thought the others would find you sooner. Ragnashuck, I thought you'd smash the tree's trunk with ice and break free. I didn't realize a storm was coming when I left you tied up there. I never bloody would have—"

"Zane," I said again. "I'm not upset."

He shook his head like I didn't get it and stepped in closer. The room was quiet; my heartbeat lifted in my ears.

"You didn't have to come in here. But thank you for telling me how you feel," I said.

Zane's fingers drifted into my hair, his thumb reaching to touch my bottom lip. "I haven't even told you yet," he said.

Warmth hit my cheeks, and I fumbled for the window latch beside us. When cool air rushed in, he took my hand and pressed my palm against his heart.

It was thudding. Racing.

Zane kept my hand there as he looked at me—really looked at me. And I knew. I knew, without a shadow of a doubt, that the boy who had always struggled to say his feelings out loud loved me. Maybe he always had. Maybe I'd always known.

And maybe…Maybe this was a moment I had been waiting for without realizing it.

"I love you too," I rasped.

The edge of his mouth tugged upward, just a little. "I know," he said. My hair ruffled in the night breeze—he brushed it away from my face. "You can't seem to stop saving me," he whispered. "It's backwards."

He leaned in, and his lips came against mine. It was soft and sweet, and I couldn't stop my own heart from picking up speed, setting off into a race against his.

My heart.

Oh, my heart.

It was full.

The Patrolmen were cleaning the bank at first light, but Zane did the most. He was sweeping when I came down. I watched him dart around to take tasks away from others, and for a moment I was back at The Steam Hollow Corner Café.

But my smile faded.

The bank's windows were shattered and patched up with boards. The front doors were barricaded with chairs and Patrol staffs. Three tellers' desks had been smashed right down the middle. There'd been too much blowing snow and smoke to see all the damage before.

Zane's voice lifted, "Are you telling me that she had all these great Patrolmen to choose from, and she picked *you*?!"

"Lovely, isn't it?" Nicholas brushed a hand down his clean bankers coat.

"I never technically picked you. I just needed you," I hurried over and cut in to clarify.

"Come now, Trite. You picked me. You came all the way to the palace to *pick* me. And I dare say, I think I've done a pretty good job of being your Patrolman," Nicholas said.

"Tell me he's bloody joking," Zane begged me.

Nicholas pretended to yawn even though his eyes stayed open a crack, watching Zane.

"I'll not have it," Zane said. "Ragnashuck, pick *anyone*

but him."

"He's not my Patrolman," I said again, and Nicholas laughed.

"Ragnashuck, sweetheart. I stayed at your side when you needed a folk. I sacrificed my beautiful face for you. I even saved you from him," he nodded toward Zane. "Sounds like a Patrolman to me." He studied his nails.

Zane pinched his lips together.

"Besides, Cohen. You should *feel* our growing bond. It's extraordinary—"

"Stop it," I said to Nicholas. "I know what you're doing. And Zane isn't going to fall for—"

"Let's quarrel for her." Zane turned to Nicholas.

"Hmm?" Nicholas feigned surprise. "A quarrel? How unexpected." His silvery eyes glimmered.

"You're *not* doing that. I completely and utterly forbid it." I stepped between them. "Zane, he's baiting you."

"I don't care what he's doing. The ashworm wants you too much, Trite. Don't you know he becomes obsessed with what he wants?" Zane's irises flared cerulean. "He doesn't care if the most powerful female in Winter is a witch or a Trite, he'll latch on and never let go."

Nicholas threw his head back and hooted a laugh. "Oh, the irony. If only you knew who the obsessed one was." He didn't hide his thumb jabbing in my direction.

"Mr. Zane! Time to patch up your wounds, I'm afraid!" Apple called from the hallway.

"Delightful." Nicholas shewed him with a flick of his hand. "Scuttle off, then."

I flattened my palm against Zane's chest before he could react. "Just go with Apple," I said. "I'll set Nicholas straight."

"*Nicholas*?" Zane blinked deliberately.

"Yes, that's my name." Nicholas smiled.

Zane exhaled beneath my hand and left for the hall without another word.

"Phew." Nicholas wiped a hand across his forehead. "He took the news better than I expected—"

"What are you doing?"

His nose crinkled. "What ever do you mean?"

"Don't be ridiculous."

Nicholas grunted and folded his arms. "Nosy commonblood," he muttered. He took in a deep, drawn-out breath and took his sweet time letting it out again. "Fine then."

He stepped in, towering over me with eyes twinkling like the madman he'd always pretended to be. "Can't you guess?"

My heel slid back a step. "Good grief…*are* you obsessed with me?"

"What? Ragnashuck, no!" His face was repulsed. "You're too sweet for me, Trite; like a tart with too much sugar. Didn't I tell you not to get your hopes up? I prefer someone a little more…"

I tried not scowl. "Mean?" I guessed.

"Precisely. I'll find someone mean. And *she* will raise my daughter."

I rolled my eyes and rubbed my forehead. "So…you *don't* need something from me?"

"Oh, fine. You can come too if you insist." He glanced at his nails again. "We can hide in a cave when the Night Beast takes over Winter. We'll be merry and drink tea, and you can protect us."

I started laughing, but Nicholas didn't. My laughter brought Zane to glance at us from the hall, and I steeled myself, shaking the humour from my face.

"I take back what I said before," I said to Nicholas.

"Oh?"

"You really are a madman." I bit my lip to hide my smile as I headed for the hall. But a wood-shuddering knock pounded on the barricaded bank doors, and everyone froze. Apple, though, rushed to them—Zane tried to grab her, but she was at the entrance in a heartbeat, shoving the chairs aside. "Wait!" I yelled as the doors flung open. Apple's gasp filled the entryway.

In walked Cane in a *green* cape, and Porethius; her dual-bladed sword, wet with snow, strapped to her back. Both were stained with blood.

When Scarlet appeared in the hall, she raced to meet Cane. He caught her in one arm.

I followed Porethius, the tremor returning to my hands as I fell into step beside her.

"Porethius," I said, and she slowed. "Have you heard anything about…" My throat swelled, and even though I thought I had no tears left, moisture filled my vision. "Porethius, I saw a vision of Orphan Island burning. Was it fake?"

She stopped walking and turned to face me, her wings drooping slightly.

"It was a lie, wasn't it?" I asked again when she didn't answer. "*Porethius*."

The fairy's strong hand fell to my shoulder.

"It wasn't fake, Carrier," she said. "The island is destroyed."

CHAPTER, THE TWENTY-FIFTH

The night felt long as I stared at the swimming serpentine bodies in the sky through my window. Occasionally a stream of moonlight would break through the nest.

"Where are you, Kaley?" I whispered to the darkness.

The bank had grown so cold with the smashed windows and unlit fires, I could see my breath.

I thought I'd be the first one up in the morning, but when I pulled on a knit sweater and came to the staircase with the steaming blessed teapot in my arms, I heard hoots and hollers below. I descended just as Apple rushed from the hall.

"Oh, there you are!" She released a heavy breath. "I was just coming to wake you, friend."

"What's going on?" My gaze flickered toward the meeting room where light spilled into the hallway.

"Well…we've been thinking of how to cheer everyone

up, you know—Timblewon and I—and I recognize that we should have stopped them, but everyone seemed so merry as soon as it all started."

"As soon as what started?"

She pursed her lips. "They're playing Trixten Moon for you!" she blurted.

I blinked. It didn't settle in until Kilen shouted from the meeting room, "Whip his scotcher, Zane!"

"Oh no."

I swept past Apple to put an end to whatever shenanigans Zane had instigated as another Patrolman piped up, "You foolish spinbugs. I'm placing my rings on Nicholas. He always wins!"

I marched into the meeting room and stopped at the table where cards lay flat and bells rested in piles. Zane sat on one side of the table, Nicholas on the other.

"Ah! Welcome, common-blood." Nicholas didn't look up when he said it. He laid a card upon the others, and Patrolmen reacted with *ooohs* and *aaahs*. "It seems you've caught us mid-quarrel. I'm about to dissolve your former Patrolman's chances, I'm afraid. Then it seems you'll be all mine." He placed a bell atop his card.

I dropped the teapot onto the table with a clatter, and they both finally looked up at me.

"Stop this. It's ridiculous."

"Too late for that, Trite." Zane flicked a bell onto an upturned card. "A deal has been made."

"What deal?" I considered flipping the table so they'd lose everything upon it.

But Zane avoided my gaze. So did Nicholas.

"If Nicholas wins, he gets to be your sole Patrolman and

Cohen can't speak a word to you for two full quarters," Kilen piped up.

My jaw dropped. "What…?"

Nicholas's smile widened. "Isn't it lovely, Trite? It's more than enough time for us to figure out *our* relationship."

"What relationship?! I'm not running away with you, Nicholas! I'm not going to hide in a cave and raise your daughter!" I blurted, and everyone in the room went quiet. Nicholas's smile vanished.

Zane lifted his electric eyes to Nicholas. "What did she just say?"

Nicholas moved a blue card to a new spot in his hand with slow movements like I hadn't spoken.

"Sorry, I didn't mean to shout that…" I stepped around the table, but Nicholas raised a finger to halt me before I came any closer, and a pang of guilt moved through my chest. "Nicholas, I wasn't planning on telling everyone about your daughter—"

"Shhh. Silence, common-blood. Let me steal you once and for all, and then we'll discuss it."

It looked like Zane was about to say something, but he dropped his gaze to his cards. An unexpected smile broke out across his face. He tossed a few bells onto playable cards in the middle of the table then picked up his last card and flicked it into the air. It spun, and everyone held their breath as it slowed and fell flat.

Cheers erupted, and some Patrolmen moaned as they dug into their pockets for rings.

But Nicholas stared at the table, mouth twitching.

"There you have it, ashworm. She's mine." Zane slid his chair back and stood, but Nicholas slapped a hand over the cards.

"Not so fast, snow pirate!" he snapped, and the room hushed. "It's not possible that you bested me."

Zane's mouth curled. "What kind of magician can't spot a trick right in front of him?" he asked. "I cheated."

Nicholas stood abruptly.

"You only said I had to beat you," Zane rounded the table and extended his hand, "*Cheat.*"

Nicholas's mouth pinched, but he took Zane's hand slowly and shook it. "Well played." He tightened his grip around Zane's fingers. "But I assure you, I'll find a way to bury your merriment in the snow." His silvery eyes narrowed. "I always do."

Zane's smile turned roguish.

Nicholas tossed his hand and headed for the door. "Now, I have somewhere to be, I'm afraid. I wish you all the best of luck."

"You're leaving?" I called after him, but he didn't seem to hear me.

Nicholas stopped in the doorway with a puzzled face. He turned his ear toward the hall.

Cold wind flitted into the room, brushing the cards off the table and blowing out the candles. Everyone looked at each other in the dark. Warmth crept down to my fingertips, and my symbols flickered as something in the bank rumbled.

"Did anyone else hear that?" Kilen asked from the quiet.

A deep creaking lifted from the building. The cold brushed in again, fluttering the ends of Zane's hair. His eyes met mine.

"Ragnashuck…" Kilen's whisper filled the darkness before an ear-splitting crack of thunder echoed, and something began banging against the walls and roof of the building.

"Find your weapons!" Mirkra shouted.

But then *his* voice filled my ears, my lungs, my mind, my soul.

"Followers of Truth." The beastly strand wove with all the voices of those he'd used as vessels; Mara Rouge, Quinten, Asteroth, and others. *"Your end is here."*

Apple released a cry.

Zane took my hand and interlocked our fingers. "I'm here, Helen," he whispered.

"Bow to me, and you shall be spared."

The cold left the bank.

The candles flickered back to life.

Terror filled the faces in the room.

Nicholas was gone.

"Why…" Wanda lifted her large eyes to the rest of us, "…hasn't Elowin put a stop to this?"

Bang!

Everyone jumped as something slammed into the roof and grains of wood and plaster fell from the ceiling.

I looked at the glowing columns on my flesh. I knew why.

Bang!

Porethius landed outside the door, bracing a hand against the doorframe. Cane slid in past her, followed by Scarlet.

A Patrol staff flew across the room and snapped into splinters against the wall. Wanda leaned forward, heaving and gripping her knees. "I can't hide away anymore! Can any of you?" She glanced around with red-rimmed eyes.

Bang! Everyone jumped again.

"It's supposed to be me," I said in answer to her first question. "That's why Elowin hasn't come. I have to face Nightflesh."

Porethius's gaze settled on me.

"Nightflesh crushes hope. I bring hope," I said. "I think this is how it was always supposed to end."

Apple began crying.

Cane tugged his mahogany hair. "Elowin spoke of an army," he said. "This isn't a big one, but I just fought a war with one folk plus one fairy against hundreds. Kingsblood, numbers don't matter, do they, Plum?"

Porethius was still looking at me, but she nodded. "I'm ready to face him with you, Carrier." Her wings fluttered, and my throat swelled.

"I want to go face him alone," I admitted.

Zane released a heavy breath. "Ragnashuck, Trite."

"Absolutely not. We're Elowin's army. Therefore, I'll dedicate my last strides to you, and to the Truth in my heart." Cane tightened his emerald cape.

"I'm done hiding. No matter what it costs," Wanda agreed, and Mirkra nodded beside her.

I looked at each one of them.

The room emitted the scents of tea, tears, and shattered wood. But there was a spark of hope—a quiet burning ember beneath the noise and ash. And one resilient spark was all I needed.

"To war, then," I said.

Heads nodded.

There was no cheering.

Bang!

Porethius slid the dual-bladed sword from her back.

"First, I'll deal with that *thing* striking the roof," she said.

But the distant hiss of a snake filled my ears. When I looked around, I realized the others couldn't hear it. It was like a tether hooked around my throat where the blackness had tried to strangle me.

Tug, tug, tug.

"I know where he is," I realized.

Porethius stopped at the door, and all the heads in the room turned.

"Nightflesh is standing on the ashes of the library. He's waiting for us in the Blossom Fields."

PART VI

AN INTERRUPTION

'Twas a roaring sea of hungry souls in the arena above. Driar listened to their chants while he marched to his gate in the tunnels, the golden sword of his father strapped to his hip and padding his thigh. He thought of a good measure of things as he slipped from the servants' tunnel into the arena's mirror-covered basement halls.

"I suppose you think Forrester will defeat you today since he is better at… well… *everything*," a fluttery voice said through the dark, and Driar halted outside the gate. He looked back the way he had come. He had been careful to not be followed.

"Ragnashuck, Driar. You march like a thrashing polar bear. Tsk tsk. Didn't I tell you to walk on your toes?" Nicholas sauntered 'round the corner, and Driar blinked at the silver-buttoned black coat he wore. He did not recognize the logo on the sleeve.

"You came," he said.

"I didn't want to."

"How did you get in here?"

"I'm sneaky."

"If they catch you in the palace, you'll wish you'd stayed missing. Didn't you see the WANTED posters on your scuttle in?"

Nicholas smiled. "Of course. They're gorgeous."

The young Red Prince stared at the former magician. "I suppose I'm relieved you're here. If I lose the quarrel—"

"Don't lose, you fool. I didn't waste all my precious time just to see you get turned to snow."

Driar made a face. "For a moment I thought perhaps you cared."

"Well, for a moment…I suppose I did." Nicholas turned the hooked staff in his fingers. "But I'd rather not see you destroyed for other reasons too."

Driar relaxed and smiled. "You'd miss me—"

"It would be embarrassing," Nicholas clarified. "For me."

The young prince folded his arms. "Kingsblood, Nicholas. I know your heart warmed in Polar Territory. Can't you say one kind thing before I go in there and get turned to snow?"

"Hmm." Nicholas huffed. "You have nice hair today. It resembles pearls and icing."

Driar grunted and pushed past him to reach the gate. "I probably won't see you again after it's over," he said.

"I'll be long gone by then," Nicholas promised without

turning 'round. But he called after the prince. "Try a trick," he said. "Forrester hates those."

Driar looked back at the folk who taught him to swing a sword, tell a lie, and to make a diversion. "I was proud of what you did," he said to Nicholas's back. "When I heard you disappeared, I knew you'd gone after that Trite woman's baby to make sure she lived. I knew only the Truth in your heart could make you do that."

The tunnel was quiet. Driar spied his teacher's reflection in the metal walls.

"Did the Crimson Court ever suspect us of destroying the ice palace?" Nicholas changed the subject.

Driar released a soft laugh. "Not yet."

Nicholas's mouth twisted into a smile.

A loud horn burst over the arena, and Nicholas did turn then. He settled his wild, silver gaze on Driar and uttered a single word: "Win."

The gate slid open, and a river of light gilded Driar. With one last nod to the ostentatious magician, the young prince left Nicholas in the tunnel and turned to embrace the arena—the same arena he had watched prisoners be tormented in since the early seasons of his timestring.

'Twas time for one Red Prince to turn to snow.

THE QUARREL

OF

HEIRS

The pounding of heels against floorboards echoed loudly through the arena, flooding in with the smells of rotten plums and warm nerves. One prince stood on each side of the freshly painted gold ring.

The heir appeared as calm as a bird gliding o'er a serene meadow, but between the strength of Forrester's shoulders, Driar could see boiling fury.

"Princes." The head Director of Tournaments' voice heated the air. Red roses were tossed toward Forrester by the noblewomen in the rows closest to him. "Draw your swords, and let the quarrel commence!"

Forrester sliced the air with his copper-plated sword as he drew it, and spectators screamed praises. His ivory hair glistened beneath where his coronet had been replaced by an obsidian band of kingly spokes.

Driar looked 'round at the crowd. Not a single folk remained seated.

When he brought his lavender gaze back to his brother, he took the handle of his sword and tore it out. The sunlight in the glass ceiling rolled to the end of the golden blade, and murmurs filled the coliseum.

Forrester's feral purple gaze fastened onto the blade.

Driar swung.

Forrester snapped backward, spinning 'round and returning with a strike. The sound of ringing metal echoed up to the ceiling when Driar blocked the heavy blow. Forrester looked down at the interlocked blades, his brows twitching inward.

Both princes shoved, and both staggered back a step or three.

"Driar, Driar, Driar," Forrester scolded as he stalked

'round the golden circle. "What have you done?" His mouth curled upward. "Did you get your beloved brother *Cane* to teach you how to block a sword like that? Do you think I haven't learned of his involvement in your scheme?"

"Kingsblood, you're clever! How did you figure it out?" Driar had never spoken to Forrester with sarcasm before, and Forrester's smile fell.

"Your name will be erased from this kingdom. I'll trample upon your snow before this crowd once you're dead. They will laugh."

Shouts and booing lifted from the spectators' seats. They began chanting for the princes to fight. Forrester raised his sword, waiting for Driar to make the next move.

Driar mimicked Forrester's prowling steps as he slid a hand into his pocket and drew out a handful of black pearls. Forrester's gaze followed as Driar tossed not one, not two, but six pearls into the air one by one.

Driar continued to walk, continued to catch, and continued to toss the pearls with one hand as his gaze fixed on Forrester.

Fury blotted the heir's light features with pink. "Is this a jest to you, Brother? Are you the new palace fool?"

A slow smile crept o'er Driar's face.

Nobles began to laugh, and Forrester glared back at them.

"Enough!" he shouted. He charged, and Driar sidestepped, tapping the copper sword away, all the while juggling pearls.

Forrester growled as he caught his footing and yanked a gemstone-encrusted dagger from his boot.

"Let me spin you a story," Driar said.

Forrester charged him again, but Driar's feet moved like a springing snow frog, and he threw one of the pearls. Forrester gawked as it struck his eye.

"Once upon a Winter's eve, the Crimson Queen disappeared without telling a soul. The Court tried to hide that their queen ran away. They claimed she was on vacation. But she wasn't, was she?"

Forrester seethed a bitter laugh. "Quinten drove her off, not me."

"But you made sure she stayed away. Just like you made sure Tegan stayed away. Just like you made sure Cane would stay away, and eventually would have made sure I stayed away. You, Brother, bury souls and slay folk for *fun*."

The copper sword glimmered as Forrester rolled it in his hand. "Drop your pearls, Brother. Come here and let me slice you open to show this Court the flimsy snow you're made of."

"I'm not finished my story," Driar said.

"You're finished."

Forrester dove too fast, and Driar's gems clattered to the ground as he blocked. The pearls bounced, one shooting across the floor toward the gate he had come through.

The nobles screamed Forrester's name as he swung his weapon.

Driar twisted away with glistening temples, and a ripping sound filled the arena as Forrester's blade split his cape. Forrester grabbed a fistful of fabric and thrust his weapon into Driar's side.

Driar inhaled; the crowd shrieked. Some clapped.

He tasted blood.

In the side of his vision, Forrester's ivory hair

glimmered as he raised his copper sword. Driar broke free with a spin, coughing up snowflakes. He dragged the golden sword behind him as he stumbled back a step or three.

"Do you need a moment, Brother?" Forrester laughed, and the arena roared along with him.

A black pearl rolled across the arena floor. It bumped Driar's boot, and the prince's eyes flickered up to the gate he had come through. He swallowed icy snow and tangy blood as he reached into his pocket a time again.

"I did not finish my story," he rasped as Forrester re-aimed his blade and growled, charging across the golden circle toward Driar's back. Driar yanked his hand from his pocket and dropped what was in it.

The tiny taps of twenty black pearls hitting the floor blended into the hollers of the Red Kingdom nobles waving their flags and blowing their horns. Rather than spin 'round to defend himself, Driar watched the crowd. When Forrester stepped onto the mess of pearls, he wobbled. The crowd's flags drooped.

Driar turned, golden blade poised, and *thrusted.*

Forrester's round purple eyes came face-to-face with Driar, the golden sword impaled through his middle.

The arena fell silent as snow sprinkled Driar's boots.

Forrester lifted his wavering stare to the hushed crowd. As whispers rose o'er the seats from one end of the arena to the other, he murmured, "Curse you, Brother. How did you keep from selling your soul to the blackness like the rest of us?"

"Books. I read once that the Truth would set me free. And I suppose I decided to believe it," Driar answered.

A swell of anger crossed Forrester's face. "I shall perish

spitting out spells upon your future, your allies, and your off-spring—"

"You didn't let me finish my story," Driar interrupted.

Forrester grit his bloodstained teeth and weakly tried to raise his gemstone dagger to Driar's throat.

"The end," Driar finished.

He tore the golden blade back out, and a body of snow puffed o'er the arena floor.

The air was frozen.

And then, cheering erupted.

Whatever roses remained were flung to Driar. He stared at the glistening white heap of flakes at his boots until the spectators began chanting his name:

"King Driar! King Driar! King Driar!"

"Long live the Crimson King!"

His throat bobbed. He kicked through the roses, crushing the petals and wreathes beneath his heels as he made his way to the locked doors at the arena's side. They were flung open for him, and the doormen elves bowed low.

Driar marched up the stairs, his torn crimson cape rippling at his back, his own snow sprinkling the stones as he ascended to the hall. He ignored the adoring shouts, the ladies' flirtatious waves, and the gifts extended toward him as he passed the Court.

He marched until he made it to the throne room. The entirety of the Crimson Court flooded in behind him, filling every corner with loud cheering and flattering smiles.

When Driar reached the throne, he paused. For there, sitting in the exact middle of the seat, rested a black pearl. A brief smile touched his lips. He took the pearl and shoved it in his pocket before leaning his golden sword against the dais and turning to face the subjects of the Red Kingdom.

"Scribes, take notes," he called out. "Release these messages in the newssheets at tomorrow's dawn. We will no longer be fighting whatever wars my late brother has pledged us to. We will also not condemn those who speak the name of the Dead King." Faces fell 'round the room, and the cheering fizzled out. But Driar went on. "And last, we will unlock the sections of our palace library where the wisdom of the sacred truths has been hidden away."

The entire room had become as silent as a graveyard. Driar's fingers tapped against the black pearl in his pocket.

He sat down on the throne.

The silence dragged on until, from the back, someone clapped. A few more joined in. Driar spotted Ember's ring-adorned hands colliding, and the rest of the younger Red Princes followed suit.

Slowly, the throne room filled with applause and mild cheers, and Driar's shoulders relaxed. "And um…would someone mind pointing me in the direction of a glass of water?" he asked.

A scream turned the room cold.

Court members scurried out of the way for a man with long, diamond-white hair and pure black eyes to pass through. He held a staff with a glowing red flame in his long, crooked fingers.

"It's the prophet!" someone said, and Driar's hands tightened on the armrests as he glanced toward the golden sword he had leaned against the dais.

"Asteroth Ryuu!" The name was whispered through the room.

"I have failed to put my pledged prince on the Crimson

throne not once, but twice now." Asteroth's voice was interwoven with a sinister growl. "If you are not for me, Driar Sollo Crimson-Norsebin, then you are against me. And every folk against me shall fall."

Nobles pressed back against the walls as the room filled with smoke and screams. People's eyes swelled from the heat; they dropped to cover their faces.

Asteroth pointed his staff at Driar's chest. "You are unworthy."

Driar saw a black coat tearing from the crowd before he squeezed his eyes shut and beckoned all his truths to bring him peace as he braced. But loud reactions forced him to peek and see the former Court magician standing before him.

Nicholas's staff needled toward Asteroth's throat.

Asteroth's staff remained aimed at Driar.

"Remember that you were nothing more than a scribe when I found you. All the power you have is because of me," Nicholas warned.

But Asteroth did not blink. He did not re-aim his weapon.

He fired.

Driar ducked, but a lap of fire tore through his shoulder with the heat and pain of a murderous stroke.

Nicholas drove himself against the once-prophet, forcing the second fire strike into the ceiling. The pair smashed through a window and disappeared, sending crimson stained-glass across the floor, and letting in a rush of wind.

CHAPTER, THE TWENTY-SIXTH

Why do people change?

Why would someone toss their reputation to the wind and choose to believe in nonsense? Why would they decide to let people think they're crazy? Why would any respectable scientist, doctor, or theologian suddenly believe in the impossible?

Why would someone join a losing side? Are they prone to illogical thinking? Did they lose their minds? Are they impulsive?

Or do they see something that others don't? Do they believe the losing side isn't really losing? Do they catch a glimpse of something unexplainable? Do they feel a change in themselves that they can't describe with science, evidence, or words?

Why would someone leave the way they've always done things and take a step of faith toward something different?

Why does anyone with something to lose risk all they have?

Why do people change?

What did they find?

Four years ago, I couldn't have answered those questions.

THE END OF WINTER

Blossom dust rolled between my fingers. The field that had once smelled of sugar, apples, and pie was now cloaked with the stench of ash. When I closed my eyes, I could envision a library that once boasted glorious stained glass, curved balconies, and warm fires sitting atop a hill.

Once, Zane had sat across from me in this field and told me to try to remember the Truth. He'd been convinced I must have heard it somewhere before; that it found everyone at least once in their lifetime, and everyone had a chance to choose it.

I didn't see Nightflesh when I opened my eyes again.

But I saw his army.

The once-white valley was filled with misty, obsidian-skinned creatures barring their teeth and thrashing on leashes. Feastbeggars floated at the army's edges offering snow-rippling whispers. The sky was polluted with smoky, serpentine bodies coiling restlessly, some breaking free and plunging down to snap at anything that moved.

"Pray the Ruby Legion doesn't show up," Cane said beside me. "If they don't come, it'll mean a thing has gone right in the Red Kingdom. And we'll only have to face half of the Beast's army."

"The horrid half," Zane said from my other side as he eyed the slithering sky.

The others waited further back. We were a small group of twenty Patrolmen, a fairy, a speedster, and a disowned prince.

Porethius hovered in the sky with banners hanging from her thighs that read: ELOWIN IS KING OF ALL WINTER KINGS, AND LORD OF ALL WINTER LORDS. A serpent eyed her from the clouds.

"I regret letting everyone else come," I admitted. "None of us will survive this."

I thought of the friends who'd already died for us to be here. I thought of all the slain Carriers of Truth since the beginning.

I thought of Emily at home who'd spend the rest of her days waiting for a friend that would never return.

I thought of Winston.

"Nightflesh won't risk leaving a single believer alive," I whispered.

"I imagine not." Cane glanced down and kicked the snow. "But there's still no sign of the Ruby Legion, so perhaps there is hope for Winter in the seasons after we're gone. Maybe…" his jaw slid to the side, "maybe someday the Truth will be able to rise again."

My fingers warmed. "Isn't that what all this was for? Were we foolish to think we'd be there when it happened?" I looked over at my Patrolman.

"I'd hoped," Zane admitted. "But this is how the Patrol lived and died. Fighting for the Truth to rise again."

Cane nodded.

Zane's gloved fingers slid between mine. "But I'm not afraid," he said, though his face didn't show it. "Are you, Helen?"

My stomach clenched. My mind told me to run and force the others to leave too.

"No," I said.

I ignored the barking across the field and studied his bright eyes.

The phantom hook around my neck tugged, and I tripped into the snow as burning seared down my throat.

Zane dropped to a knee and grabbed my shoulders. "What's he bloody doing?" he asked.

"I think he's trying to pull me to him."

The sound of Cane drawing his sword filled the air. "It's begun then," he said.

Zane lifted me as the ice crawled from his Patrol staff. The air changed, like it had gone from thin to heavy, and the slithering in the sky quickened. The black army shuffled and parted.

Nightflesh emerged.

His hollow helmet tilted toward us. A low growl rumbled across the snow, and a breath of cold wind blew back my hair. Nightflesh's rusted metal wings began to flap, and he lifted from the snow.

Onyx patches of flesh soared up from his army and slapped onto his body. He lifted higher as the flesh enclosed over him, giving him a face, covering his armour, and filling in his broken wings with veins.

"Ragnashuck."

"Kingsblood," the boys murmured at the same time.

Nightflesh took off toward the mountains on his new wings. A puff of snow sprayed from the mountaintop in the distance where he landed, and the mountains grumbled. Blue ice ripped from the stone, attaching itself to Nightflesh. His wings and glassy body grew so large, I could see them from the valley, along with the hind legs that formed at his back.

"He's a bloody *dragon*."

Nightflesh's body stomped around the mountain's peak, unsettling the snow, and sending an avalanche down the slope toward the field. A sharp, blood-chilling howl came from the dragon, and he lifted back into the sky, flapping over his army.

The Patrols sent a wall of ice toward the valley's edge to stop the avalanche. But shrieks rose from the dark army as they crouched to pounce. I aimed my hands toward them instead.

"Glory to Elowin," Zane said.

"Glory to Elowin." Cane held his sword out as the gnashing creatures were released. They barked and raced toward us.

I exhaled a shuddering breath as a war cry from the Patrols sounded at my back.

Porethius soared down, sword pointed, and landed in the midst of the army where I couldn't see. Sky serpents hissed and broke from the cloud nest to dive after her. I thrust my hands forward, and a wave of snow kicked the closest creatures off their feet.

Patrolmen skated past me. Creatures met them in a clash of metal, teeth, and Patrol staffs. Wanda sprang into the sky, jumping past the first line of creatures. She turned and fired snow into their eyes when they spun for her. I saw her be grabbed. I saw her go down.

Feastbeggars swept in from both sides, attacking Cane at my left and Zane at my right.

A serpent plunged and snapped its fangs before I could move. My hands glowed, my orb a hot stone on my chest. I buried the snake, but it burst through the snow, hollow slit eyes staring down as it hissed, ice fangs elongating, and I stumbled a step back.

I conjured snow eels that tore up from the field and wrapped around the serpent, strangling it and pinning it into the snow. I shoved the whole mess of snow and smoke backward as the snake thrashed. But another serpent dove over it with its jaws wide, and I screamed at Cane, "Look out!"

Cane whirled with his sword raised, but the serpent snapped over the former Red Prince, weapon and all.

In a burst of white snow, Cane disappeared.

My hand was still held out toward him. My dull heart thuds echoed in my ears. Cane's emerald cape rolled away in the wind.

I pulled my watery eyes back to the Patrolmen being dragged down into the snow. Kilen screamed and growled as creatures yanked him onto his back by the fabric of his sleeves. He was swallowed into the hoard, and my hand flew up again; I blasted ice needles into the ripples of dark flesh, and black blood hit the snow as creatures rolled away.

I raced over, but I didn't see Kilen. My eyes darted over the snow as I kicked away a moaning creature to look beneath. Kilen was gone.

This was a mistake.

Ginger wailed to my left—the Greed grappled at his legs, tying them together so he couldn't run.

I clenched my fists and dragged my moist gaze to where Nightflesh prowled over the snow, snapping his jaws and releasing ear-piercing growls. The hook around my throat tugged, and he turned his dragon head toward me, his black eyes narrowing.

"Don't you see, Carrier? All of this is about my duel with you."

I moved toward him, thrusting an icicle through a feast-beggar in my way.

"I shall destroy you in the end."

I lifted the snow around me and let it hover like a lion waiting to pounce.

"And so shall they all fall..."

Mirkra's shout came from my right as he tore away from ghastly hands, springing into the sky with snow spilling from a gash where a Greed arrow had pierced his heart. He was only in the air for a second before bursting into a flurry. His empty, raven-black uniform flittered down to the ground.

"You are unworthy..."

Ice slammed my wrist, binding together to form a shield, and a cold handle hit my palm; a sword weighed down my grip.

"Unworthy!"

I didn't see the serpent dive down from the sky.

I didn't see Zane sweep in to throw himself over me.

I just felt warm arms wrap my waist, peppermint flood my senses, and the dark, consuming mouth of smoke snapping shut around us.

The day we defeated Mara Rouge at Wentchester Cove:

Outside the cave, I wasn't hit with frightening images of scarlet armour and grey flesh. All that was left was messy snow, doubled over gnome bodies, and large footprints where the army had been.

Zane stood before the Patrol in raven black. Water dripped from them into murky puddles in the snow, and two or three broken staffs lay at their feet.

Mikal was there, his once-calm head of hair a furry mess now.

Zane hugged his arms to himself. "If Elowin is alive, why didn't he save the other Carriers? Why didn't he destroy Mara Rouge all those seasons ago when she attacked us? Why did Elowin let our hope wither?" He tucked his staff into his elbow as he spoke in a quiet voice. "We nearly lost everything."

A sad smile touched Mikal's face. "It wasn't yet his time to return. It still isn't, I gather. And maybe he never lost his faith in your abilities, even on the days you lost your faith in his."

☾

I sat in the brightly coloured Waterloo Children's Therapy office. Every wall was a different colour: pink, fluorescent yellow, mint green, and sky blue. My mother spoke in hushed tones, but I could hear her through the cracked-open glass service window the receptionist forgot to close. My small feet stuck off the end of the purple chair, and my pink stuffed bunny was across my lap.

"She has no trouble learning. She already reads novels and flips through encyclopedias. She just hasn't been able to relate to other kids since her father left," my mother said. "I'm worried my husband's choice has ruined her childhood."

I tied my bunny's ears together, clapping the toes of my shoes as I did it.

The therapist clicked her pen. "Children are stronger than you think. Take her outside to climb some trees."

There was another long pause. "Helen doesn't climb trees."

The pen stopped clicking.

"Then take her to the library if that's the only thing she likes. Maybe she can read about how to climb a tree. And maybe one day, after she's read about it enough, she'll decide she wants to climb one on her own," the therapist said. "Kids are capable. Give them a book, and they'll go on an adventure. Give them a stick, and they'll turn it into a sword. Give them a bit of confidence, and they'll fight their monsters on their own."

My symbols flickered in the darkness. Black mist and wind smothered me. Tentacles slashed overhead, and I could. *Not*. Breathe.

I blinked up at the eye of the dark, whirling tornado above.

Zane trembled over me, holding my face against his chest. The song inside him twisted off tune, and he released an anguished noise as a dark limb slashed his back. Then his shoulder. But he dug his fingers into the snow, anchored.

"Zane, don't do this!" My pleas were swallowed by the roaring wind. I grabbed his arm as a tentacle soared down, but it struck him, tearing him off of me. He got swept away in the current of cloud before I could catch his sleeve, bright eyes disappearing into the blackness. I screamed after him, scrambling to my feet, but the tentacle pushed me back down.

The limbs all webbed together, twisting to form one giant snake of black smoke with glowing eyes. It arched its neck, a tentacle emerging from its open mouth in place of a tongue as it released a deafening hiss. The wind sliced at my vision, and a tear rolled into the snow.

"Why do you cry, *my love*?"

My rapid breathing slowed.

Quinten.

His voice boomed against the walls of wind and smoke.

The viper's tall, wide eyes brightened, mutating to a sharp amethyst as its body hardened into obsidian snake flesh. I dragged myself back on wobbly elbows.

A loud, crazed laugh filled the twisting tunnel, snapping by my ear like Mara Rouge was crouched beside me. Sounds of clashing metal and screams raced in; Wanda, Mirkra, Ginger, Kilen. "You didn't save us!" they cried. I slammed my palms against my ears.

"I'm not afraid of you." I said it to the witch just like I'd said it in her ice dome all those years ago.

"Why not, *my love*?" Quinten again.

I dragged my gaze up to the angled snake head.

"Because I'm not alone."

My hands drove upward and with them came a white whirlwind, rivalling the black one. My throat constricted—smoke and bad memories stabbed through me. But then there were other voices:

"I'm with you, Helen." Zane's voice came from the swelling white.

"You're not alone," Apple said.

"I love you, Helen." My mother.

"I'd do it all again for you, Helen." Kaley.

"You're my family." Emily.

"Don't you remember the stories?" Grandma. "I used to read you many stories."

Fresh tears broke away, heating my cheeks as my whirlwind pushed against the tornado. The viper bit at the snow, swallowing it in massive bites.

"Get up, Trite. You're almost there."

I reached for my cracked ice shield, and I hoisted it over my head as the snake spat my snow back at me. It flooded down like rain, pelting the glassy surface.

Wasn't I supposed to do this? Wasn't I the one Winter had supplied with what it needed to survive? "I can do this…" I whispered through dry lips. My whirlwind got tangled into the smoke, disintegrating.

"I *can*…"

But no. I couldn't do this.

I was Helen Bell, the Trite.

A peg out of its shell.

I was the child who couldn't climb trees. The child who'd never been able to catch up to the other kids when they ran. The child who'd lost everyone I'd tried to keep and had always been overlooked. Who was I to think I could do this?

A cube of ice slammed against my temple.

I was flat in the snow when a bright light came against my eyelids. Through my brain fog, I realized it was my orb that was glowing so bright. The serpent was thrashing overhead. Threads of snow and ice burst up from the ground and whipped its face. I didn't know how long I'd been out—if it had been seconds or minutes.

I tilted my head. I saw children.

Twelve-year-olds, maybe. Some younger.

Bulbs of light glowed at their chests, and the tallest one swung a Patrol staff, slicing into the tornado with ice-drawn blades. Small hands and stubborn hearts sent the snow around the viper's neck. I thought I was dreaming.

"Mr. Leutenski!" a boy shouted, pointing at where I was lying on my back.

Caramel-topaz eyes and an impossibly wide smile appeared over me.

"Ragnashuck, I bet you didn't see this coming, did you?" he said. And then, "Move your scotcher, Trite!"

Lucas's hair was longer; he didn't seem real. But he yanked me to my feet.

"Get out of here." He shoved a Patrol staff into my hand and pointed.

I blinked at Lucas. I looked at the children battling the serpent.

My hand tightened around the staff.

"Go!" Lucas shouted again, pushing me into a skate. I spun and plunged into the wall of wind and smoke. It swept me off my feet, sending me flying out the other side into the sky, and my stomach lurched into my throat.

Violet wings and dark hair flashed in the clouds, and I was caught by strong arms. Porethius spiralled past the tornado and flung me toward a snow drift. I slammed into it and rolled, clawing to a stop with burning fingers as smoke serpents snatched her by her wings. They shredded them with ice fangs and dropped the fairy into a freefall. She landed in the snow, and I pulled myself up, lifting a trembling arm as feastbeggars lunged for her. But Porethius was swallowed by the hoard, and shards of her remaining violet wings slipped out, blowing away with the wind.

"P…" *Porethius*.

My hand shook violently, held out toward where Porethius had been. I curled my fingers and gripped them into a fist as a presence arrived at my back.

"Turn," his beastly voice said.

I inched around, but Nightflesh wasn't who I saw.

Zane's face was bruised and covered in blood. They had him on his knees, his hands fastened tightly behind his back. Snow gushed from a gash between his neck and shoulder.

He teetered, lashes fluttering. The electricity in his eyes was patched with slate, but he dragged his gaze up to me.

I might have started begging. I heard myself shouting, but my words hitched when Nightflesh's mist dove for the tornado where flashes of light told me the children and Lucas still fought. The spiralling storm solidified into obsidian rock, crunching together to trap them in, frozen.

A silent beat passed.

Then it collapsed.

I had no voice left to scream.

It was over too fast; the children—*Lucas*. Every light dimmed out until it was only a mound of dark stones.

My weak pulse beat in my ears.

Nightflesh spoke:

"YOU."

“SHOULD.”

“HAVE.”

“MY.”

“DEAL.”

A gnome lifted Zane's icy Patrol staff, and before I could blink, the creature speared it into Zane's back. Zane's tired, lovely blue eyes stayed on me until they flickered to slate, and his body folded over.

My sobs shattered the silence as I stumbled to him. I reached for my Patrolman as he combusted into a flurry of snow, and the flakes seeped through my fingers.

"Zane." I cried it again and again like it might bring him back. I gripped his empty Patrol jacket.

Nightflesh's scratched, deformed sabatons crushed Zane's snowy remains, and I lifted my eyes to the monstrous dragon.

"The saints have failed."

I didn't shudder as a sharp limb of smoke lifted over me. I didn't look away as it plunged down. I barely felt it stab through my body.

I'd once wondered what would happen to me if I died in Winter.

In my last moment, I lifted my hand and watched my fingers turn to snow.

I'd thought death would look like hollow darkness.

But it was white.

Everything was white.

YOU HAVE REACHED
THE END

the bell that should have alerted her that someone had entered. She simply turned ‘round, and he was there.

A youthful being in a bland cloak sat in the corner’s chair. There was certainly more than one colour in his remarkably bright eyes. A basket rested atop the table at his side, and in it…

A baby.

“Who are you?” she asked the fellow.

A smile danced o’er his mouth. “I am the end,” he said in a voice that could form rivers and open shy blossoms. “I am the beginning too.”

Emily did not know what to say to that. “Can I…get you anything?” She half-pointed to the menu on the wall.

But the youthful being stood and carried the basket to the counter as the baby stirred in her pink swaddle. “She needs a guardian, Miss Parker. Might you be willing to guard her?”

This close, Emily became lost in the mineral topaz, the deepest green, and the purple of an evening sky within his irises. She answered without a thought. “Yes, of course.” Her gaze dropped to the baby in the basket with big round eyes, sucking on its fingers. A tuft of unbrushed hair peeked from beneath a hat.

“You need a bath and a brush,” Emily concluded as she stroked the baby’s cheek. The baby clasped her hand ‘round Emily’s thumb, and Emily’s heart did a spin.

“Please give this to your guest when he’s awake,” the fellow said, sliding a card o’er the counter. But Emily was focused on the big-eyed baby with the teeniest of fingers.

So, she said, “What’s the baby’s name?”

The café was empty when she glanced up.

The baby released a tiny sound, and Emily noticed the child's hair was dark like hers, and she had the eyes of one who might grow to be a glorious troublemaker.

Emily scooted 'round the counter and went to the door. She looked out at the rainy streets but did not see the fellow outside.

She came back and noticed the card on the counter. It looked to be made of *pure gold*. When she lifted it, a shallow inscription glimmered beneath the café lights:

MASTER KEY

"Master key?" she mumbled and looked back toward the door a time again. "What's that supposed to mean? And what guest?"

And that was that.

A pinch and a dip away, a youthful being with eyes a kaleidoscope of colours walked into a cathedral. Cloaked by the hood of a common Trite beggar, he passed through the sanctuary, entered a hall, and came to a staircase which he climbed all the way to a great bell hanging in a steeple. Once there, he swung himself o'er the brick rail and landed on a ledge before a great, magnificent clock that could be seen by the entire city.

'Twas only a few hours wrong.

The being greeted the clock and wound the hour hand

evaporated in Asteroth's flames, and in the blink of an eye, the ice beneath Nicholas's feet melted too.

Nicholas dropped deep into a pool, his body consumed. The water above him sealed back into ice, and he pounded on it with his fist, spotting his Patrol staff frozen into the rink. Crackling sounded in the pool's depths, and Nicholas realized the water was solidifying around him.

He drew his silver gaze up to the man with diamond-white hair, watching.

But another set of footprints arrived on the rink as Nicholas's breath ran out, his merry thoughts turned to ashes, and his ankles pinched in the ice.

And so, he said a thing he had not uttered in many seasons.

"Glory to Elowin," he whispered to the waters as ice covered his face, his chest, his outstretched arm reaching toward the Patrol staff.

A hand dipped into the ice. 'Twas as though the ice itself parted for it. The hand clasped onto Nicholas's, and the ice 'round him released its hold like the snapping of chains. Nicholas was pulled from the pit and found his feet on solid ground.

A pale-faced Asteroth Ryuu held his scepter toward the fellow with the helping hand, and Nicholas whirled to see who it was.

"I dare say, it took you long enough," he said when he saw the youthful being with eyes of a rainbow, dressed in a rugged Trite cloak. "My daughter?" Nicholas asked as he reached to lift his freed Patrol staff from the ground.

"Posineon is well cared for."

When the being spoke, Asteroth's body trembled. His

flesh turned into that of a grey monster, and he screamed to all of Winter, “He’s back! He’s back!” Asteroth’s voice changed from man to Beast. “You’ve lost, *Son of the White Kingdom*!”

Nicholas blinked at the once-prophet whose eyes could not settle on pure black or silver. “Is that what might have happened to me?” he asked the being in revulsion.

“Jolly Cheat, son of *mine*. No one leaves my company with their heart still beating,” the Beast snarled from within Asteroth.

“That’s where your lies end, I’m afraid,” Nicholas said, wiping cold water from his temples.

But Asteroth released an ear-piercing growl.

“Death to Nicholas Saint, who is unworthy. Who is his past. Who is stained with the sin of his seasons.” The Beast’s sound radiated across the Winter wind, and Nicholas saw visions of it enter each home—press across each mind. He felt a mere flit of fear as he imagined all of Winter coming for him.

But the cloaked being at his back spoke a time again. “Would you like to say goodbye before you go?”

Nicholas stared at Asteroth Ryuu—the *thing* he could have become—and at the Beast within him. And he said, “Goodbye, old ways.”

Nicholas did not wait to see what would happen. He turned and marched toward the unblemished snow, and he skated, leaving Asteroth Ryuu to the True King of Winter.

CHAPTER, THE TWENTY-SEVENTH

For a moment, I was in a white pool. There was no sound apart from faint singing in the distance—a choir calling me onward—and the faint giggles of prayers carrying whispers in the wind. Then my feet were on a solid surface.

The floor below me was a smooth, even crystal, encasing a river of liquid colours that trickled on by. I watched it, mesmerized, until I realized my dirty battle clothes were gone. Instead, I was clothed in white, like all my stains had been washed away. Faint memories of a fight were somewhere within me, but the trouble seemed far away now.

A soft pattering of footsteps rippled over the crystal floor, making the river beneath it dance. When I lifted my eyes, I could hardly behold the creature that came forward.

A lion of light and glass approached. Inside his clear

body were so many colours, I didn't recognize many of them. Sparkling icicles created his mane, clinking together quietly in a sweet, comforting tune. His eyes were the colours of honey and flower fields and quartz—and they were familiar.

"Elowin?" I tried his name.

The great lion stopped before me, so large I could hardly see the top of him. He was a mountain, a fortress, a stronghold of power. He was the greatest thing I had ever seen with my own eyes.

The light and colours within him trickled out, creating a human-shaped body of light that stood before me. He had the same face from when he'd lifted me from the Midnight Forest years ago. The face I'd carried in my heart.

He spoke, not in human words, but in a quiet voice that pressed against my soul and filled me from within.

"Well done," he said. *"You have been on a long journey, Trite. Welcome home."*

Pride filled my chest, but as I turned and glanced behind me toward the endless white, those faint memories of battle returned. "But…I failed," I realized. "I lost the fight."

The smile that Elowin had when I turned back filled all the white space and sent the river below us twirling off in spirals.

"You won," he corrected. *"You believed."*

"But… Winter…"

"Winter was, and always has been, mine."

"I was supposed to defeat Nightflesh," I said. "But he destroyed me in the end, like he said he would."

Elowin's presence turned warmer, and I felt it brush along my skin. His colours swirled around him in transparent ribbons.

"No, Trite. I am supposed to defeat Nightflesh." The music around us grew louder and I tried to look past him toward where I was sure it was coming from. It sounded like a choir. But Elowin spoke again, taking my attention back from whatever lay beyond where we stood. *"You were only supposed to believe. You won your own heart. You believed right until the end."*

I stared at him as my chest filled with warmth and a strange relief. My body relaxed like I was given permission to rest for the first time since before I could remember.

"But you're too late. Nightflesh already took Winter," I said. "Everyone…" A fresh sweep of worry filled me as the memories became sharper. "The Patrol. Lucas. *Zane…*"

The river beneath my feet sped up. My eyes darted down to it as Elowin said something else that took me a moment to hear, *"How great it is then, that I created time itself."*

The next second, I was falling, rushing backward into a previous moment. I dropped into Winter and was carried back to the second Nightflesh struck me, then I was pulled further to when Zane was turned to snow, and I saw his eyes turn back from slate to blue. I was propelled backward even further—into the sky where Porethius caught me, back into the whirlwind of smoke where I'd met Lucas. I was tugged through the snow where Mirkra had combusted, past where Kilen had disappeared, and I landed in my own boots, back on the ground in the place where I'd first stood on the Blossom Fields.

I heard the echo of my own voice say, "Nightflesh won't risk leaving a single believer alive."

Sounds of distant growling filled my ears. Cold wind

touched my face, and I blinked at the army of darkness back on its own side, waiting. The coiling smoke serpents filled the sky.

"I imagine not." Cane's voice came from my left, and I whipped my head toward him. "But there's still no sign of the Ruby Legion, so perhaps there is hope for Winter in the seasons after we're gone. Maybe…Maybe someday, the Truth will be able to rise again."

He said that before.

"Cane?" I whispered, and he glanced over, lifting a mahogany brow.

Was I dreaming?

Was I dead?

Hadn't I watched Cane turn to snow?

I lifted my arm and stared at the thick fabric of my sleeve, marked with tiny stains and sprinkled with snow.

A Patrol staff gently nudged my shoulder. "What's going on, Helen?"

My heart seized at his voice.

I turned, and Zane was there. He stood over me, his bright, electric blue eyes darting between mine.

"Helen?" Zane's expression was odd. "Something is…different," he whispered.

"I watched you die," I rasped.

He went quiet. I looked over Zane's shoulder and my heart swelled at the sight of Kilen, Wanda, Mirkra, Ginger, and all the others stationed exactly where they'd been before the fight had begun.

"I remember," Zane said, and my gaze darted back to him. "I remember we were failing. I remember losing you in the smoke. I remember being caught by the Greed and pinned down. I remember being heartwrenched that they were going to make you watch what they would do to me…"

"Kingsblood, what in all of Winter are you two talking about?" Cane appeared beside us.

We both looked at him.

"You don't *remember*?" I asked, and Cane folded his arms.

"Should I remember something, Carrier?" He squinted. "Something happened, didn't it?" His burgundy eyes darted to the restless serpents in the sky.

I grabbed Cane's bicep.

"We *lost*."

The former Red Prince blinked. Finally, he glanced off to think, then up at Porethius hovering below the clouds.

"I don't bloody get it. Why are we back here where it started?" Zane looked around.

The army of creatures began to stir, and my skin tightened when I remembered what happened next. "He's coming."

The sky rumbled and the snakes split away from the nest, weaving around each other's bodies.

"Don't turn your back to those, Cane." I pointed to the sky.

A melody slipped over the fields. "Do you hear that?" Zane asked. There hadn't been singing last time. He pointed a gloved finger to the valley's edge.

Hundreds of children marched down the hillside on small feet, ringing handbells and bellowing out a song. Dwarves were scattered among them, harmonizing, and I gasped when a green-eyed Trite girl appeared beside Lucas with a braid that almost reached her hips.

Thoughts of the whirlwind turning to rock and crushing them inside made my legs jerk to run toward them, but Zane caught my waist and pulled my back against his chest.

"Wait, Helen," he said. "There's a thing or three different. Something is going on."

Lucas stopped when he reached us, but the children passed to fall in line with the Patrol. Patrolmen leaned forward to stare, gaping at the orbs glowing at the children's throats. Kaley caught my eye. She gave me a nod that said it all.

"Are you sure it's a good idea to bring the sputtlepuns?" was all Zane said to Lucas in greeting.

"Oh, of course not," Lucas said, forcing a nervous laugh. "But they won't listen to me. They watched the Night Beast kill their fairies. Also, their uncontainable childlike faith is feverishly potent. Now, tell me how much you missed me while I was gone."

There was a beat of silence. Then Zane said, "I missed you."

"Of course you did. I missed you too." And then, "Did you apologize to Helen yet?"

Another beat of silence. "I did."

I shot Lucas a look, and he grinned.

The creatures of darkness shifted and parted. Nightflesh emerged in capes of smoke and mist, and dread sailed through me.

He was already a dragon.

Nightflesh's wild black eyes peered from his helmet. His monstrous ice and metal body stopped before his army, and he spread his wings wide, blanketing the field in shadow.

Cane drew his sword, and I looked at Zane, who looked

back.

"Why isn't he attacking?" Cane asked.

I swallowed, glancing up at the snake pit. "He will."

We waited as the feastbeggars drifted around the valley to trap us in like last time.

"Don't you see, believers? You have been separated from the king you chose." Nightflesh's deep dragon voice shuddered the snow, and Zane flinched. *"You are alone."* His whisper crept into my head. *"Prepare to die alone a time again."*

I squeezed my eyes shut, trying to drown out his voice. But I saw new visions of Zane being killed, Lucas and the children, Porethius, the Patrols, Cane, Ginger, and everyone else.

"Get out of my head."

Rumbling laughter flitted over the field as the phantom hook at my throat tugged.

A new voice entered my mind, cool and sweet like a quiet river. *"No power of hell, no scheme of folk can separate you from me. You were never alone."*

Nightflesh's laughter stopped.

My eyes peeled open.

High-pitched cries lifted behind me. Children raced by, kicking up ashes and blossom dust. When I spun, my gaze found someone at the valley's edge behind us. His long, battered hood drifted in the wind. When he lifted his shadowed face, a thousand colours filled the valley from his eyes, illuminating the slope where it was written in the snow:

I AM THEIRS AND THEY ARE MINE

The Patrols charged after the children. Zane broke into a skate. Cane tossed aside a charging feastbeggar to my left.

The dragon growled out a dark, bone-shivering spell, and blackness lifted around him like a swarm of locusts, catching one of the children into its cloud.

Nightflesh struck.

The darkness thundered across the field and my body flew backward.

Zane leapt, slamming his staff over Nightflesh's helmet as a limb of darkness grabbed his ankle and dragged my Patrolman down, winding around his body again and again. Nightflesh's helmet rolled off into the snow.

I jumped to my feet and raced across the field, shooting all the pellets of snow I could muster. Nightflesh's smoke limb flicked them away.

Zane freed a hand and reached for his Patrol staff. I pushed the snow to roll it toward him, but a serpent plunged down from the sky and snapped at me, driving me back, and Zane was dragged over jagged ice.

Someone appeared in a black bankers coat and stopped above the staff. Nicholas's silvery eyes were wild as he kicked it to Zane. My Patrolman snatched it up and sliced through the blackness in one motion. He fell from Nightflesh's grip.

My friends were lost to the magnitude of creatures. Greed and gnomes marched in over the hills in numbers too great to count, and snowsquatches ripped up from the ground across the valley, roaring and morphing into different forms.

Nightflesh slammed Zane and Nicholas into the snow, and mist drove against their eyes and into their mouths. I charged Nightflesh, but a warm voice pressed against my head: "*Wait.*" I slid to a stop and looked back at Elowin on the hillside. "*Help is coming,*" he said.

The sky glowed behind him, blue and white piercing through the grey cloud. Gold dust sprinkled out as it peeled apart, and a roar sounded from the heavens so loud that the fighting in the valley slowed to a stop.

In the bright light, *thousands* of people stood in luminescent armour—white like pearls. They carried dual-bladed swords, glowing like a sunrise. They leapt down from the great tear in the heavens, landing on their boots in the snow, and they raced past with a war cry like music. I thought I spotted someone I knew, but he was gone into the mix again before I could be sure.

It had looked like Wren Stallone.

Thousands of shining faces charged the army of darkness. Patrolmen watched in awe and tears, some pointing.

I didn't realize Zane was beside me until he grabbed my arm, and I glimpsed a man in the crowd who was unmistakably Mikal Migraithe.

Mikal marched beside another man who looked exactly like him with his same buttery hair and eyes, and beside them was Edward Haid—the Prince of the Pines. "Zane." I clasped my hand over my mouth.

But Zane had gone still beside me.

I followed his gaze to where a teenager with messy light-blond hair stood looking back at him from bronze eyes. The boy had a smile with a touch of humour, intensely warm. He waved.

Zane didn't blink. When he finally lifted his gloved hand, it was barely a wave. His electric eyes pinked as the boy smiled again with the happiest look I'd ever seen.

Neither of them glanced away until someone patted the boy on his shoulder, and he cast Zane one last smile as he turned to race with the others.

Victory shouts filled the valley as all the believers since the beginning of time—the Carriers of Truth, the martyrs, the fallen Patrolmen, families, and fairies—uprooted the snow where the dark creatures were.

"He was building an army," I whispered to myself as it dawned on me that Elowin's army had been outside of Winter all along.

"It's Eliot!" Kilen pointed to a boy with curly, bobbing hair running at full strength. A girl raced beside him on strong legs with dime-grey eyes and a dainty mouth that I recognized from the day she threw me off my feet in Waterloo and handed me a curious glass ball.

The bright army slammed into the darkness like a light blasting over a city at night, and I saw eight misty limbs lift from Nightflesh's dragon body to strike.

Back on his hill, Elowin pulled off his tattered cloak.

Suddenly, the snowsquatches across the valley halted. As one, they turned and bowed to where Elowin stood. The ground shook as they dropped until every snow being Nightflesh had created acknowledged the True King of Winter.

Silver-winged birds tore over the hills and speared the smoky sky, pecking at the thrashing snakes. Elowin leapt after them, transforming into a bird with colourful eyes and flapping toward Nightflesh at the speed of a shooting star.

Nightflesh pumped his own wings of metal and ice to lift, but the martyrs in white grabbed him from all sides, pulling at his arms, his sabatons, his misty limbs, and dragging him back down into the snow. The dragon growled and screamed as his ice was shattered and all the flesh he'd stolen ripped away from him.

Above, Elowin transformed again from a bird into the great white and glass lion, magnificent in size and sparkling, and as he landed amidst the creatures of darkness, he let out a mighty roar.

The sound echoed all the way to the mountains in the distance, and the mountains roared back. Songs erupted from the birds as they devoured the snakes in the sky, and I watched in awe as the beings in white destroyed the dark army.

I didn't know what to do.

Should I help?

Should I just watch?

Zane's hand slid into mine, and we stayed that way.

After a moment, my legs shook, and I toppled to sit. Zane sank down beside me, dragging his Patrol staff over his lap. I shuddered as my heart settled.

The battle was over in minutes.

Some of the creatures that had fought alongside the Beast began to disintegrate, some into snow, and others into charred bits of ash that floated away with the breeze.

Nightflesh was nowhere to be seen.

Someone dropped into the snow beside me. Kaley reached over and took my other hand.

A moment later, Apple appeared from her hiding place, sat down, and took Kaley's hand. Then, Cane tumbled to his knees and offered Apple his ring-adorned hand. Kilen scooted over, and Lucas fell to his seat on Kilen's other side, and soon the rest of the Patrolmen surrounded us, followed by the dwarves. We sat there, the believers, hand in hand.

Silent as it all came to an end.

Sunlight rolled over the valley, glistening off the few uncrushed blossoms still standing proudly across the field. When the light reached Elowin, he glowed like a torch.

The army in white began to fizzle away, and Zane squeezed my hand. The group of us watched the friends we once knew jump toward the rift in the sky and go back to where they belonged. A place we couldn't follow them to, *yet*.

But Elowin remained. He shrank back down to a human form and turned toward us. He looked right at me. I felt his smile in my soul. It was the sort of smile a proud father gave a daughter.

The ground began to rumble, and the dwarves murmured. When the valley jolted, we all hopped to our feet.

Colours leaked from Elowin like ink in water as he lifted into the sky, sparkling and painting the clouds floral pink, ripe cerulean, violet, and orange. A steeple lifted from the snow and spread into a collection of high peaks and spiralling staircases, curved balconies and stained glass, with snow spilling from glittering arches and oval windows as it emptied.

"It's the library!" Kilen shrieked. He began to dance, pulling at his hair and running around in circles. Ginger chased him doing the same.

The building grew wider, rising from the ashes with all its former glory, but it kept rising when it was complete, detaching from the ground and leaving a deep cavern in the valley. The remains of the creatures of darkness fell down into the depths of Winter as the library lifted into the sky, following Elowin to the clouds. The pit below sealed over with ice and snow, and a fresh wind blew seeds from the surrounding blossoms over it.

Light burst across the sky when the library finally stopped moving, and white clouds formed at the building's base. I shielded my eyes to watch as Elowin's flowing colours painted the clouds the same colours as the heavens, and the library disappeared, camouflaging into the sky.

"How do we get up? Jumping contest?" Kilen looked at Zane, and Zane smirked.

"Look!" Apple pointed to an icy spiral staircase spinning up from the ground. The same colours seeped along its decorative banister and blended it into the landscape.

"Race you up, spinbugs!" Lucas went sprinting, shoving Kilen into the snow on his way by. A dozen children raced after him and he lifted them onto the staircase one by one.

A spread of multicoloured wings rippled out from Elowin, and he became a shooting star in the sky, sailing over Winter in a burst of light toward the closing rift in the heavens.

In the distance, music slipped through the blue mountains, brushing over the Blossom Fields with a tune I knew in my heart. The dwarves began to hum along with it, and flurries lifted off the ground like ballet dancers, twirling and leaping and sprinkling us with snow. Trees around the valley shed their cinders and began to sprout new buds.

Everything was living. It was a new Winter.

I marvelled at it until a loud *toot* filled the air, and glittering smoke washed over us as a great, red-painted train came sliding to a halt over the fresh ice. From the engine car, Cornelius Britley emerged with an axe and began hacking away at the metal chains restraining the wheels of his locomotive. The dark links snapped and bounced into the snow. He wiped a bead of sweat from below his top hat as he turned to us with a charming bow.

"I have one last reservation today. My mum has been released from the Crimson Court and needs a ride, you see. But I came here as soon as I heard." He glanced up to where the library was hidden away. "Care for a quick lift, dwarves?" he called, nodding up to the sky. "All aboard!"

The dwarves cheered and began racing for the train. I meant to follow, but Zane attached his Patrol staff to his back. He grabbed my waist and jumped, turning us into a bullet speeding toward the sky and landing us in a frost-covered courtyard that surrounded the library. Patrolmen who'd already made the leap were rushing inside the massive arches. I looked over a glass rail to where the train was beginning to chug far below, lifting into the air.

"Is this real?" I whispered to Zane.

We stared at each other. He didn't let my waist go, even when Lucas made it to the top of the ice stairs and rushed by us with the flock of children.

Zane bit his lip and smiled.

"Can we make this quick, sweetheart?" Nicholas appeared and nudged Zane away. "You and I need to get back to our world, I'm afraid. I have a thing there to return to." He took my wrist with a tug.

"*Our* world?" I raised a brow.

Zane took Nicholas's hand and removed it from my arm.

So, Nicholas took my *other* wrist and pulled me to the arch. Zane bit down on his next words as he slid his fingers between mine.

The three of us walked into the library like that.

Scents of cinnamon sugar, fresh pine, and thick paper manuscripts washed over us as we entered. Lights prismed through the stained-glass windows, casting colours along the walls where fireplaces and bookshelves warmed every nook. Children and Patrolmen sprinted down hallways, climbed staircases, and poked their heads over balcony rails as they discovered the new library—completely different and yet entirely familiar. I heard books telling their stories as they were opened by the children.

Lucas ran out to the courtyard and leapt off its edge into the sky. A moment later, he came back up with Kaley in his arms. He pecked her on the mouth, and I started.

Beside me, Zane said, "How long were they in that time pocket?"

I blinked as Lucas yanked Kaley into the library, shouting, "Come see, darling!" I wasn't ready when he grabbed my arm on the way by. "You too, Trite! I have a thing to show you!"

I was torn from Zane and Nicholas as Lucas ran with us through the curves of the grand room and up a triad of mosaicked stairs.

Silk curtains fluttered in our wake as we burst through a set of heavy doors into a tall room where sunlight streamed through triangular windows on either side. The bookshelf at the back stretched several floors high with gold-railed balconies.

In the middle of the room rested a large wooden desk. A copper nameplate sat atop it, and on it was the name: BELL.

Carefully inscribed below in a smaller font were the words:

Head Librarian

Kaley and I exchanged a look.

"Now tell me, which one of you is this glorious room meant for?" Lucas asked us, stroking a dramatic finger over the desk to feel its richness. He tapped the nameplate.

"It's for you," I told Kaley, a smile cracking my face. "You did it, Kaley. You brought back the Carriers of Truth. You turned the island into the library and taught the wisdom you've learned to all those kids."

But Kaley shook her head. "No, Helen. I liked being a teacher, and I want to still help when I can, but I'd rather go back and forth between our worlds and find more kids who would be a good fit to learn what we know. Like a scout." She flashed Lucas a smile.

Even though I was thrilled with the idea, my face fell. I hadn't expected to be the one to keep the library going. I imagined I'd always come back to Winter whenever I could. But even after all these years of my heart being split between two places, I didn't know if I could leave the Trite world behind. I still had Emily to think about. I still had The Steam Hollow Corner Café.

"I don't think it's for me either," I admitted.

Nicholas picked up the nameplate and studied it. "Hmm. What a muddle. Well, time to go home I think, common-blood…" Nicholas's words faded, and the nameplate slipped from his hand, hitting the desk with a clatter.

"Posineon?!" He shouted it so loud, I jumped.

A stunned, wide-eyed Emily Parker stood by an open closet door with a swaddled baby in her arms. Whiffs of coffee and Waterloo smog sailed into the room, and I recognized the wallpaper in the hallway behind her.

"Em? How did you—"

Nicholas marched toward her and reached for the baby, but Emily *kicked* him.

"Get back!" she shouted as Nicholas stumbled into the desk. Just as quickly, he sprang up again and pointed a threatening finger at her face.

"That's *my* daughter!" he snapped.

"Pffft!" Emily grunted. "How do I know that? She doesn't look anything like you!"

Nicholas's jaw tightened. "She's *mine*. Give her back before I show you what a cruel, calculating Rime Folk can do."

"Hey, don't talk to her like that." Someone else stepped through the door, and Kaley gasped.

Winston stood at Emily's side, frowning at Nicholas. He wasn't teetering. His eyes weren't half closed. He looked showered, fed, and his clothes were clean.

"Who in all of Winter are *you*?" Nicholas demanded.

"That's my brother!" Kaley and I said at once.

Nicholas threw his hands up. "Oh, for the love of… There's *another* one of you?"

Winston's throat bobbed when he spotted me and Kaley. He reached into his pocket and pulled out a golden key card. "This is how we got here," he said. "It didn't work until a few seconds ago. But I've been trying it every day."

"Ragnashuck," Lucas said, plucking the card from Winston's hand to see. "This is the master key to the library!" He held it up. "That's who the desk is for! Your beloved *brother*!"

Winston's cheeks flushed. "I don't know what you're

talking about—"

"Give me back my Trite baby, *now*!" Nicholas shouted at Emily.

"You don't know how to raise a Trite." Emily looked him up and down. "How will you teach her to hold her own against high school girls, or to do her hair, or how to kick mean boys in the shins—"

"Don't test me, common-blood," Nicholas warned.

"Do your worst, you weird *elf*!" Emily snapped, and Lucas snorted a laugh.

Nicholas stared at Emily for a moment. "*You*," he sauntered over with a twinkle in his wild eyes, "are *mean*."

Winston took the card back from Lucas and walked to me and Kaley with hunched shoulders. He opened his mouth to say something, but he just sighed instead.

I threw my arms around him. His arms wrapped me too, only lifting to rewrap when Kaley joined us. None of us spoke.

Patrolmen filed into the room with shuffling footsteps, followed by the dwarves, Ginger, Cane and Scarlet, and Porethius. Porethius folded her arms and flashed me a brilliant smile.

Nicholas huffed impatiently by the closet door.

When I detached from my siblings, I looked at Winston. "Kaley and I will stay for a few days to help get you settled. I'm not ready to go home anyway after everything," I said, and Winston cracked a weak smile.

"Emily is doing a terrible job at running the café without you," he admitted.

"Hey!" Emily protested, and Nicholas sneered.

"If what the reindeer guy says about me is true,"

Winston nodded back toward Lucas, "then I'm the one who has to stay. Which is for the best because I'm in a bit of trouble in Waterloo." My brother glanced down at his golden key card. "But I'll open this door every week," he promised. "We can have muffins and coffee."

I glanced past my brother to where Zane ran a hand through his pecan hair. "I think I'll be coming back here a lot," I confessed.

"Then this isn't goodbye forever. It's just 'see you soon'." Winston swallowed and put his arms around Kaley's and my shoulders to walk us to the closet door. Emily nodded a quick goodbye to everyone and left, patting the baby on the head. Nicholas sprang after her, and they disappeared down the café hallway.

My gaze sailed to Zane fidgeting with his Patrol staff.

Lucas took Kaley's hand in his. "Don't stay with the Trites too long, darling. And don't you dare meet some young, dull-eyed Trite boy while you're away," he warned.

Kaley laughed and waved him off as she went through. "I'm coming back as soon as I sort things out at home. Watch your language in front of the kids while I'm gone."

Lucas released a long, heavy, sad breath. "Not a chance," he said.

"Wait!" Apple's shout echoed through the room as she came speeding in with an armful of books. "I'm coming, friends! I promised to make my infamous chocolates for the Trites, remember?" She flung her hair out of her face to look at me. "I rather like having all these doors to the dead world, but perhaps we should do a thing about it, don't you agree, friend? I'm not sure anyone else will think to fix this mess."

Before I could answer, she was through the closet door

and hustling down the café hallway with her books, loose papers falling out the whole way.

I hovered, feeling Zane's eyes on me. Finally, he said to everyone watching, "Give us a pinch?"

Kilen raced over and stole a hug, and the others shouted their goodbyes. But, like Winston had said, it wasn't goodbye forever. It wouldn't even be goodbye for long. I smiled and watched them leave; Patrolmen poking the squealing children. Lucas linked an arm through Winston's, and Winston scowled, casting me a pleading look as the Rime boy led him away.

"Even just a week apart feels like a good measure too long," Zane said when they were gone. He tugged off his gloves and pushed my rebellious hair out of my face. "Even if I stay here, it'll never end for us, Helen," he said.

"What do you mean?"

A slow smile spread across his face, blue electricity sparking in his eyes. "You know precisely what I mean, Trite. I promised I'd keep you and I together. So, you'll marry me, right? I see no other way."

I started, taking a step back and almost tripping over my feet. But Zane followed and grabbed my arms to steady me, his dimples threatening to show. "That's what's going to happen for us. Maybe not today, or tomorrow, or the season or three next. But you will one day, right, Trite? That's what'll happen?"

My mouth hung open. "I…I don't know—"

"Yes, you do." He laughed and guided me toward the closet door. He shoved me a little to get me through it, and I stared back at him, knowing that as soon as that door shut, he'd be sealed away.

Zane began to close it, but my hand flashed out, palm flat against the wood.

He pursed his lips, staring. Staring, staring, staring. “Ragnashuck,” he finally whispered. “Tell me I’m right before you go. Tell me all this bloody discomfort in my chest will be done with.” He slapped a hand over his heart.

I made a face. “That’s what this is about? You just want to be rid of the discomfort you feel when we’re apart? You can’t think of *any other reason* you’d want to be with me forever?”

His smile widened, and he reached through the doorway to flick my nose. “Nope.”

He swung the door shut, and my chest deflated.

But the latch never clicked.

I lifted a hand toward it just as the door flew back open, and Zane marched through. He slammed the door shut behind him, blue eyes glowing in the dim café hallway.

I held up a finger between us and backed up. “That proposal sucked,” I whispered.

He flicked my hand aside and grabbed my Carrier coat, pulling me against him. But he paused with his lips barely touching mine. “Stubborn Trite,” he muttered. “Making me beg. After I carried you around for four bloody seasons—”

He caught my wrist before I could smack him, and he kissed me with a grin.

THE PEBBLE PAPER

YESTERMORNING THE CRIMSON COURT'S PROPHETESS WAS APPREHENDED BY THE RUBY LEGION AFTER WITNESSES BROUGHT FORTH TESTIMONY OF HER WRONGDOINGS. HOWEVER, FOLLOWING HER EVENING TRIAL, THE PROPHETESS ESCAPED HER PRISON AND SEEMS TO HAVE VANISHED INTO THE SCARLET CITY. ON THE BACK OF THIS NEWSSHEET IS A SKETCH OF THE PROPHETESS SUBMITTED BY THE INFAMOUS CHOCOLATIER, APPLE DOUGH. (DO ADMIRE THE ARTISTRY AND DETAIL WHEN YOU LOOK AT IT.)

THE BOUNTY FOR THE PROPHETESS'S CAPTURE HAS BEEN SET AT SEVEN HUNDRED FIFTY PLUS FIVE RINGS. IF YOU CROSS A WOMAN WITH AN ASHWORM TATTOO ON HER NECK, PLEASE REPORT IT TO THE RUBY LEGION. (OR, IF YOU FANCY IT, THROW A PIE IN HER DIRECTION AND SEE IF SHE NOTICES. IF SHE GETS ANGRY AND SPUTTERS CRUEL SPELLS AT YOU FOR IT, SHE IS LIKELY THE WOMAN WE ARE LOOKING FOR.)

IN BRIGHTER NEWS, THE CRIMSON KING IS SETTLING INTO HIS POSITION WITH GRACE DESPITE THE RUMOURS THAT THE COURT IS URGING HIM

TO SEARCH FOR A WIFE. SHOULD THE COURT HAVE THEIR WAY, TRIALS MAY BE PUT IN PLACE TO FIND A WORTHY MATCH FOR KING DRIAR. (OH, WHAT FUN THAT WOULD BE. CAN YOU IMAGINE?)

SINCERELY,
YOUR NEW EDITOR-IN-CHIEF,
CORA THIMBLE

CHAPTER, THE TWENTY-EIGHTH

It was chaos when twenty Patrolmen decided to come through the door only five days after we'd shut it. Winston should have known better than to open it for them, but Lucas had bribed him by gifting him his own shiny Patrol staff. The door that linked our café to Winston's office in the Winter library was proving to be a problem I was preparing to scold my brother for.

Patrolmen fluttered around the café, creating a situation that was going to take me ages to explain to the customers who kept getting their cups and snacks knocked around by Rime Folk they couldn't see.

Mirkra snooped through the cupboard for something to eat behind the counter, and I tried to keep my face composed as Mrs. Shellwinger ordered her morning coffee to go. I stepped around Mirkra's thick arms as I reached for the to-go cups, but I made sure I kicked the Patrolman in his curled-toe boot on my way back. Winston hadn't just let them all through, he'd shut the door so I couldn't send them back until he opened it again.

"I have an idea." Apple came to the counter the second Mrs. Shellwinger left. "I think we should put together a special group to hunt down all the unsanctioned doors and peepholes in the area and sew them shut with invisible thread. What do you think, friend?"

"Didn't Zane say there were over six hundred of them? How would we find them all?" I shut the cash register.

Apple reached for a chocolate from the pedestal display. "Oh, I have an idea or three." She flashed me a dark-chocolate smile and her large silver earrings swayed.

Zane appeared and tugged the towel from his shoulder as he reached around me to clean the counters, sliding his hands into my space as he did—running his fingers over my fingertips, brushing his shoulder against mine, standing behind me and reaching beneath my arm instead of stepping around me like a normal person.

"You're going to start rumours." I fought a smile.

"I certainly hope so." He leaned around and planted a kiss on my cheek. "I'd hate for my Carrier to have it easy in her boring Trite life."

The bell on the door chimed, but I barely heard it over the noise of the Rime Folk in the café.

A man with sunken eyes and unshaved stubble approached the counter. When his dark eyes met mine, he studied me, taking in my facial features most of all.

"I'm looking for Winston Bell," the man said, and Zane slowed his movements beside me.

"He's not here," I told him.

Zane casually tossed the towel back over his shoulder and picked up a dishcloth.

"We know he was living here," the man said.

The bell rang again, and three more men entered. They sauntered toward the counter, one folding burly arms. Zane kept his eyes on the counter as he wiped it, but a muscle feathered in his jaw.

Emily came from the hallway with Posineon, but Nicholas flung an arm out to stop her. His silvery eyes took in the men, and he pulled Emily—and the baby—back the way they'd come.

Suddenly Zane slapped the towel down on the counter, and I jumped. The man's dark eyes fired over to him.

"She said he's not here. Are you bloody deaf?" Zane asked.

One of the men pulled out a knife that he held casually behind his folded hands. I stole a glance at the café's entrance where I realized the men had turned the *closed* sign around and had locked the door after they came in.

"You won't find Winston. Not here," I said again.

But the man's lip curled into a sneer. "Didn't Bell have a sister?" he asked the others, looking me over again.

Suddenly Zane burst out laughing, his high tenor filling the café.

The man's stare darkened, and I felt heat rush into my fingers, but Zane let out a long, melodramatic sigh. "This is going to be fun." He settled his electric gaze on them. "Blink twice, ashworms."

The four men raised their eyebrows. But confusion filled their expressions when their eyes beheld twenty Patrolmen strolling through the café toward them like a flock of ravens.

Lucas walked up to the closest man, a half-eaten chocolate in his fingers. "Season's greetings," he said and shoved the rest of the chocolate into his mouth.

The man released a vulgar curse, spinning around as the clicking of Patrolmen unlatching their staffs filled the café.

Zane's dimples faded, his electric eyes turning ice blue.

"Now," he said, "move your merry scotchers."

EPILOGUE

A prayer is how this story began. 'Twas a thought no larger than a button, no tastier than honey or hope, slipping out into the midnight hush by the mouth of a mother only moments before she passed. And this is what it said:

"I know I haven't always been devout, but I do believe. Please help my kids to survive after I've left; especially Helen, because she's going to take it the hardest when I'm gone. Help her to fight her battles, and to know that she's not alone."

And so, the prayer battled the elements to survive, slipping past every power and force that tried to stop it. 'Twas one prayer that changed everything. As one prayer can and will.

Those feisty little things have a certain magic; the means

to shift mountains off a path, to see a blind one healed, to transform the atmosphere, and to take back a household.

Never underestimate a prayer spoken into the midnight hush.

Those prayers fight their way into the ears of Heaven, you see.

THE END
THE SECOND, AND FINAL ONE

(Or is it?)

If you loved this book, please consider leaving a review on your favourite bookstore website(s).
It makes such a big difference when you do!

BOOKS BY JENNIFER KROPF

The Winter Souls Collection:
A Soul as Cold as Frost
A Heart as Red as Paint
A Crown as Sharp as Pines
A Beast as Dark as Night
Carols and Spies, Princes and Pies

Humourous Fantasy:
Welcome to Fae Cafe

Co-Author Anthologies:
Enchanted Waters
Enchanted Forests

ACKNOWLEDGEMENTS

I'm a gross mess of tears as I'm writing this final 'acknowledgements section' for the last (official) book of this series. This series has been through a lot: Book 1 has gone through rewrites, ISBN changes, and republishing since I first published it back in 2020. I learned so many things from *A Soul as Cold as Frost*, but every experience has taught me valuable lessons about life, courage, my own faith, and being an author. As a mother who prays for her children, I found myself experiencing emotional struggles throughout this journey, but especially now as Helen's story is coming to an end. This story started because Helen's mother prayed for her. That idea was the springboard for everything else.

Okay, here we go:

To Phil, the one who talks me through the hard days, who prays for our family, and who supports me with unconditional love: You are the reason I get to do this. You are the reason I haven't quit yet. Thank you.

To my kids: I wish I could say, "Read more books and maybe you'll end up being an author like me!" but I didn't read books until my adult years. My storytelling when I was little was much more about getting out of trouble than trying to entertain others. So instead, I'll say, chase your dreams, because you can learn to do anything once you decide to do it.

To my parents and siblings: In case I haven't said it enough, you guys really did create a family environment that made me believe anything was possible. (Seriously, who has people in their life who actually believe them when they say absurd things like, "I'm going to go hop on a plane and live in South Africa for four months. Bye!" or, "I'm going to be a New York Times Bestselling Author some day.")

To my content editor Jesse Calder: Thank you for reading my trashy first draft even though it was the FIRST DRAFT and people should never see that horrendous garbage. Thank you for calling me out on every speck of lazy writing and not letting me get away with it. If it weren't for you, this book would really suck.

To my line editor and proof-reader Melissa Cole: I got so lucky the afternoon you told me you were starting an editing company. To this day I still don't know how that worked out so well for me but working with you will always be my favourite.

To all my family and friends who wanted to "talk book" with me and showed so much enthusiasm for my work, thank you!!

And to God: There's just too much to say here without writing another whole book about it. Thank you for being the anchor.

I know that Winter is just a fantasy world I created, but Helen's life struggles were ones that real people go through, and that's what made her story powerful. I know there's not a person on planet earth who will have been affected by this story as much as I have as the writer, but for any of you who are feeling the weight of this series ending like I am, just know that Helen's ending is only paving the way for new stories to rise.

Winter is not done with you yet.

ABOUT THE AUTHOR

Jennifer Kropf lives in a small town in Ontario, Canada. She writes cozy fantasy novels and designs fantasy-themed journals. She loves books, coffee, knit sweaters, and K-dramas and hoards a massive mug collection. Her favourite authors are C. S. Lewis, Stephanie Garber, and Marissa Meyer.

Join her email list at JenniferKropf.com to stay updated on all of her new books.

Made in United States
Troutdale, OR
12/12/2023